CARMILLA
The former queen of Termine Kingdom who was taken prisoner by Grandleon.

GRANDLEON
The powerful Beast Emperor who rules over the continent of Rhadral.

SEIYA RYUUGUUIN
The overly cautious hero summoned by Rista.

RISTARTE
The novice goddess who summoned Seiya once again to save Ixphoria.

RASTI
The Goddess of Shapeshifting, who teaches Seiya how to shapeshift.

ZET
The Goddess of Warfare, who "teaches" Seiya the secret of Status Limit Break...

THE HERO IS OVERPOWERED BUT OVERLY CAUTIOUS

STORY **LIGHT TUCHIHI**

ILLUS. SAORI TOYOTA

3

YEN ON

NEW YORK

THE HERO IS OVERPOWERED BUT OVERLY CAUTIOUS 3

LIGHT TUCHIHI

Translation by Matt Rutsohn
Cover art by Saori Toyota

KONO YUSHA GA ORE TUEEE KUSENI SHINCHO SUGIRU Vol. 3
©Light Tuchihi, Saori Toyota 2017
First published in Japan in 2017 by KADOKAWA CORPORATION, Tokyo.
English translation rights arranged with KADOKAWA CORPORATION, Tokyo, through
TUTTLE-MORI AGENCY, INC., Tokyo.

English translation © 2020 by Yen Press, LLC

Yen On
150 West 30th Street, 19th Floor
New York, NY 10001

Visit us at yenpress.com • facebook.com/yenpress • twitter.com/yenpress • yenpress.tumblr.com
instagram.com/yenpress

First Yen On Edition: April 2020

Yen On is an imprint of Yen Press, LLC.
The Yen On name and logo are trademarks of Yen Press, LLC.

Library of Congress Cataloging-in-Publication Data
Names: Tuchihi, Light, author. I Toyota, Saori, illustrator. I Rutsohn, Matt, translator.
Title: The hero is overpowered but overly cautious / Light Tuchihi ;
illustration by Saori Toyota ; translation by Matt Rutsohn ; cover art by Saori Toyota.
Other titles: Kono yuusha ga ore tueee kuse ni shinchou sugiru. English
Description: First Yen On edition. I New York : Yen On, 2019–
Identifiers: LCCN 2019013049 I ISBN 9781975356880 (v. 1 ; pbk.) I ISBN 9781975356903 (v. 2 ; pbk.) I
ISBN 9781975356927 (v. 3 ; pbk.)
Subjects: GSAFD: Fantasy fiction.
Classification: LCC PL876.U34 K5613 2019 I DDC 895.63/6—dc23
LC record available at https://lccn.loc.gov/2019013049

ISBNs: 978-1-9753-5692-7 (paperback)
978-1-9753-5693-4 (ebook)

10 9 8 7 6 5 4 3 2 1

LSC-C

Printed in the United States of America

CONTENTS

The Hero Is Overpowered but Overly Cautious 3

PROLOGUE
A Reunion and a Change

Panting, I draw a magic circle on the floor of the spacious room, which is white as far as the eye can see. After receiving the list of Heroes from Great Goddess Ishtar, I sprinted all the way to the Hero Summoning Chamber in the sanctuary as quickly as I could.

Since I broke the rules of the unified spirit world when we saved Gaeabrande, I was put in charge of saving the world of Ixphoria, an SS-ranked world, next. Ranking higher than Gaeabrande, Ixphoria has already become a world overrun by demons. But even so, I feel no despair. Brimming with emotion, I chant the summoning spell while gazing at the Hero's status written on the list. I thought I had run out of tears, but the corners of my eyes begin to burn anew.

I'm sure Seiya has lost all the memories of our adventure together after his stats were reset. But that's okay. I'll be able to see him again, and that's all that matters. I read the Hero's name aloud. Before long, the magic circle expels a powerful light, summoning the Hero from the human realm.

He has a tall, fit body with youthful black locks of hair hanging over his masculine face. Just like when I first summoned him, Seiya Ryuuguuin is wearing a T-shirt and jeans while emitting a powerful, godlike aura. I thought I would never see this overly cautious Hero again, and yet here we are, reunited.

Seiya...!

I desperately hold myself back as I unconsciously reach out to touch him.

Ristarte! No! Pull yourself together! Seiya doesn't remember anything about you!

I tell myself even as the corners of my lips fight to curl upward. After standing up straight and making myself presentable, as a goddess should, I turn my gaze to Seiya once more.

Let's start over and take our time. Right…Seiya?

I introduce myself to Seiya the same way I did the first time we met.

"It is a pleasure to finally meet you. I am Ristarte, a goddess of this unified spirit world. I have summoned you to this dimension for a certain mission. Seiya Ryuuguuin, you shall become the Hero who saves the parallel world Ixphoria from the evil clutches of the Demon Lord."

…Silence follows, as expected. Seiya casts me a dubious look just like he did the last time he was suddenly summoned to this world. It feels very nostalgic to me, though.

After a few moments, he finally speaks up.

"Rista. What's gotten into you?"

"…Huh?"

W-wait. What? Huh? Wait. Did he just call me Rista? Huh? Why?

"You already told me all that last time. Or do you have to say that every time you summon a Hero?"

Wh-wh-wh-what?!

My mouth flaps open and shut like a fish out of water.

"Y-you… You remember me? But when Heroes are summoned, their memories of the past world are supposed to be erased. Why…?"

"Beats me. I remember everything, though."

I suddenly think back to my conversation with Ishtar.

"This will be an exception."

Did she mean…that she would allow Seiya to keep his memories?! Th-that's the only way this makes sense! What a wonderful arrangement!

I am so moved, I begin to tremble when…

"Hang on. After all that training I did, my stats went back down to level one… This is ridiculous. Please tell me there's some way to fix this system."

Seiya fires off complaints, but that's so like him. Seeing the Hero just

how I remember him causes the urges I had been fighting back to spill out from within.

"*Waaah!* Seiyaaaaa! I missed yooooooou!"

Casting aside my dignified demeanor as a goddess, I leap into Seiya's arms, bury my face in his chest, and start crying.

"I thought your soul was destroyed after the battle! I thought I'd never see you again! You acted so tough in front of everyone, but in reality, you were in so much pain!"

After bawling my eyes out, I eventually take my face off his chest.

"Ah!"

His clothes are stained with my tears. Well, not only my tears. Some stuff came out of my nose and mouth and… Well, there's a lot of me on his shirt.

Eeeep! O-oh no… I—I completely lost control of myself! He's gonna hit me; I just know it…!

I promptly cover my face with my hands, but Seiya doesn't hit me.

"Huh? Y-you're not mad? I completely ruined your shirt, though."

"I don't care."

"Huh? Really? Wh-why?"

"…Rista."

Seiya looks at me, and his face becomes serious.

"I remember you desperately trying to save me, too. Also, when I was on the verge of death in return for using Gate of Valhalla, I remembered how much you meant to me in my past life."

"D-do you really mean that?"

"I do."

"Y-you care about me?"

"Yes. Stop making me repeat myself. I mean, I came back this time for you. I heard Ishtar's voice in my head, and she told me you were going to have to save a world even deadlier than Gaeabrande as punishment for saving me."

"O-oh… Um… C-could you give me a second?"

I turn away so that Seiya can't see my face, then I crouch.

Whoo-hoooooo! Wh-wh-what is going on?! I went from hell to heaven! From despair to euphoria! I'm drowning in an indescribable feeling of joy! But… even then, I shake my head.

W-wait! He's probably just teasing me! Yeah! He's probably trying to get me to let my guard down so that he can kick me! There's only one way to find out...!

My heart pounding in my chest, I approach Seiya.

"A-ahem... Hey."

I casually wrap my arm around his. Seiya's expression doesn't change. He doesn't even say a word, but he doesn't look like he's going to attack me, either.

Impossible! He doesn't want me to stop?! Th-then that means— Wait! I can't let my guard down just yet! I need to experiment further!

With my arm still around his, I hit Seiya with the puppy-dog eyes.

"Hey, Seiya. Let's go visit Mash and Elulu the next time we're free. They really wanted us all to go to that hot spring together, remember?"

The old Seiya would have said, *I don't care*, but he immediately replies with:

"Yeah, that sounds good."

I got a "sounds good"!

"I really put them through a lot. I actually wish I could go see them now if possible."

Th-this is really happening! H-he's finally... He has finally...

Fireworks bloom in my heart like beautiful flaming flowers of passion. He has finally opened up to me!! Just you wait, Mash and Elulu! You're going to be blown away when you see just how lovey-dovey we are now!

"But that's going to have to wait until after we finish our mission. The next world is going to be even more difficult than Gaeabrande, right? I'll need to be even more cautious this time around."

Thereupon, Seiya looks ahead with a sharp gaze.

"Time to train."

"Whaaaaaat?! Already?!"

"Yeah. I'm going to start with basic training just like last time."

Seiya shoots me a look. He doesn't even need to say a word because I know what he wants to say. He wants me to get out of the Summoning Chamber.

"Y-yeah, I'm used to this by now."

His stoic personality sure hasn't changed a bit. *Tch.* I wanted to hold hands and cuddle, but...

Just like last time, I use my goddess powers of creation to create a simple toilet and bed before handing Seiya the buzzer.

"Buzz me when you're ready, okay?"

Right as I, looking a little dejected, start to leave, Seiya calls out to me.

"Rista, could you bring me something to eat later?"

"...Okay!!"

"Aria, Aria, Aria! Listen to this! Seiya is sooo sweet now! He doesn't punch me or kick me or crush my boobs anymore!"

"Th-that's wonderful... Wait, just what has he put you through...?"

I frantically ramble about Seiya in Ariadoa's room. She has red hair. Her boobs are bigger than mine, and she has way more goddess experience than I do. She's like my big sister.

Aria listens to me, letting out a chuckle here and there.

"Seiya still has his memories thanks to Great Goddess Ishtar. She must have gotten in touch with all the highest-ranking deities at the heart of the spirit world and worked something out for you. It looks like I have to apologize to her for my behavior earlier as well."

Aria suddenly pauses and furrows her brow.

"Um... Rista? Are you listening?"

"Y-yeah! I'm listening! I'm listening! I need to thank Great Goddess Ishtar, right? I know!"

"H-hey, Rista... Make sure to keep yourself in check, okay? I know you two used to be in love with each other, but Seiya is a human, and you're a goddess."

"Ha-ha-ha! Oh, Aria! Come on! I get it! I'll be fine!"

"Are you sure? Do you really get it?"

Aria lets out a deep sigh for some reason.

"I'm worried about you. I wish I could go with you. A painful past awaits you in Ixphoria. Even if you don't remember, your soul might when you get there..."

I decide to crack a joke in spite of her concern.

"Don't worry! I'll be fine! I have my sweet, loving darling from a past, past, past world with me! Anyway, talk to you later, Aria!"

"R-Rista?! What happened to thanking Great Goddess Ishtar?!"

"Sorry! I'll do it tomorrow!"

After retiring from Aria's room, I head straight for the kitchen.

The next day, I make rice balls for Seiya's breakfast and proceed to the Summoning Chamber when I see Cerceus the Divine Blade and the Goddess of War, Adenela, standing in the hallway. Cerceus, who is very muscular, is actually a meek god who likes baking cakes. Adenela is a little creepy and always looks like she's about to keel over, but she's hundreds of times stronger than Cerceus.

"Morning, Cerceus! Your muscles are looking great as always! The bags under your eyes look wonderful as well, Adenela!"

When I cheerfully greet them, Adenela glares at me with a fed-up expression.

"Wh-what a change. W-well, I get that you're h-happy that Seiya's alive, but…"

However, my excitement isn't only due to that. Yesterday, I actually made Seiya stew for dinner and checked how much he changed again. Like feeding a wild animal, I scooped up some stew with a spoon and nervously pointed it toward Seiya's mouth.

"S-Seiya! O-open wide! Here, say 'ahh.'"

The anxiety nearly killed me. I was almost expecting to take an uppercut to the jaw. That negative thought crossed my mind, but…Seiya put his mouth around the spoon and chewed the stew in silence.

"I-is it good?"

"Yeah, it's great."

…And that's why I'm in such a good mood today. Plus, I'm about to go to Seiya's room and feed him the rice balls I made. I'm so excited, I can't help smiling.

However, contrary to my mood, Cerceus hangs his head.

"So that Hero's back, huh? Don't tell me I'm going to have to train with him again… *Sigh*…"

"Don't worry, Cerceus! Seiya is a lot nicer than he used to be!"

"What?! S-seriously?!"

"Yep! A lot happened in Gaeabrande, and it helped Seiya grow as a person!"

"W-well, isn't that something? ...Hmm? Hold on! Now that I think about it, his stats were reset, so he should be weaker than me right now! Ha! There's no reason for me to be afraid anymore! Heh-heh-heh... Ha-ha-ha-haaa!"

As Cerceus cackles...

"You're sure in a good mood, Cerceus."

Seiya stands behind him with his arms crossed.

"Ha-ha...ha... Eeeeeek!"

"Hey, Cerceus, I may be weaker than you right now, but don't let it go to your head. I'll catch up with you in no time and make sure you'll never be able to bake another cake again."

"Wh-wh-whatever could you mean? Oh, come on! I was only kidding! Anyway, forget about that! Welcome back, Seiya! Glad to see you're doing well!"

What happened to that confidence he had two seconds ago? Excessively rubbing his hands together, Cerceus tries to ingratiate himself with Seiya.

"Wait, Seiya. Did you come over here to ask Cerceus to train with you?"

"Yeah, I decided to cut basic training short this time. Figured it'd be more productive to train with one of the gods here."

"U-um... I've got a cake to bake, so I don't think I can help... Plus, I've got a slight fever...and diarrhea...and my joints hurt... Actually, I think I'm gonna die soon..."

Seiya pats Cerceus on the shoulder in the midst of his obvious excuses.

"Relax, Cerceus. I'll let you take breaks. You can use that time to bake cakes."

"What?! R-really?! You're gonna give me time to bake?!"

"Of course. From now on, I'm going to respect your free time and put that above my training."

I whisper to Cerceus:

"See? Seiya's a lot nicer now!"

"Y-yeah, you're right! He really is!"

But that's when Seiya sternly declares:

"You get one minute every five hours to rest, and you get to sleep once every three days for three hours. Got it?"

"…?! That's ridiculous! What kind of sweatshop training is this?! The conditions are beyond unreasonable! When will I have time to bake?! I can't even beat an egg in under a minute!"

Cerceus shakes my shoulders, tears in his eyes.

"What part of Seiya is 'a lot nicer now'?! His tyrannical personality has gotten even worse!"

Wh-what the…? That's weird. I thought he was nicer now…

Out of nowhere, Adenela pushes Cerceus out of the way and tries to strike up conversation with Seiya.

"S-S-Seiya, forget C-Cerceus and t-train with m-me."

I'm taken aback when I see her. She's blushing like a maiden in love! What the…?! I'm pretty sure she knows about our relationship in a past life! Was her love for Seiya suddenly rekindled?! This *is* the first time she's seen him in a while, after all…

I watch in suspense, but Seiya simply stares at Adenela as if bored.

"Yep. You're just as spooky as ever, Adenela. The more I look at you, the worse it gets."

"Y-yes…! I—I love you…!"

What the…?! Is she even listening to what he's saying?! She even looks happy to hear him say that! What's going on anyway?! Seiya's just as awful to her as he used to be!

And then Seiya looks back at me, and his cold expression warms a bit.

"Oh, hey. I've got an idea, Rista. I can train with Cerceus and Adenela at the same time. That way, I can shorten the amount of time I need."

Cerceus lets out an "Eek!" but I smile and nod back at Seiya.

"Y-yeah! That's a great idea!"

Seiya turns on his heel, but he looks back at me once more.

"Let me know when the food's ready, Rista. We can eat together in your room. Is that okay?"

"Y-yeah! Of course!"

Dragging poor Cerceus along, Seiya and Adenela head toward the Summoning Chamber while I just stare in blank amazement.

Ohhh! So that's what's going on! Seiya's only nice to me! Hee-hee-hee! Why do I feel so superior to everyone else now?! But it does make sense! After all, we were tied by the red thread of fate in a past life! Not only that, but we worked together to defeat the Demon Lord of Gaeabrande! I mean, how much more in love can you get?!

A few hours go by before Seiya actually shows up in my room. I welcome him with the feast I lovingly prepared.

"How's the rice ball?"

"It's good."

"And the salad?"

"It's good."

Oh my gosh! I am sooo happy! He won't say anything other than "*It's good,*" but regardless…I'm on cloud nine!

As I watch him dig in to my home cooking, my heart suddenly starts to race.

I—I could probably kiss him, and he wouldn't get that mad. Sh-should I do it?! I missed my chance last time, so should I do it now?! Just a kiss on the cheek! Ahhh! *Hff…! Hff…! Hff…! Hff…!*

But all of a sudden, the door flies open without a knock, and Adenela barges inside.

"S-Seiya! C-Cerceus r-ran off again!"

"Okay. I'll be right there. Looks like he needs to be disciplined."

After gulping down the rest of his meal, Seiya leaves the room with Adenela.

Sigh. *Looks like I missed my chance again. But…whatever! There's no need to rush! I'll have plenty of opportunities from now on! Hmm… I can't wait to go to Ixphoria! Saving SS-ranked or even SSS-ranked parallel worlds should be a walk in the park now! After all, I have my dear, sweet Seiya by my side, and we're madly in love!*

…That was the happiest I had ever been. But, of course, it didn't last long. As expected, my feelings would soon be crushed, ripped to shreds, and left to fade away into nothingness.

CHAPTER 1
Invasion

The day after Seiya started training with Cerceus and Adenela, it occurs to me that I forgot to thank Ishtar, so I quickly head to her room. After knocking, I open the door and immediately bow.

"I'm so sorry I didn't come to thank you sooner, Great Goddess Ishtar!"

"Oh, it's no trouble at all."

Just as I expected, she doesn't hold it against me. She sweetly smiles at me while sitting in her wooden chair, knitting.

"Allowing the Hero to be summoned with his memories intact was the least I could do. The rest is up to you and Seiya Ryuuguuin."

"Thank you so very much!"

After I convey just how grateful I am from the bottom of my heart, Ishtar stops knitting and looks at me.

"I really wish I could help you more, but when I think about Ixphoria... my head gets cloudy, and I cannot see into the future. The Demon Lord of Gaeabrande possessed evil powers that got in the way of my power of precognition, but it appears this Demon Lord's powers exceed even that."

Ishtar's expression then slightly tenses.

"After defeating the Hero, the Demon Lord destroyed the world and received a blessing from a dark dimension. The Demon Lord—and indeed all monsters that live in Ixphoria—has possibly gained powers that far exceed the creatures of other parallel words. In addition, you will not be able to use your healing powers during this mission. It is easy to imagine just how difficult this will be. However—"

"I have Seiya by my side, so I'll be okay!" I suddenly declare.

The Great Goddess's troubled expression becomes a warm smile, and she laughs.

"Yes, you will be. After overcoming a past rife with regret, Seiya Ryuuguuin has become not only physically strong but mentally strong as well. His level of raw talent is certainly unique. But he does have a weakness. His growth speed is both an advantage and a disadvantage. Before long, his attributes will reach their limit just as they did in Gaeabrande. Even then, I know he will overcome this obstacle and save Ixphoria. I believe in him just as you do."

Ishtar gives me a gracious smile.

"Ixphoria is an SS-ranked world now, Rista. You are free to let Seiya Ryuuguuin train in the unified spirit world until he is ready to depart."

After another deep bow, I retire from the Great Goddess's room.

Thanks to my talk with Ishtar, I was able to look to the future with unclouded vision. Seiya might have gotten nicer, but I can't keep doting on him every second of the day. I won't be able to use my healing abilities this time around, so I need to find another way I can help. I want to be able to help the man I love, and that feeling is eating away at me.

While Seiya trains, I decide to go have a chat with Aria so that I can learn more about Ixphoria. It may be a world forgotten to me, but the memories are probably vividly carved in her mind. I feel bad asking her about the world she failed to save, but this is something I have to know if I want to make things right.

Aria seems hesitant to speak at first, but she slowly opens up.

"Rista, even now, I sometimes wonder what's going on in Ixphoria, so I peer into the crystal ball…"

She tells me that what she sees in the crystal ball is frightening. The world rests in the palm of the Demon Lord's hand. Entire continents have fallen under control of the demons. Humans have become little more than slaves or toys…or food.

"Great Goddess Ishtar exploited an opening in the Demon Lord's magic and was able to create a starting point for you in a town known as Galvano. This town essentially creates and produces obedient slaves, but that's exactly why it's a relatively decent place for humans to live. At the very least, they won't be used as toys or food…"

"So that's our starting point, huh?"

I nod while taking notes. Before I realize it, Aria is smiling broadly at me.

"You're really taking this seriously. I was a little worried at first, but it looks like you're going to be okay."

"Yeah, I just want to make myself useful so I can help Seiya."

Aria places a finger on her chin and ponders for a few moments until she gently claps her hands together as if she's had an epiphany.

"That's it! Rista! I'll teach you the special ability Appraise! You can use it to check the condition of items and equipment!"

"'Appraise'? D-do I really need an ability like that…?"

"Ixphoria is ruled by the Demon Lord. Unlike other parallel worlds, there are almost no item or weapon shops run by humans. You will need to take care of getting items and weapons yourself, so you definitely need to learn Appraise!"

I was worried I wouldn't be able to learn it, but it actually wasn't that hard once I got the hang of it. You basically just need to look at objects the same way you look at people when you use Scan. I ended up mastering it in two days.

I use Appraise on the flowerpot in Aria's room to test it out.

Vase: a container for holding flowers. This vase appears to be made out of a ceramic material rare in the spirit world. Can be sold at a high price.

Those words suddenly appear in my head.

Wow! This is kind of fun! It reminds me of those video games people play in Seiya's world!

"You can adjust the writing style and customize Appraise to your liking."

Ha-ha-ha! I wonder what Seiya's going to say when he sees this!

I skip all the way to the Summoning Chamber after leaving Aria's room.

When I throw open the door, Seiya is glistening with sweat while trading wooden-sword blows with Adenela. Meanwhile, Cerceus is at his side, passed out due to exhaustion.

"Oh, Rista."

Seiya glances at me and stops sparring.

"Ah! I'm so sorry! I interrupted your training session!"

"I don't mind if it's you, Rista."

He's sooo sweet!

"Seiya! Aria taught me the special ability Appraise! I can see how effective items and weapons are now!"

"That'll come in handy. Use it well."

His praise makes it feel like all the hard work I put into learning it was worth it! It feels so good, I might melt.

That's when I suddenly get an idea.

Wh-what if I use Appraise on Seiya?

I secretly use Appraise while reciting, "Show me what I want to know most about Seiya." Then I see the following information appear before my very eyes:

☆RISTA'S LOVE APPRAISAL☆

-Your love rating with Seiya:	90 points
-Seiya thinks you're:	a very important person in his life.
-A tidbit of advice:	Keep doing what you're doing, and you'll be crossing the finish line in no time! Good luck!

Whooooooa! This Appraise ability is amaaaziiing! Ninety points? That means we're basically joined at the hip! And I'll be crossing the finish line in no time?! Is that my subconscious giving me advice?! I—I don't really know what's going on, but this Appraise ability is…AMAAAAAAZING!

Noticing me staring at him, Seiya curiously tilts his head.

"Hmm? Something wrong?"

"O-oh…! No! Nothing! Oh-ho-ho-ho!"

"Did you want to see my status or something?"

"Oh, yeah. I really want to, but…"

Seiya was extremely against the idea of me seeing his stats last time in fear of the information being leaked, so he persistently used the ability Fake Out to hide his attributes, but…

"It's fine. I'll show you."

Yeah baby!! I wanna see it all!! The finish line is in sight, and there's no turning back!

I use Scan and catch a glimpse of Seiya's status without Fake Out.

SEIYA RYUUGUUIN

LV: 51

HP: 145,683   MP: 25,622

ATK: 72,888   DEF: 67,693   SPD: 65,007   MAG: 28,765   GRW: 669

Resistance: Fire, Wind, Water, Lightning, Ice, Earth, Holy, Dark, Poison, Paralysis, Sleep, Curse, Instant Death, Status Ailments

Special Abilities: Fire Magic (LV: MAX), Explosion Magic (LV: 8), Magic Sword (LV: 9), EXP Boost (LV: 15), Scan (LV: 18), Fake Out (LV: 20), Synthesis (LV: 7)

Skills: Hellfire, Maximum Inferno, Phoenix Drive, Phoenix Thrust, Eternal Sword

Personality: Overly Cautious

"I—I can't believe what I'm seeing!"

His attack power is already over 70,000, and his HP is almost 150,000! He's already strong enough to take on a C-ranked world. I'm sure SS-ranked worlds are hard, but I feel like he's ready. However, as if reading my mind, Seiya shakes his head.

"This isn't enough. At the very least, I need to be at the level I was when I defeated the Great Mother of Dragons."

"Y-you mean max level?!"

"Yeah. The problem is what to do after that, though. If I don't surpass this limit, then I'm going to hit a wall in Ixphoria just like I did last time."

Seiya seems to have the same worries as Ishtar. Obviously, he'll have to hit his limit before he can even think about surpassing it. I'm guessing that's why Seiya wants to reach the max level as soon as possible.

"By the way, I still haven't learned Flight, Atomic Split Slash, or Wind Blade, even though I learned those on a lower level before. What's going on?"

"Special abilities and skills change depending on the principles of the parallel world. It looks like Flight can't be learned in Ixphoria. It also looks like the magic system is more fragmented than Gaeabrande. It appears you'll only be able to use fire magic this time."

"That's going to make things difficult."

"I know. I guess that's one of the things that makes this an SS-ranked world. But it isn't all bad. It looks like you'll be able to learn skills and abilities in Ixphoria that you weren't able to learn in Gaeabrande."

Seiya and Adenela resume training after our conversation. Unlike Cerceus, Adenela is tough. She doesn't even seem tired as she fiercely crosses swords with Seiya. Watching them battle was making me feel impatient all over again. I wanted to do something for Seiya. I wanted to help out with more than just this Appraise ability.

——*That's it!*

The idea suddenly hit me. I should adjust the gate's location to put Seiya in the best possible starting position. Since it's my first time going to this world as a goddess—a low-level one at that—I probably won't be able to make any fine adjustments without actually creating a gate. I make sure I'm away from the others as I begin to chant the spell to materialize the gate to Ixphoria. That's when Seiya suddenly looks over at me.

"Rista, what are you doing? I'm still not prepared."

"Oh, this? I'm just making some adjustments! Even though we're starting in a relatively safe town, I want to make sure the gate is in the safest area possible."

"I appreciate the thought, but…are you sure a monster isn't going to suddenly leap out from that door?"

"Don't worry! There's a powerful force field around the gate! It'll be fine!"

However…

Creeeeeeeeeak…

The gate suddenly starts to creak open on its own.

…Huh?

I stare in a daze, instead of surprise, at the door opening on its own. Standing behind it is a humanoid beast with the face of a wolf. Its muscular body is covered in silver fur. It steps into the room very naturally as if it was nothing out of the ordinary.

"Greetings, goddess of another dimension. And farewell."

Only when I hear the deep voice speak in a human tongue do I realize that my life is in danger. But by that point, the werewolf's sharp claws are already on the verge of piercing my throat.

CHAPTER 2
A Strange Feeling

Both the Divine Blade and the Goddess of War—two masters of combat—are present, but the unexpected turn of events seems to have made their minds go blank just like mine. They merely stand in mute shock.

Right before the werewolf's claws pierce my throat, I reflexively shut my eyes. As my vision becomes a world of darkness, I hear a dull sound following an intense impact. I fall to the floor, but it's strange. It wasn't my throat but my shoulders and back that were hit. When I timidly open my eyes, I see Seiya on top of me. He was the only one who reacted to the situation. He protected me before the enemy's sharp claws could slice through my throat.

"Seiya!"

But Seiya continues to limply lie on top of me without even budging.

D-did he let himself get hit by those claws to protect me?!

I take a quick glance but don't see any blood. I wish I could make sure he's okay, but there is a coldhearted voice echoing down from above.

"So this is the Hero who was summoned to save Ixphoria?"

The werewolf's eyes cast an eerie glow, changing his target from me to Seiya. As he lifts an arm into the air, his sharp claws begin emitting a jet-black aura. My instincts deny its existence. It's the same feeling I got when the emperor used the God Eater against me. There is no way I could ever forget this feeling. It's...

…Chain Destruction!

"…Die," the werewolf says in a cold, deep voice as his claws close in on Seiya.

N-no…!

I immediately throw myself on top of Seiya, reversing roles. Watching the werewolf about to strike…

"Eeeeek!"

Cerceus lets out a scream.

I'm prepared to have my soul destroyed—an eternal death…but that's when I suddenly hear the ear-piercing clang of metal hitting metal. The werewolf's claws reach neither Seiya nor me. When I look up, I see Adenela blocking the enemy's claws with a real sword that she had sheathed at her waist. Her eyes open wide as she glares at the werewolf.

"S-stay back, you f-filthy mutt…!"

The werewolf pushes her sword back, creates some distance between them, and licks his claws.

"So you're a goddess as well…which makes you our enemy."

The werewolf's claws extend in the blink of an eye. His nails the length of short swords, the werewolf gets into a battle stance to attack Adenela as she guards Seiya and me.

"Slash Disorder."

I hear cracking and creaking coming from Adenela, as if she were dislocating her joints.

"U-Ultimate Eternal Sword!"

As Adenela points the tip of her blade at the werewolf, I yell out:

"Adenela, watch out! His claws are imbued with Chain Destruction! If he fatally wounds us, our souls will be destroyed!"

But only Cerceus reacts to my warning.

"What?! If he hits us with those claws, we're really going to die?! P-please tell me you're joking! Gods can't die!"

"I'm only warning you because it *can* kill gods!"

"Noooooo! This can't be happening! I don't wanna die!" cries the Divine Blade, obviously not as tough as he looks. On the other hand, Adenela, the Goddess of War, smirks.

"Heh-heh-heh-heh! Th-there's nothing more exciting…th-than fighting to the death!"

Without a hint of hesitation, Adenela rushes toward the enemy like a carnivore nimbly leaping at its prey before unleashing Ultimate Eternal Sword. Despite the original Eternal Sword being one-handed compared to Seiya's dual-wielding version, it's so fast that afterimages of her blade are carved into the air!

And yet…the werewolf is somehow knocking each strike away with both hands! It's an unbelievable sight. Sparks fly as blades cross again and again, reminiscent of Seiya's battle in Gaeabrande against the emperor.

…Before long, I hear the dull sound of flesh being sliced open. When I look over, Adenela has backed up a few steps while covering her stomach with her free hand. Fresh blood pours out, trickling between her fingers and down her side.

"Adenela?!"

"Th-this can't be happening! The Goddess of War's Ultimate Eternal Sword lost?! What in the world is that thing?!"

While keeping an eye out for the werewolf's next attack, Adenela says to me:

"D-don't worry. I-it's just a scratch…"

The werewolf appears to have been hit by one of Adenela's attacks as well. Drips of black blood flow from a cut on his cheek. Nevertheless, it's painfully clear that Adenela was hurt worse. Unable to watch any longer, I wildly shake Cerceus.

"C-Cerceus! Valkyrie! Go get Valkyrie!"

"O-okay!"

Cerceus starts to take off, but…

"Th-that won't be necessary," Adenela softly mutters. "U-unlike the reaper, ph-physical attacks work on him. S-so there's n-no need to worry."

Adenela then raises her voice while clumsily stuttering:

"O-o-order!"

Crack! Creak! Adenela's right arm lets out a pop as it twists and turns, transforming.

"Whoa?! H-her arm…! What is that?! It's gross! And creepy! It's greepy!"

Cerceus swiftly hides behind me. While I glare at him in disgust, Adenela's arm transforms into something else. Her forearm illuminates as it becomes a shining silver blade. Her lips curl so wide that they almost touch her ears.

"Heh-heh-heh-heh-heh! D-Divine Sword: Soaring Falcon!"

I swallow my breath.

"Sh-she changed her arm...into a sword?"

Leaning forward, she hangs her sword-arm by her side as it gently sways. She defenselessly approaches the werewolf. Then...she mutters:

"U-Unlimited Eternal Sword...!"

In the blink of an eye, a storm of blades soars toward the werewolf, despite Adenela seemingly not moving a muscle.

"Mn...!"

The enemy's confident grin twists.

The standard Eternal Sword attack alternates among chopping, countering, horizontally slicing, and thrusting at an incredible speed. The exponentially quicker Ultimate Eternal Sword is no less impressive. However, Unlimited Eternal Sword is an attack that specializes solely in thrusting. In addition, her right arm, which turned into a Divine Sword after she used Soaring Falcon, slowly becomes finer as it reaches the tip, like a rapier, making it perfect for consecutive thrusting attacks.

Without a shield, it would be impossible for the werewolf to completely avoid the flurry of strikes, despite being able to outdo Ultimate Eternal Sword. The sword pierces his body each time he is unable to dodge. The werewolf leaps to the side to get away, but the Soaring Falcon curves like a whip as if Adenela was waiting for this moment. The instant the sword curls around his right arm, it gets sliced clean off.

"Gwooooooh!"

Fresh black blood pours out of the werewolf's wound as he screams.

"S-Soaring Falcon has enough p-power to do more than j-just thrusting attacks."

Wow! So this is Adenela at full power!

The tables have turned. After losing an arm, the werewolf slowly steps away from Adenela.

"Tch!"

After clicking his tongue, the werewolf turns on his heel and begins heading toward the gate from which he emerged. Cerceus yells:

"He's getting away!"

The werewolf then turns and grins smugly.

"This is fine. I've already left my mark."

His mark? What does that mean?

"I—I won't let you escape…"

Adenela charges the werewolf, closing the distance in the blink of an eye as her left arm transforms into a Japanese sword even longer than Soaring Falcon while making an ear-wrenching sound.

"D-Divine Sword: Homing Swallow…!"

Out of nowhere, Adenela begins cackling like a witch.

"Hee-hee-hee-hee-hee-hee! D-Dual Unlimited Eternal Blade…!"

With both arms transformed into swords, Adenela leaps at the werewolf as he tries to make his getaway. The werewolf's face hardens at the sight of the encroaching Goddess of War.

"D-d-d-die…!"

"A-Adenela, wait! We need him alive so we can get inform—"

But my words don't reach her. Her left sword-arm tears into the enemy's back as her right sword-arm immediately begins thrusting at lightning speed.

"Hee-hee-hee-hee-hee-hee-hee-hee!"

Copious amounts of black blood splatter across the Summoning Chamber as the werewolf is skewered and sliced to bits!

Dual Unlimited Eternal Blade…! Adenela's inimitable ultimate attack where she turns both arms into swords using Order!

Blood spurts from the enemy's body like a fountain, even getting a drop on Cerceus's cheek despite his being halfway across the room.

"Ahhhhhh! I can't take it anymore! I just want to go back to my room and drink a warm cup of chamomile tea!"

Cerceus screams pathetically, but it's hard to blame him. We are basically being forced to watch a one-sided slaughter. A few seconds go by until the werewolf is nothing more than a pile of flesh.

"Hee-hee-hee…hee-hee-hee-hee-hee!"

After bathing in the blood of her prey, Adenela looks back at Cerceus's and my frightened expressions as if she has awoken from a trance.

"…Oops."

Humanity suddenly returns to her eyes, and she looks down at the sad puddle of viscera that was once a monster.

"L-looks like I did it again…"

She awkwardly mutters as her arms suddenly change back to normal. After that, she points down toward my knees.

"Um… I-is… Is Seiya…o-okay?"

"Y-yes… He doesn't look like he was cut…"

The werewolf's claws didn't seem to touch his body. But then why…?

"I've already left my mark."

Why did he say something like that…?

Wait—!

Alarmed, I shake Seiya's body.

"Seiya! Seiya, wake up!"

But I end up worrying for nothing.

"Mn…"

Though moaning, Seiya sits up with a hand on his head.

"Thank goodness! Are you okay?!"

"Yeah, I'm fine. I'm just feeling a bit light-headed."

"Y-you are?! You should rest! Here, lie down!"

"I'm fine. More importantly, what happened to that werewolf?"

"Oh… Um… Adenela kind of…k-killed him…"

"…What?"

Seiya turns his gaze to the lifeless lump of meat on the ground, then knits his brow. Meanwhile, there isn't even a hint of Adenela's fit of passion left as she miserably lowers her head like a little girl who just broke a vase. Adenela understands how Seiya is. She's clearly prepared to be scolded by the cautious Hero, since she slaughtered the enemy without getting any information from him first.

"I-I'm sorry…"

Seiya approaches the apologetic goddess before speaking to her in a surprisingly gentle voice.

"Don't be sorry. You did the right thing. If you hadn't killed him, he would have killed me. I owe you one."

"S-Seiya…! I—I love you! I love you so much!"

The bags under Adenela's eyes suddenly vanish, and her eyes sparkle like a little schoolgirl's.

I raise my voice, sensing that Adenela's young, innocent girl act is about to go south.

"A-anyway, we need to report what happened to Great Goddess Ishtar! I mean, this is serious! The first enemy to attack the unified spirit world was a user of Chain Destruction!"

Cerceus repeatedly nods in silence. Seiya glances at him, then says:

"Could I ask you to go in my place? There's still something I need to do here."

Oh… He's going to use Hellfire on the werewolf until there's nothing left, isn't he?

I thought the usual cleanup ritual was about to start. But instead, Seiya grabs me by the arm and jerks me over.

Huh?! Wh-what the…?! Is he mad at me?! He must be! If I hadn't created that gate, then the werewolf would have never gotten in here! O-oh no! Everything was going so well between us until I messed things up!

But I've gotten worked up over nothing again. Seiya isn't mad at me. He simply tugs at my arm and rushes me.

"Come on. We don't have any time to waste. We're going to Ixphoria."

"What?! What about burning the body?! And weren't you still in the middle of training?!"

"I've trained enough."

"H-hold on! Seiya?!"

Seiya drags me over toward the gate to Ixphoria. Both Cerceus and Adenela stare at Seiya with their eyes wide, taken aback by his unexpected behavior.

S-Seiya is overly cautious, so if he says he's ready to go, then he must be… Plus, he's already over level fifty, so we'll be fine…right?

Seiya places a hand on the gate, then says:

"Let's go, Goddess."

"'G-Goddess'?! Are you referring to me?!"

"We must hurry to save the world. Innocent lives are being lost as we speak."

Hearing those uncharacteristic words come out of his mouth makes me extremely uncomfortable. Overcome with a strange feeling, I gaze at the Hero's profile as he walks through the gate.

"S-Seiya, are you sure you're ready to go?! Are you *perfectly prepared*?!"

"Of course…"

The Hero doesn't even glance at me. He gazes into the distance and says:

"Everything's gonna be okay."

CHAPTER 3
Reckless

Upon exiting the gate, we find ourselves in a dim room. The floors and walls are nothing more than wooden boards stuck together, and the window has no glass. The room seems capable of accommodating four to five people, but there are holes here and there on the floor, and the tables, chairs, and other furniture are all old and degraded. It appears to be an abandoned shack. Usually, I would want to investigate the place a little more, but something is really bothering me. I turn to the Hero still wearing jeans and a T-shirt.

"Seiya! You just called me 'Goddess' back there, didn't you? And you didn't say that you were perfectly prepared. Instead, you said, 'Everything's gonna be okay.'"

He used to say his catchphrase all the time, which is why the worries in my heart are beginning to swirl around and grow.

"I know this may sound crazy, but...you remember who I am, right?"

"You're the goddess assigned to guide me, and I'm the Hero summoned to save Ixphoria...right?"

"Y-yeah, but...what's my name? Can you remember my name?"

"It was something like...Miso Tart, wasn't it?"

"...?! It's Ristarte! How does that even sound close to 'Miso Tart'?! What about Gaeabrande?! Do you remember what happened there?!"

"'Gaeabrande'? Never even heard of it."

H-he hasn't forgotten his objective! He even recognizes that I'm a goddess! But…this is…!

I decide to use Scan to check his status, since interrogating him won't get me anywhere.

SEIYA RYUUGUUIN

LV: 51

HP: 90,854/145,683...

He lost a lot of HP! It looks like that werewolf's attack did hit him!

But what makes my eyes bulge is the unfamiliar condition under his attributes.

<Condition: Amnesia>

A-a-amnesia?! Ohhh! So that's why he can't remember anything and doesn't seem all there!

What convinces me, though, is what it says after "Personality" on his status screen. Instead of the usual "Overly Cautious," it now reads…

Personality: Reckless

I feel light-headed. Of course, what first comes to mind is what the were-wolf said before he died. *"I've already left my mark."* It looks like this is what he meant. He gave the Hero a status ailment, thus reducing our fighting strength. More importantly…this is the first time I've ever seen this status ailment! I don't know if I'd be able to treat it even if I could use my healing ability! Ahhh! What am I going to do now?! It's not fair! Ishtar let Seiya keep his memories, and we were so in love! After all that…!

Suddenly curious about Seiya's feelings for me, I used my Love Appraise ability on Seiya.

☆RISTA'S LOVE APPRAISAL☆

-Your love rating with Seiya:　　40 points

-Seiya thinks you're:　　just there.

-A tidbit of advice:　　Hmm... He's barely even aware of your existence. But if he gets his memories back, maybe...

"…?! His affection level is less than half of what it was?! 'Just there'?!"

Seiya shoots me a dubious glare as I scream.

"What are you talking about?"

"I-it's nothing… Don't worry about it…"

Y-yeah, everything's gonna be fine! Once his amnesia is cured, he'll be back to normal! It's nothing to worry about! Anyway, now that we've figured out the problem, we should head back to the spirit world and ask Ishtar how to cure him!

"Seiya, we're heading back to the unified spirit world for now!"

"Why? We just got here."

"Just trust me!"

"You're not making any sense."

The roles reverse once again, and this time, I grab Seiya by the wrist and drag him behind me. Then I reopen the gate to the spirit world and take a step inside when…

Bam!

I take a powerful blow to the forehead.

"Owww! Ow, ow, ow!"

Holding my head, I see a concrete-like white wall in front of me.

"Wh-what is this?! Why is there a wall inside the gate?!"

Thinking it's some sort of mistake, I get rid of the gate and create another…only to discover that there's still a wall inside.

"How are we gonna get back home now?! This is ridiculous! How come we could use the gate to get here but not to leave?!"

This doesn't make any sense! B-but I learned Appraise exactly for times like this! I stare hard at the white wall until a message appears.

A wall that blocks off other dimensions. It was created by an evil sorcerer's spell. Looks like it can only be destroyed by defeating the spellcaster or destroying the magic item making the wall.

I customized Appraise to speak like me, but what it says sends a chill down my spine.

"W-we can't go back to the unified spirit world?! Wait! That means we have to continue our journey in Ixphoria like this?!"

I freeze in blank amazement as if I've just lost my soul, unlike Seiya, who is standing by the window, enthusiastically waving me over.

"Hey, Goddess. Come over here. Check that out."

Still stunned, I drag my feet across the creaking wooden floors and look out the glassless window.

The first things that catch my eye are the purple sky and demolished buildings. The stagnant air greets my nostrils. Galvano is in such ruin, it's hard to believe this is the first town of our journey. After that...I gasp. Slightly in the distance are two beastkin stalking the streets! One has the face of a dog while the other looks like a cat! In their hands are chains, which are tied to naked humans walking on all fours!

"Wh-what is going on?!"

It's the complete opposite of any normal world! The beasts are walking humans like pets!

More importantly, they're the first monsters we've encountered in Ixphoria. I make sure to remain hidden while I use Scan.

BEASTKIN (DOG TYPE)

LV: 35

HP: 56,274   MP: 0

ATK: 28,754   DEF: 27,895...

BEASTKIN (CAT TYPE)

LV: 37

HP: 58,887   MP: 0

ATK: 30,008   DEF: 29,574...

"What?!"

Y-you've gotta be kidding me! We just got here, and we're already running into enemies with stats like this?! Oh...wait! They must be high-ranking enemies like the four generals in Gaeabrande! It looks like we've already run into two mini bosses!

But...

"Yo. I see you've got yourself another filthy pet."

"Still better than that wretched thing *mew* keep at home."

"Are you two even feeding those things? They're nothing but skin and bones. At this rate, they'll be dead in no time."

A beastkin with a bird's face, a beastkin with a boar's face—beastkin speaking human tongue begin to gather in the streets one by one. There's even another group of beastkin talking slightly in the distance! To make matters worse, they're all at an extremely high level! The place is crawling with enemies who have around 50,000 HP and over 30,000 ATK!

"I was wrong...! Even the small-fry enemies in this world are superstrong!"

And there are so many of them, to boot! Even though I just took a quick glance so I wouldn't get caught, I saw a few dozen! There are probably hundreds of them living in this town!

"Wh-what a terrifying world!"

My body begins trembling, and I look to the Hero for guidance, but... Seiya isn't there.

"...Huh?"

Seiya already has a hand on the door. Eyes popping wide and startled out of my wits, I scream:

"What do you think you're doing?!"

Seiya calmly replies:

"I'm gonna go fight them. Do you seriously expect me to watch them chain up humans and treat them like pets? Those monsters are dead."

"But you're unarmed, and you don't have any armor!"

"What's wrong with fighting with my bare hands in jeans and a T-shirt?"

"Everything! You're not going to a friend's sleepover! This is an SS-ranked world! There's no way you can take on a powerful horde of monsters like that without any equipment!"

I peel Seiya away from the door, dragging him back to the center of the room.

"Relax for a bit, will ya?! You're severely ill! So just sit back and wait until your amnesia has healed!"

"I'm fine. I don't have amnesia."

"You can't even remember my name!"

"Yeah, I can. Rice Tart, right?"

"Ristarte! You weren't even close!"

I get a terrible headache as I raise my voice. With a hand on my temple, I shake my head.

"Listen, Seiya. The werewolf did a number on you, and you're not at your best. Not only do you have amnesia, but your 140,000 HP is now barely at 90,000. I want to heal you, but I can't use any healing spells this time. So come on...just rest for a while, okay?"

"I don't think it matters how much HP I have, but...*sigh*. You're one cautious goddess."

What the...?! I—I can't even describe how annoying it is being called "cautious" by Seiya! The old Seiya would have immediately healed himself even if he had lost only one HP!

Regardless, it looks like he gave up trying to leave. Instead, he's busily looking out the window.

"H-hey, if you're gonna keep looking out the window like that, do you think you could be a little more subtle about it? Someone's gonna see you if you keep sticking your head out the window."

I watch the reckless Hero with bated breath until his eyes light up as if he found something.

"There's a new beastkin."

"What...?"

I approach the window and slowly peek outside. Just as Seiya claimed, a massive beastkin boldly stands with his arms crossed before the group of monsters walking their naked human pets.

He looks twice as big as the others. He's stout, with the horrific face of a pig. Unlike the other unarmed beastkin, the colossal orc is wearing a steel breastplate. Every time he moves, I can see the giant ax-like weapon on his back. The orc's imposing aura is clearly different from the others. He glares at the cat and dog beastkin.

"What is wrong with you twooo? Ya need to take better care of yer slaves. Look how skinny those poor things are. Are ya feeding 'em enooough?"

After the orc speaks in a drawling voice, the cat and dog beastkin look at each other before bowing.

"F-forgive us, Lord Bunogeos."

"How many times are ya feeding them a daaay?"

"I—I feed mine once a day..."

"*Meow...* I only feed mine once at night as well..."

"Ya numbskulls. Ya need to feed 'em three times a daaay. Make sure to give 'em a bath every once in a while as well. Neeever forget that it's our job to make good slaves for the Demon Lord."

Despite his appearance, he seems to care more about the humans than the other beastkin. He must be a pretty high-ranking orc, given how the surrounding monsters respect him. He's still an orc, though. I doubt he's much stronger than his furry friends.

When I casually use Scan just to make sure...I'm speechless.

BEAST BUNOGEOS

LV: 67

HP: 338,547   MP: 0

ATK: 300,019   DEF: 258,344   SPD: 77,777   MAG: 794   GRW: 674

Resistance: Fire, Wind, Water, Lightning, Ice, Earth, Holy, Dark, Poison, Paralysis, Sleep, Instant Death, Status Ailments

Special Abilities: Dark God's Blessing (LV: MAX), Total Magic Nullification (LV: MAX)

Skills: God Chopper, Vacuum Shredder

Personality: Short-tempered

Th-th-this can't be happening! He has basically the same stats as the powered-up emperor who Seiya barely managed to defeat! And Total Magic Nullification?! It seems we can't count on using magic to damage him! Th-this can't be real! Gae-abrande looks like a joke compared to this place! Common sense means nothing here!

The naked humans being walked by the dog and cat beastkin appear to be adults. Their rib cages are sticking out. They're filthy, and they look weak. They're probably being treated like garbage. Tears roll down the woman's face, and the man clings to the kind orc.

"Oh, Lord Bunogeos! Thank you! Thank you so much!"

The orc's expression clouds over the moment the unclothed man touches his foot while expressing gratitude.

"…Ya touched me."

"Huh?"

"Ya touched me."

Suddenly baring his fangs, Bunogeos screams:

"Ya filthy humaaaaaan! How dare ya touch me with yer shit-stained haaands!"

"Eek!"

The man yells and removes his hand, but Bunogeos has already lifted the giant ax on his back into the air. An ominous black aura radiates from the weapon.

"Th-that's Chain Destruction! He has a weapon that can destroy our souls, too?!"

I shudder. The slave outside pitifully begs for his life.

"Forgive me! Please forgive me!"

But his words do not reach the reddened orc through his rage. Bunogeos mercilessly swings his ax, blood spraying as he splits the man in half.

"Ahhhhhh!!"

The woman screams before hiding behind her owner's—the cat-faced beastkin's—legs. As if her scream brought Bunogeos back to his senses, he suddenly puts on an embarrassed expression.

"Whoops. Looks like I killed another one. Ah, whatever. There are plenty more where that came from."

After witnessing the terrifying event, the man to my side begins trembling with rage.

"He's going to pay for that."

Seiya's usual calm expression is twisted with rage as he starts heading for the door.

"S-Seiya?! Calm down! This isn't like you!"

"Someone was just killed right in front of me. There's no way I'm going to sit back and watch."

"Listen, Seiya! If you go out there, you're going to die! His stats were slightly better than yours, you know?!"

"It's fine. I can take him."

"Based on what?! Check his stats! Not even your beloved fire magic is going to do much damage to him!"

"I saw his status, which is exactly why I feel I can take him."

"...Huh?"

"Goddess, did you notice something when you saw his status?"

"'Notice something'?"

Seiya lets out his usual "Hmph."

"Think back to his speed."

"W-well, it was lower than his attack and defense, so I don't think focusing on his speed is a bad idea. But even then, your speed is only sixty-five thousand. All your stats are lower than his."

"That's not what I'm talking about."

Seiya gives me a piercing gaze, and I swallow air.

O-oh! He must have a plan! Seiya always comes up with unbelievable strategies to defeat powerful enemies! He may have become more reckless, but he has still got a good head on his shoulders!

"Tell me the strategy you came up with, Seiya!"

Seiya smugly replies:

"His speed is 77,777. In other words, a matching set of sevens. Plus, seven is a lucky number."

"...Huh?"

"You get it now? ...I can handle him!"

"...?! Wait, hold on! What kind of stupid reasoning is that?! If that's all it took to win, then everybody would be doing it!"

I'm gonna win 'cause seven's my lucky number! is something a stupid elementary school kid would say. I feel beyond disgusted and just want to cry. Regardless, the reckless Hero heads to the door.

"I can't let that pig get away with this. I'm gonna end him."

"Stop! You can't! He's going to kill you! Listen, Seiya! He has a weapon that can destroy our souls! Normally, the Hero will return to their own world if they die, but if he kills you, you'll never be able to return to your world! You could die."

"So what? Death isn't something to be feared. Death is an inevitable part of life, so why not face it head-on and accept it? All right, I've made up my mind. This is where I die."

H-how reckless can you get?! How am I gonna stop him now?!

Seiya is worked up after seeing Bunogeos kill the slave. He heads for the door, paying no heed to my calls.

"Stooooooooop!"

I manage to attach myself to his waist, but he doesn't stop.

Ahhhhhh! Why?! Can things get any worse?! I'm starting to miss when he used to be overly cautious!

"I'm not kidding! Stop! Pleeeease!"

Driven into a corner, I scream and beg as tears flow down my cheeks. Seiya looks at me, then shows a hint of concern.

"What's wrong, Goddess? Why are you crying?"

"B-because...*sniffle*...you won't...*sniffle*...listen to anything I say...!"

Seiya scratches his head.

"Sorry. I didn't mean to trouble you. It looks like I got a little too worked up."

Huh...? S-Seiya's apologizing?

Seiya regains his cool and takes a seat on the floor.

H-huh, I guess Seiya's naturally just kind when his personality is reckless, unlike when he's overly cautious...

While I wipe away my tears, Seiya lowers his head to me.

"I'm sorry. I'll do whatever you think is best."

"Good. As long as you understand, then we won't have a problem. Thanks, Seiya..."

"Please forgive my behavior, Racetrack."

"...?! How many times do I have to tell you! It's Ristarte! You're doing that on purpose, aren't you?!"

I cried, got angry—I'm an emotional wreck.

Rattle! Rattle! Rattle! I suddenly hear the floor begin to rattle, and my body starts to violently shake.

"Wh-wh-wh-what's going on?!"

Thereupon, the floor in the corner of the room starts to rise until someone in filthy, tattered clothes comes crawling out.

"A-an enemy attack?!"

Seiya gets into a fighting stance, and I promptly hide behind him. But the filthy person simply stares. Before long, they remove their hood, revealing an old man with white hair.

"Hurry. This way."

The old man points to the hole in the floor from which he came.

"There aren't any terrifying beastkin in here. Now, come. You must hurry."

The old man urges us to move, but I'm hesitant. I mean, he just randomly came crawling out from beneath the floorboards. There's no way I can trust him that easily. But Seiya wastes no time.

"He seems like a good guy. Let's go."

"H-hold up! Seiya?!"

I whisper:

"Don't you think this is just a little suspicious?! He came crawling out from beneath the floorboards! You shouldn't trust people so easily!"

"He could have jumped down from the ceiling for all I care. Everything starts with trust."

"Sure, but this is an SS-ranked world, so—"

"It's going to be okay. Look at that old man's clear eyes."

I sense no hint of evil when I take a hard look at the old man's eyes. If anything, they're…

As I hesitate, the mysterious visitor takes out a pendant of a cross that hung under his tattered clothes.

"There is no need to worry. I am Luke, Galvano's priest. Well, I *was* a priest until the town turned into…what I'm sure you saw."

The priest's lips slightly curl.

"I experienced a faint yet divine revelation a few days ago. The Lord told me that a Hero would appear in this ruined world to save it… And then you two appeared in this shack, which leads to our underground shelter."

Th-there's a secret underground shelter below this shack?! That sounds a little too conven— Oh! Ishtar adjusted our starting point so we would end up in this shack! Then she gave divine revelation to this priest!

Father Luke cheerfully smiles as he waves us over.

"Now, come. Join me in our underground settlement, Little Light."

CHAPTER 4
Little Light

We follow Father Luke into the hole in the floor to find a staircase made from packed dirt. After heading a few steps underground, I hear a sound coming from above, and the opened floor begins to automatically close. Furthermore, the steps disappear from the staircase behind us as we continue to descend.

"Is this...magic?"

"Yes, this is Eich's earth magic. There are a few other entrances to our underground settlement within the town, but they are made so that the beastkin won't be able to come inside even if they find them."

It looks like they had some mage named Eich use their earth magic to create an entire settlement for humans underground. With just enough heat, earth magic can create vast underground caverns. However, you would still need the extremely rare and unique gift to do so. Father Luke regards my expression and smiles as if he knows what I'm thinking.

"Eich is the younger sister of the legendary mage Colt. That's why."

Colt...I'm pretty sure that was the name of the sorcerer who fought by Seiya's side against Ixphoria's Demon Lord...and was devoured by the Demon Lord just like I was in my past life...

Every few steps, there is a light on the wall to the side of the staircase. Unlike lamps or torches, these lights are buried in the dirt and illuminated like glowing rocks. I can only assume they're glowstones.

While walking down what seems like an endless staircase, Seiya asks the priest:

"Why did you decide to hide underground, though? Wouldn't you be able to skip town if you used that earth magic?"

"We cannot leave Galvano. As long as Bunogeos has the spell stone, any human who steps outside of the town will turn to ash. Regardless, even if we could escape, there is no place in Ixphoria where humans can live in peace."

"Oh! Maybe that magic item's the reason we can't return to the unified spirit world!"

After explaining how there was a wall inside the gate, Father Luke tells me I'm probably right.

"Bunogeos, the monster who holds the spell stone, was created after the Demon Lord took over the world and received the Dark God's Blessing. He now works for the Beast Emperor Grandleon, who rules over this continent of Rhadral."

I'm taken aback by what I hear.

"W-wait, wait, wait! Bunogeos isn't the boss of this continent?"

"Bunogeos only rules this town. The one who rules over the continent is Grandleon, a monster with powers that far surpass Bunogeos's."

But Bunogeos already has better stats than the four generals in Gaeabrande! Is he telling me the ruler here is even stronger than that?!

Oblivious to my concerns, Seiya bumps his chest with a fist.

"Hmph. A worthy opponent."

"Oh, Chosen One! We are ever blessed by your presence!"

The priest seems ecstatic, and…um…I hate to be the bearer of bad news, but this Hero is all talk. He wouldn't even be able to defeat Bunogeos in his current state. He'd be utterly destroyed. No doubt.

"We have arrived."

The long staircase finally comes to an end, and we now stand before a giant double door. As if giving a secret signal, the priest thumps the door with the metal door knocker with absolutely no rhythm. With that, the door opens before us.

"Whoa…!"

I gasp in admiration as I gaze inside. The settlement is so vast that it's hard to believe we're underground. The high ceiling sports countless glowstones, illuminating the private houses lined up below. I can even see luscious green fields with crops in the distance. Seiya nods as if impressed.

"Hmm. Impressive. It's like an entire other town underground."

"We grow our own crops, and while they aren't much, we're self-sufficient. The food we grow isn't exactly the healthiest, though, due to the glowstones being our only light source..."

It appears everyone was told in advance that the priest was going to bring us here. Dozens of men and women of all ages line up before us. I smile and wave at them, but they don't respond.

"H-huh?"

The people of Gaeabrande had great respect for the Goddess and Hero, but everyone here glares at us distantly. Just as I start to feel a little uncomfortable, a young man outfitted in steel armor emerges from the crowd and approaches us. He has short hair and a piercing gaze.

"This is Braht, the leader of Little Light—"

Even though the priest is introducing him, the young man continues walking straight for Seiya, then grabs him by the collar. In a threatening tone, he says:

"That face... I knew it! You're still alive?!"

"Wh-what do you think you're doing?!"

The priest is taken aback as well.

"Braht?! What is the meaning of this?!"

Braht's eyes are locked on Seiya, but he yells to the priest:

"Father Luke! You don't know?! This is the Hero who lost to the Demon Lord a year ago!"

"What?!"

Father Luke gasps. Braht then continues spewing hatred.

"I hear that Colt and Princess Tiana from the Kingdom of Termine were killed by the Demon Lord as well! But the Hero ran away and went into hiding! And yet he has the audacity to show his face here like nothing happened?!"

After I died as Princess Tiana, I was reborn as a goddess and spent the last hundred years in the spirit world where the flow of time moves more slowly. That's why I look completely different from the Princess Tiana I saw in the crystal ball. But for Seiya, all this happened only one year ago. His appearance has hardly changed. In other words, everyone who has ever met Seiya will instantly recognize him.

Braht violently pushes Seiya back.

"Seiya?!"

I rush over to help him up, but the other townspeople behind me start yelling as well.

"H-he's right! I saw the last Hero a year ago, and that's the same guy!"

"You're right! *Leave it to me*, my ass! You talked a big game, but then you lost to the Demon Lord and Ixphoria was destroyed!"

"It's all your fault! My family is dead because of you!"

Almost everyone in the settlement begins pelting Seiya with insults and complaints, and before I know it, we're surrounded by people with clubs and rakes.

Wh-what?! Not only are the abnormally strong enemies our enemies, but all the humans living in Ixphoria are as well?! I-is this what it means to be an SS-ranked world?! What's Seiya going to do?!

But Seiya looks back at me in a relaxed manner.

"Hey, Goddess, is what these people are saying true? Have I been to this world before?"

Keeping it a secret won't help anything. I tell him the truth.

"Yes… This is the second time you've come to Ixphoria, and the first time you came…you failed."

"I see…"

Seiya instantly throws his head to the ground.

Whaaaaaat?!

I never imagined he'd ever do that! *That* rude Hero is bowing before them! And he speaks up in a deeply troubled voice, to boot!

"I'm sorry. I beg your forgiveness."

N-no! I can't take it anymore! I don't want to see Seiya groveling! What he's doing might be admirable, but…but…I don't want to see him like this!

The townspeople briefly fall silent in reaction to Seiya's sudden apology, but it isn't long before a man begins trembling.

"Th-this is bullshit! Apologizing isn't going to fix what you've done!"

"Colt and Princess Tiana are dead because of you! You killed them!"

"Yeah!"

Somebody throws a rock at Seiya, which he doesn't even attempt to dodge. The rock hitting his head starts a ripple effect, and in the blink of an eye, the people of Little Light raise their hands against him.

"H-hey?! Stop! Stop it!"

"Shaddup!"

I try to end the violence, but somebody pushes me to the ground.

"I told you to stop! Don't you dare lay another hand on Seiya!"

I scream, but the violence doesn't abate. Old women coldly glare at me as I panic.

"Hmph. Some 'goddess' you are. You're no different from us humans."

"That redheaded goddess from last time was worthless, too. I heard the Demon Lord ate her. How pathetic."

"Don't you dare talk about Aria that way!"

When I glare at her, she looks back at me with an even fiercer stare.

"The world wouldn't have been destroyed if you 'goddesses' weren't so useless!"

The old men slowly approach me.

Ahhh! Are they gonna hit me, too?!

As I shiver in fear, Seiya manages to get up and stand in front of me.

"Stop. This is my fault."

"S-Seiya…!"

"Leave Recycle Bin out of this."

Who are you calling "Recycle Bin"?! He's getting worse with each guess!

At any rate, it looks like he made the townspeople even angrier by defending me, and they start hitting him again. Seiya's at level 50. His defense is high, so the damage should be minimal…but even so, I can't watch.

Why is this happening?! We came to save this world! What did we do to deserve this?! As the tears begin to well in my eyes…

"Enough."

A high, dignified voice radiates, and the townspeople instantly freeze. They turn their gazes at a young girl of tender years. She's dressed in rags like the others, except for the accessories around her dainty arms.

Out of nowhere, somebody murmurs:

"Eich!"

"Everyone, that is enough. My brother, Colt, wouldn't have wanted this."

Eich, the mage who used her earth magic to create this settlement, is even younger than I imagined. If I had to guess, I'd say she's around six or seven years old. The girl, who is even younger than Elulu, silences the entire settlement with only a few words.

"Th-thank you…"

I thank her, but she gives me a frigid stare.

"Goddess, Hero, I would like to thank you for coming. However, I do not expect anything from you, for there is no one who can defeat the Demon Lord Ultimaeus."

Demon Lord…Ultimaeus…!

The moment I hear the Demon Lord's name, an indescribable chill shoots through my entire body. My soul must be reacting to the name of the monster who killed me in a past life.

"This world is beyond saving."

Eich turns on her heel and leaves. The citizens spit at us and click their tongues before leaving as well. Only Father Luke, Braht, a battered and bruised Hero, and I remain. Braht shoots me a glance.

"Goddess…Recycle Bin, was it?"

"No, it's Ristarte…"

"Whatever. What I want to know is if you're serious about defeating the Demon Lord and saving this world."

"That's…the plan…"

"And what can you do?"

I want to tell him that I have the ability to heal, but that power is currently sealed away.

"…Appraisal."

A look of disgust flashes across Braht's face.

"Great. So can I. Is that seriously all you can do?"

"I—I have wings. I can fly."

I should be able to use Rista Wing if I can just get permission from Ishtar!

"Order!"

I yell out, but nothing happens.

…Yep. I figured it wouldn't work. I've lost contact with Ishtar. It was pretty obvious that this would be the case, seeing as I can't even return to the spirit world.

"You're useless!"

As his stare bores a hole in my heart, I sharpen my tone.

"I—I can't die! Goddesses can't die!"

"So you're immortal? Is that true?"

Braht looks to Father Luke by my side for answers instead of me. He nods.

"According to legend, gods cannot die. I believe she is telling the truth."

Heh! How do you like them apples? So what does he think about me now? Oh…! B-but now that I think about it, I could die if the enemy uses Chain Destruction…and that werewolf and Bunogeos can both use it, so…

I decide to tell the truth.

"Actually, I can die sometimes."

"…?! 'Sometimes'?! What does that even mean?! So you're not immortal after all!" Braht screams out.

A few moments go by, and he heaves a sigh as he scratches his head.

"A goddess who can 'sometimes' die and a Hero who failed once already. What a joke. Looks like the heavens have no intention of saving Ixphoria."

Braht turns his cold gaze on us again.

"But you're going to make yourselves useful now that you're here. You claim you're here to defeat the Demon Lord, so at the very least, you can kill Bunogeos, right?"

"Th-that's, uh…"

Seiya was already at max level when he defeated the powered-up emperor in Gaeabrande, so there is absolutely no way he's going to be able to defeat Bunogeos, who boasts similar stats. He's only at level 50.

"All right. I'll go take care of him."

Seiya, who was probably listening the entire time, sits up despite being bruised and battered.

"Bunogeos created a market on the outskirts of town to buy and sell humans. He raises slaves there. Go defeat him and free the slaves."

Whether or not we can defeat Bunogeos is beside the point. For now, we just need to get out of here as soon as possible. However, the outside world is swarming with powerful monsters.

"At least let us prepare!"

I beg Braht. If we're going to leave Little Light, we'll need some weapons and armor.

Braht scoffs. He then pats Father Luke on the shoulder before taking off. Wearing a gentle smile, Father Luke points at a man sitting on a mat slightly in the distance.

"That's the item shop."

Ishtar handed me some currency before we came to Ixphoria just like she did before we left for Gaeabrande. I take the pouch of money out of my pocket and head toward the item shop…but the wares lined up on the mat are mostly either glowstones or farming tools. Other than that, all I see are daily necessities on display. I was hoping there would be something I could use to cure Seiya's amnesia, but it doesn't even look like there are any healing or antidotal herbs.

I end up just purchasing hemp clothes and get Seiya to change out of his T-shirt and jeans, if only to make sure he doesn't stand out any more than he already does.

"Hey, Father Luke, are there any weapon or armor shops around here?"

"Unfortunately not. We simply do not have the resources."

It's just like Aria said. There are no easy ways to get equipment in Ixphoria anymore. As I drop my shoulders, I hear a guttural voice call out to me.

"Hey, you. Ever think about changing your class? Just let me know if you're interested."

Father Luke introduces the old man with almost no front teeth.

"This is Enzo. He's Little Light's baptist. If you want, he can change your class for you."

Seiya gives a quizzical stare.

"Is my class not Hero?"

Enzo shakes his head.

"There aren't any Hero classes in this world… Let me have a look. Hmm… It says here you're a Spellblade and you specialize in fire magic."

Seiya learned a lot of fire magic in Gaeabrande, so it's no surprise that fire magic is part of his base class. He's already relearned powerful fire-sword attacks like Phoenix Drive and Phoenix Thrust as well.

Enzo flashes his gums.

"It's an advanced class that combines both the Warrior and Mage classes.

Heh. I guess that's why you're the Hero. But if you switch jobs, you'll be able to choose two different classes... So what'll it be?"

Personally, I wanted to ask him what other kinds of classes there were, but...

"I'll stick with what I've got."

Seiya doesn't think twice. If he was still cautious, he would have asked for details and carefully examined his choices, but... Well, I agree he shouldn't change classes as things currently are. A Spellblade is an advanced class, and there probably aren't many other jobs like it. Plus, it would probably take some time getting used to a new class, and time is something we don't have.

"All right, then. Let's head out."

Getting impatient, Seiya goes on ahead and makes his way back to Little Light's entrance. However, when we reach the door, Father Luke says, as if suddenly remembering something, "Please wait here for a moment," and jogs off. After some time passes, he comes rushing back with a sheathed blade in hand.

"Please take this sword with you. It's rusty, but it's better than nothing."

"Th-thank you so much!"

I thank the priest, and he waves. After that, I glance to my side to see Seiya's face light up as he holds the rusty sword in the air.

"Perfect. I'll have no problem winning now with this."

"You make it sound like you just got Excalibur. That thing is a rusty hunk of junk."

"Everything's gonna be okay."

"I'd rather hear you say, *I'm perfectly prepared...*"

"Why would I say that?"

"*Sigh...*"

I retire from Little Light, carrying this overpowering anxiety with me.

CHAPTER 5
The Difference in Power

After climbing stairs for what seems like forever, I can finally see a wooden board up ahead. I push up the floorboard and crawl back onto the surface with Seiya. I survey the room. The walls are dirty, and the furniture is worn out… We find ourselves once again in an abandoned shack, but it's different from the one we were in when we first met Father Luke.

I nervously approach the window and look outside, and the scenery is different from earlier as well. While we climbed up the same number of stairs, it looks like Eich's earth magic connected us to another house. Beastkin gather in the distance, making a commotion. When I strain my eyes and look ahead, I see humans lined up with shackles around their necks and wrists. That must be the slave market Braht was talking about.

"Seiya, you don't need to take what Braht said seriously. There is no way you can beat Bunogeos at your current level. The best thing you can do is find a way to save the slaves in the market. And the people of Little Light might change their minds about us if we can pull it off. Anyway—"

While looking out the window, I continue speaking to Seiya until I discover something unbelievable.

…He's casually walking down the street with the rusty sword!

"Huhhhhhh?!"

I scream and immediately rush out of the shack.

"Heeeeey!! What the hell do you think you're doing?!"

As I grab his shoulders and shake his brains into mush, he stares back at me with a puzzled look in his eyes.

"I need to defeat Bunogeos, right? How am I supposed to do that without going outside?"

"No, that's why you need to listen. We're going to free the…slaves…"

Around a dozen beastkin curiously stare at us as we argue in the middle of the main road.

"Hey… Those humans aren't wearing collars."

"Are they strays?"

Ahhhhhhhhh!! We're dooooooooomed!!

My heart hammers against my chest, but Seiya doesn't seem to be concerned in the least.

"I was going to fight them anyway, so this saves me some time."

Seiya breezily approaches the beastkin with his rusty sword leaning against his shoulder.

"Huh?! What's wrong with this human?!"

As if creeped out by Seiya's daunting behavior, the beastkin don't even draw their weapons. Instead, they part like the Red Sea, making way for Seiya. I hurriedly follow behind.

W-wait. What? Are we really just gonna be able to waltz right in and free the slaves?

But after walking a few more meters, a fox-faced beastkin screams as if he knows what we're up to.

"Hey!! Pull yourselves together! Stop them!"

"R-right!"

The fox person's orders prompt all the nearby beastkin to surround us.

Y-yeah, I guess I shouldn't be surprised… It was too good to be true…

A rhino beastkin with rugged skin stands before us, licking his lips.

"If these humans don't belong to anyone, that means…"

The fox beastkin replies:

"Exactly. Nobody's gonna get mad at us if we eat them…"

I prepare for battle as I listen to their vile conversation.

I-it looks like we have to fight!

I use Scan to check the stats of the rhino beastkin, the fox beastkin, and their three companions. It's just as I feared. Everyone's attack is over

30,000! They're all really strong! But it appears they're waiting for us to make the first move. Capitalizing on the moment, I tightly grab on to a fistful of my own hair and yank it out. While the move is painful, this is no time to complain.

"Seiya, here! Take this! You know what to do with it, right?"

"Of course."

Seiya nods, then takes the strip of blond hair and attaches it to his bangs. The blond hair glitters among his shiny black hair, giving it just the right accent.

"No!!" I scream. "Those aren't extensions, Seiya! They're for synthesizing!"

"Huh? What's that?"

"Synthesis! It's one of your abilities! That sword is rusty, but it's still a steel sword! If you synthesize it with my hair, you can make a platinum sword!"

I take his hand, then force the hair and sword into it. Thereupon, a blinding light radiates, instantly transforming the rusty blade into a divine, glittering platinum sword. Seiya's face lights up just like the platinum sword itself.

"What a wonderful sword! I bet I could defeat the Demon Lord with this!"

No, probably not. In fact, I'm worried if he's even going to be able to get himself out of this pinch.

It isn't long before the fox beastkin loses control and yells:

"I got first dibs!"

As the fox beastkin leaps in to attack…

"Eek!"

I double over in fright, but Seiya lunges before me. Almost instantly, I hear something cracking in the hand in which he's holding his platinum sword, as if his joints are dislocating.

"Eternal Sword!"

In the blink of an eye, countless afterimages of the platinum sword soar through the air, heading right for the fox beastkin. By the time the blur is gone, the enemy's body is already sliced to ribbons. Blood spews into the air as numerous chunks of meat fall to the ground.

"Y-you'll pay for that…!"

The other four beastkin lunge at Seiya to avenge their comrade! There's no way he can use Eternal Sword to stop this many enemies at once!

However...

"Maximum Inferno!"

Seiya's free hand is already engulfed in flames! Before the beastkin can even reach him, the crimson flames shoot off his arm like chains and swallow the enemies.

"Arghhh!"

Their agonizing cries ring out as they catch fire, burning as Maximum Inferno's intense heat instantly turns them into charred corpses that fall lifelessly to the ground. Seiya raises his still-burning hand into the air.

"...Get out of the way or be reduced to ash."

Seiya briskly walks ahead after the nearby beastkin, who were watching, timidly back away.

H-he killed four beastkin in the blink of an eye?! He only used Maximum Inferno in Gaeabrande to dispose of corpses and distract the enemy...so I never knew it was such a high-level spell!

While struck with admiration, I notice something... The rhino beastkin, covered in soot, was able to withstand the fire thanks to his tough skin, and he's about to charge Seiya from behind!

"Seiya, behind you! He's still alive!"

I shout out to him, but he doesn't even look back! Even then, his fiery platinum sword is already under his arm, stabbing the rhinoceros monster between the eyes!

"Phoenix Thrust...!"

After witnessing their fellow beastkin fall to the ground...

"Wh-what kind of human is this?!"

"He's too strong!"

The surrounding enemies seem to have lost all will to fight. I swallow hard.

He's very reckless now...but he still has extraordinary fighting skills! I guess regardless of what his personality is like, Seiya Ryuuguuin's talents are still one in a million!

Elated, I look ahead and see a few dozen slaves chained up.

"Seiya! We have to free the slaves over there! After that, we can head back to Little Light!"

Seiya and I rush over to the slaves.

"You're all safe now!"

While Seiya keeps watch, I remove the frightened slaves' wrist and ankle shackles. But by the time I free the last of them, the silence is suddenly broken.

"Heeeeeey! What's going on over here?"

A chill creeps up my spine when I hear the familiar, drawling tone. A massive monster pushes through the crowd of beastkin.

"Th-this can't be happening. Why now?!"

The orc—the ruler of this town—Bunogeos is headed right for us! After taking us in, he scratches the back of his neck, then casually says:

"Ohhh, are you the Hero and Goddess? It's just like what that tawny-haired demon saaaid: 'A messenger of the gods will soon arrive to free the slaves.'"

A demon with tawny hair? One who's aware of what we're doing? Was the werewolf who invaded the spirit world guided by this demon, too?

Beastkin begin circling around Seiya and me, seemingly relieved now that Bunogeos is here. It's only a few seconds until there are dozens of them. However, Bunogeos shakes his hand at them.

"You guys can fall baaack. I'll handle thiiis."

This could be our only chance! I subtly whisper to Seiya:

"Seiya! Now's our chance! Use Maximum Inferno to create a smoke screen, then grab the slaves and run!"

"Run? When the boss is already here?"

"You can't beat him, Seiya! Besides, the slaves' lives are our priority, right?!"

"Well...I guess."

I somehow manage to talk Seiya out of engaging, but Bunogeos lets out a vile chuckle as if he knows exactly what we're going to do.

"You're not gettin' away from meee. Well, you could run if you wanted, but I'd just chop this slave's head right offfff."

Before I even realize, the orc is holding a woman in tattered clothes in

one hand. She struggles in agony as he tightens his grip around her neck. That's when the Hero's piercing gaze locks onto Bunogeos.

"Goddess, I can't just abandon that hostage and run. I'm going to defeat Bunogeos here and save all the slaves."

Mn…! What he's saying is very heroic, b-but there's no way he can beat that orc!

Once he realizes that Seiya is willing to fight, Bunogeos tosses the woman behind him and reaches for the ax on his back.

"Chain Destruction…was it? Once I hit ya with this, neither yooou nor the goddess will be able to come back to liiife."

"Wh-why do you have that?! Did that demon give you that, too?!"

"That's none o' yer busineeeeess."

…While I distract Bunogeos, Seiya infuses his sword with flames. Before Bunogeos can even draw his ax…

"Die…! Phoenix Drive!"

Seiya unleashes an attack with a powerful roar, but Bunogeos deeply inhales with an air of confidence. Immediately, my hair and dress start fluttering as everything around me is sucked in. Bunogeos expels the air he inhaled directly at the charging Hero.

"Mn…!"

The powerful gale stops Seiya in his tracks and extinguishes the flames on his sword as if blowing out a birthday candle.

"Weeee-hee-hee. Wouldn't want to start a fire, now, would weee?"

Bunogeos neutralizes the magic sword through sheer force alone, but Seiya still leaps at him.

"Then how about this? Eternal Sword!"

Since he can't use Phoenix Drive anymore, Seiya switches to Adenela's special attack without missing a beat. I inwardly applaud Seiya for his quick judgment, but…

"Hmm? That ticklesss."

The orc takes each one of Seiya's consecutive hits yet shows no sign of injury. But Seiya doesn't give up. He continues attacking with Eternal Sword until his arm suddenly stops. That's when I notice…that Bunogeos is holding the platinum sword's blade!

"It doesn't really hurt, buuut…you're starting to annoy meeeeee!"

With his other thick arm, he buries a punch right into Seiya's stomach. Seiya's feet lift off the ground with a *thud*.

"Urgh…!"

"Seiya!!"

The Hero crumbles with just a single punch, and Bunogeos's expression can only be described as disgust.

"Whaaat? That's it? I didn't even need my ax. Didn't think the Hero would be this weeeak. Wait. Am I just too strooong?"

I-it was like fighting a baby! Seiya didn't stand a chance! It's exactly how I imagined it would go down, though. Seiya's attack power isn't even high enough to leave a scratch on Bunogeos. There's just too big a gap between their stats.

We're no longer in any position to save the slaves! We need to find a way to escape!

I instinctively sprint toward Seiya, but the dog beastkin stops in front of me before chopping my neck with his hand.

"Hng…!"

And just like that, I collapse at Seiya's side. As I slowly fade out of consciousness, I see the ax on Bunogeos's back out of the corner of my eye.

Oh… He's going to use that ax and destroy our souls… Our journey ends here…

"M-mn…"

How much time has passed? I place a hand on my bruised neck while sitting up. The area is dark, but I see thick iron bars before me. It looks like I'm in a cell of some sort. There's another cell next to mine…

"Seiya?!"

Seiya is curled up on the floor, disarmed and lying on his side.

"Are you okay?! Seiya, wake up!"

"Y-yeah…"

Seiya sits up as if he heard my cries. He clutches his stomach like he's in pain, but it doesn't seem to be life-threatening.

"Thank goodness you're okay!"

But without missing a beat…

"I wouldn't get so excited if I were you…"

I hear a voice coming from right behind me. I turn around to find the girl Bunogeos took hostage sitting in the corner of the cell. I'm relieved.

"Thank goodness you're okay, too! What about the other slaves?"

"No clue. Seeing as they're not here, I'm guessing Bunogeos temporarily removed the curse of the spell stone and sold them somewhere outside of town."

"Wh-what?!"

"Oh, don't worry about them. They're the lucky ones. They're still alive. We should be more worried about ourselves…"

She continues to speak as if she was talking about something mundane like the weather.

"Because you and me—we're about to be Bunogeos's food."

"H-huh?! You mean he's gonna eat us?! I thought this town produced slaves?! Bunogeos said—"

"That's what he says when others are listening. But he secretly likes to eat young women. Oh…speak of the devil. Here he comes."

The massive orc heavily drags his feet this way. First, he looks at Seiya in his cell and smirks.

"Lord Grandleon's gonna be thrilled when I hand ya over to himmm. Weeee-hee-hee."

Cheerfully rubbing his stomach, he walks over to our cell next and carefully stares at me through the iron bars like he's examining me.

"I caught the Hero. I deserve a special rewarrrd."

Drool drips down his vile chin.

"Hmm… I think I'll start with the Goddesssssss."

CHAPTER 6
The End of the World

It doesn't matter how immortal goddesses are if he swallows me whole! Once my body dissolves, I'll be sent straight back to the spirit world!

"Y-you're kidding, right?"

But Bunogeos unlocks the cell and barges right in.

"B-Bunogeos, stop!"

Seiya yells out in agony in the cell beside mine. Paying no heed to his cries, the orc grabs me by the arm and forces me to my feet. He then lowers his head below mine, huffing and puffing on my chest in excitement.

"N-no, don't…! Stop…!"

Bunogeos vulgarly stares at me as I tremble…but out of nowhere, his expression suddenly clouds over.

"Hmm? Hmmmm? Hmmmmmm? This Goddess smells sour…"

"Huh?!"

"Well, this is no goooood. Can't eat rotten foooood."

"What the—?! You're kidding, right?!"

Bunogeos lets go of me, and I crumple to the ground. I can hear Seiya call out to me with a mirthful note.

"Goddess! It's a good thing you stink, huh?"

The orc speaks up, responding to Seiya.

"I'm a foodie. I don't wanna waste space in my stomach with something rottennn."

I'm trembling, but this time not in fear.

"Who are you calling rotten?! I'm a goddess! You take that back, you pig!!"

"The nose doesn't lie. Weeee-hee-hee."

"I don't smell bad! Eat me! At least take a bite!!"

I'm so humiliated that I'd rather be eaten! Ignoring my rage-filled ramblings, Bunogeos walks over to the woman behind me.

"Yep. I'm gonna go with this one."

"What?! No, you're gonna eat *me* first!"

Furious, I stand in between them, but he casually knocks me away and picks up the woman before leaving the cell and locking it. Bunogeos places his fat finger on the woman's chin and pushes her head up as if he wants Seiya and me to watch.

"Her skin is so milky white and yummy-looking. Don'tcha agreeeee? Would be a waste making her a slaaave."

He suddenly stops rubbing her chin and stabs her cheek with a black claw coming out of his index finger.

"…!"

The woman faintly screams as red blood trickles down her cheek. Licking the blood off his finger causes the orc's lips to curl.

"Awww, yeah. That's the stuff. This is some high-quality meeeat. Wish I could enjoy it for the next couple of hours, but I'd be setting a bad example if any of the other beastkin found meee. Oh well. Guess I'll just eat her here."

His insolent behavior sends me into a fit of blind rage, but I simultaneously feel sick at the thought of him eating a human in front of me. Seiya, in the nearby cell, seems to feel the same.

"Bunogeos, stop! Get your hands off her!"

Bunogeos seems amused as he watches Seiya aggressively rattle the iron bars.

"Nooope. I'm gonna eat her, and you two are gonna watch."

"B-Bunogeos, please stop!"

I assail the bars of my cell as well, but there's no way I'll be able to break them if Seiya couldn't. The orc seems to be enjoying watching us struggle.

"You're wasting yer time. Even I'd have trouble breaking those baaarsss, so there's no way you're gonna be able to do it."

"*Tch…!*"

I punch the iron bars.

"Oh?"

Bunogeos turns a curious gaze on me.

"Why? Why did it have to be like this?! If the old Seiya were here—if the cautious Hero were here…then this would have never happened!"

The resentment slips off my tongue.

"…Goddess."

Though I failed to notice earlier, Seiya is looking at me.

"I-I'm sorry. It's not your fault. It's all my fault. I'm the one who caused your amnesia, which led to this."

"I get that I have amnesia, but…would I be able to save that woman if I had my memories back?"

Logically, I don't think a change in personality would help us get out of this tight corner, and yet, I still get this sense of hope. I feel almost as if that overly cautious, cool and collected, clear-sighted Hero would be able to reverse any situation, regardless of how grave it might seem.

"It's possible. Knowing how you failed last time on Ixphoria would help you become mentally strong to an extent."

"…I see."

Thereupon, I hear a violent bang peeling from the cell next door.

"What the…?!"

I turn to find Seiya banging his head against the iron bars!

"S-Seiya?!"

Bunogeos is also taken aback by Seiya's bizarre action.

"Uhhh… Whatcha doin' there?"

Blood pours down Seiya's forehead after repeatedly ramming his head against the bars, but even then, he doesn't stop.

"I don't care what happens to me…if it means I can save that woman."

"B-but what you're doing is reckless!"

"I'll be fine. I once fixed a TV back in my world by doing this."

"…?! Seiya, you're not a TV!"

He's out of his mind...but he's doing his best. I can feel just how desperate he is, and it breaks my heart.

...How many times has he hit his head already? Bunogeos seemed to be enjoying himself at first, but now he's yawning out of boredom.

"Well, I guess it's about time I aaate."

He looks at the slave and licks his lips. In the depth of despair...

"It's okay."

I hear a sudden voice.

"Don't worry about me."

It's the voice of the woman Bunogeos is holding.

"I'm afraid to be eaten, but once I move past the pain, I will finally be able to escape this hell..."

"Wh-what are you...?"

Even though she's about to be eaten, she gives me a gentle smile.

"The end of the world...has already come and gone. That's why..."

It's the voice of a woman who has already resigned herself.

Creak! Crack! Snap!

I hear something crumble in the cell next to mine.

"Wh-what was thaaat?"

In tandem with Bunogeos, I look over at Seiya's cell...and can't believe what I'm seeing! The hard iron bars have shattered and fallen to the floor! His head slick with blood, Seiya slowly crawls through the opening.

"How many times...am I going to repeat this? I should have figured it out last time... I can't save the world like this..."

His lower tone makes my heart skip a beat.

W-wait...?! But it has to be! He's the same person, but the air around him has gotten tense!

Seiya brushes back his blood-soaked hair, then lets out a small breath and walks over to Bunogeos.

"The hell? How did ya break those iron baaars?"

As Seiya stands right in front of Bunogeos, I use Scan and check his status.

<Condition: Normal>

*   *   *

Yes!! He healed his amnesia! The cautious Hero is back! B-but even if his personality changed, that doesn't mean his stats improved! There's no way he can defeat Bunogeos like this! What is he going to do?!

Seiya suddenly places his bloody hand on Bunogeos's thigh, and the orc's demeanor immediately changes.

"Ya filthy humaaaaaan! How dare ya touch me with yer shit-stained haaands!"

"I didn't just touch your leg. I destroyed it."

"...Huh?"

Ker-splat! Bunogeos's thigh tears right open, releasing a torrent of jet-black blood. It sounds like an overripe apple falling from a tree.

"Hmm...? Ah... Ahhhhhh!!"

Finally realizing what happened, Bunogeos's face twists in agony. After he falls to one knee and screams, Seiya talks over him with a cold air.

"First Valkyrja: Shattered Break!"

That's one of Valkyrie's techniques of destruction! H-he remembered how to do that?! But...oh! That move ignores defense! That's why he was able to break such sturdy iron bars and even use it on an enemy on a higher level than he is!

While Bunogeos crouches in pain, Seiya breaks the iron bars to my cell as well. But when I rush out to his side...

"Rista, stay back."

He signals me with his hand to move back, but I'm secretly overjoyed because he finally called me by my name!

"H-h-h-humaaan!"

Holding his wounded leg, Bunogeos stands up again.

"Impossible! How could such a weak human do this...?!"

Bunogeos shows his true colors. Red-eyed, he bares his fangs and fiercely glares at Seiya. But the Hero doesn't even blink.

"A 'weak human'? It would be in your best interest to forget the man you fought earlier."

Thereupon, flames shoot out of Seiya's body, surrounding the slave and me to protect us.

"Allow me to show you the ultimate attack I learned from the Goddess of Destruction."

"Heh. Funny! Just try it, you little shiiiiiit! I'll crush yer little skuuulll!"

...Panting, Seiya sprints up the stairs holding the woman's hand, with me following closely behind.

"Once we climb the stairs, it's a...right, I believe. After that, we'll be able to escape this dungeon..."

As the woman helps navigate Seiya through the dungeon, I ask:

"W-we're running? After all that trash talking?"

"Yeah. That move was the only Valkyrja technique I could remember, so our lives were really in danger back there."

"Oh, no wonder..."

"I bet he wasn't expecting we'd run. Even if he did and tried to chase us, it would be difficult with only one leg. We should be able to escape with no problem once we get past the other beastkin."

"Oh! Seiya, listen! We won't be able to return to the unified spirit world even if we do escape! They have a magic item that's preventing me from creating a gate!"

"I still have my memories from when I was reckless, so I understand the situation. If we can't return to the spirit world, then we'll just have to go to Little Light to prepare."

"'P-prepare'? For what?"

"Defeating the enemy, of course."

H-he plans on defeating Bunogeos without training in the spirit world?! B-but...!

Looking at his sharp, dignified profile, I think to myself:

Wh-what is this sense of security?! This is it! This is how Seiya Ryuuguuin has to be! This is the love of my life!

Almost moved to tears, I try to wrap my arm around his—but he knocks my hand away.

"What do you think you're doing? Get your hands off me."

"Huh...?"

Wh-what...? I thought he got his memories back? I-is he embarrassed? Is that it? Y-yeah... That has to be it...

CHAPTER 7
A Punch and a Promise

We run into a few beastkin along the way, but Seiya uses his fire magic to vanquish them. After escaping the dungeon, we eventually make it to the staircase leading to Little Light beneath the floorboards of the shack.

I'm glad we were able to get away from Bunogeos, but I get depressed when I think back to how they treated us in Little Light. We were unable to defeat the orc, and the only slave we saved is this woman behind us. It's better than nothing, but I can already imagine how enraged Braht and the other villagers are going to be.

Upon reaching the bottom of the staircase, I knock using the metal fitting on the door. When the doors open, the glowstones above illuminate the townspeople of the settlement, who turn their gazes toward us in unison. Braht and a couple of people his age, who I assume are his friends, approach us. He stops before us, then casts an eye on Seiya.

"So? Did you defeat Bunogeos?"

"No."

I can hear him grind his teeth after hearing Seiya's swift reply. After that, he glances at the slave we brought.

"Where are the other slaves?"

"They were sold outside of town. She's the only one I could save."

"Oh... I see..."

Braht promptly grabs Seiya by the collar, pulls his face forward, and threateningly says:

"And you call yourself a Hero!"

Before I can even get a word out, the woman we saved speaks up.

"Stop that! He saved me, you know?"

Thereupon, Braht lets go of Seiya's collar as if pushing him away.

"Yeah, you're right. He failed to defeat Bunogeos, and he came back with just one slave. What an *amazing* Hero."

Unable to sit back and listen any longer, I yell:

"H-hey! Seiya doesn't deserve to be talked to like that! He worked really hard to save her!"

But the people around Braht throw Seiya haughty expressions.

"Look at his head."

"It seems he ran away after Bunogeos gave him the beating of his life."

The next thing I know, we're surrounded by other townspeople.

"What a pathetic Hero!"

"Worthless trash!"

Once again, they begin hurling insults at Seiya. The tense atmosphere makes me anxious, but Seiya simply watches in silence. It isn't long before Braht makes another demand.

"Hey, Hero. Go back to the slave market, and this time, defeat Bunogeos."

But Seiya shakes his head.

"No. I need to prepare."

"Go."

"No."

Braht's pupils suddenly dilate. He widely draws back his arm, then screams:

"It's your fault the world ended up like this! You have no right to refuse!"

But as he throws a punch...

Wham! A powerful *thud* echoes throughout the settlement.

"Hrblbrbl...?"

The once abusive, threatening man makes a pathetic noise as his eyes roll back into his head. It makes sense, though—because the crown of his head connected with Seiya's fist!

"Shut up."

With those words, Seiya watches Braht foam at the mouth before collapsing to the ground.

Wh-wh-wh-wha—?!

My nose twitches and my mouth gapes and closes as I try to process what I just saw.

""""Whaaaaaaaaaaaat?!"""""

Braht's friends yell in unison as if speaking my heart.

"Y-y-you bastard!"

"D-do you have any idea what you've done?!"

"You couldn't save the world, you couldn't beat Bunogeos, and n-now you've raised a hand to Braht?!"

But Seiya is unapologetic.

"He was annoying. Talk shit, get hit."

He then stands before Braht's men.

"You guys are starting to annoy me, too."

He raises his fist into the air.

Wham!

"Urk!"

"Wh-what do you think you're—?"

"And one for you."

Bam!

"Oooof!"

Whack! Crack! Thwack!

Seiya uses his extraordinary strength to knock them down one by one, causing each to foam at the mouth as they lose consciousness. Eventually, a few older women come rushing over and stand in front of Seiya as if they can't take the violence anymore. They're the same women who said nasty things about Aria and me earlier.

"H-how dare you!"

"Yeah! None of this would have happened if you'd just saved the world!"

"You should be ashamed of yourselves!"

Wh-what is Seiya gonna do?! I mean, he'd never hit an old—

Crunch!

What a thud! I can't believe what I'm seeing! The Hero's fist is sinking into that old crone's crown!

"Eeeep?!"

She lets out a pitiful scream and collapses to the ground, foaming at the mouth.

"S-S-S-Seiya?! Don't you think that's overdoing it a little?!"

"Y-yeah! We're ladies, you know!"

"And?"

Whack!

"Eeeek!"

Another old lady hits the dirt. I can feel the blood slowly draining from my cheeks.

I—I can't believe him! I was kind of enjoying it at first, to be honest, though...

But...no! This is way too much! It gives me chills!

In the midst of the violence, I suddenly hear a new voice.

"Mommy!! What did you do to my mom?!"

It's an extremely young boy. Apparently, one of the women Seiya knocked out is his mother.

"Stupid Hero! You big dummy!"

The kid spits out insults while peppering Seiya with a flurry of fists.

S-Seiya, don't...! You would never do something like that, right?! I know you! I know you're actually a sweet guy deep down inside!

Whack!

"Ffff?!"

The boy shares his mother's fate as he's delivered a swift strike to the dome. After his eyes roll into the back of his head and he falls to the ground, Seiya sputters:

"Talk shit, get hit. No exceptions."

He doesn't even show mercy to kids!! Wh-what's next?! Stealing candy from babies?! What's gonna happen now?!

I shudder, the people of Little Light riot, and Seiya beats each head like a drum.

"This is getting tedious. Everyone, line up for your knuckle sandwiches."

A man who appears to be in his forties standing before Seiya tries to explain himself.

"I—I didn't say anything! I-it was them! They're the ones who were insulting y—"

"Shut up."

Bam!

"I-I've always thought you were handsome. You know, we should—"

"Nice try."

Bam!

"P-please forgive m—"

"Nope."

Bam!

Everyone tries to make excuses, but Seiya's fists aren't having it. Nevertheless, I've seen enough.

"Seiyaaaa! Stop! That's enough!!"

Bam!

"Ohwee…?!"

I take a powerful fist to the pate. My eyes roll back in my head, and I start to lose consciousness but somehow manage to stay awake.

"H-h-heeey! Why did you hit me?!"

But Seiya doesn't even seem sorry. If anything, he's glaring at me like I'm the enemy.

"…Rista."

"Huh?! Y-y-yes?!"

Though he never really shows his emotions, Seiya's face is bright red.

"I am heavily regretting everything thus far. Trusting you in the spirit world and letting you into the Summoning Chamber were huge mistakes. Because of that, I have to fix this world's problems without even getting a chance to prepare properly."

Eek! H-he's pissed! Please don't tell me he was angry because of me and took it out on the townspeople!

"The plan was to raise my level in the spirit world until I was at max level. Then I was going to ask Aria to help me train and learn some new abilities before coming here."

A tense, rage-induced atmosphere flows through the air. I decide to apologize for now.

"I-I'm sorry! I'm so sorry, Seiya…!"

As I sincerely lower my head, Seiya insists:

"No, Rista. This isn't your fault. It's mine."

"S-Seiya…!"

Thank goodness! I knew he was a nice guy! It looks like he's already forgiven me! But I guess I shouldn't be surprised! Our destinies are tied together by the red thread of fate and— Aaack?!

Seiya clenches his teeth like an ogre.

"This is all my fault for being so soft! I should have never trusted some*thing* like you!"

"'Some*thing*'?! Are you referring to me?!"

"What else would I be talking about?"

His eyes are as cold as ice, just like they were back in Gaeabrande.

"W-wait, wait, wait! Seiya! Hold on! Have you forgotten the deep bond we had in a past life—?"

"Save it. We may have been lovers in a past life, but that doesn't mean we need to be together in this one. Besides, you're a goddess, and I'm a human. It's not even up for debate."

"S-Seiya?! Tell me you're joking!"

"I'll continue saving this world, but only because of our past and unfortunate bond. But don't get the wrong idea. This isn't love. It's my duty."

"'Unfortunate bond'…! 'Duty'…!"

H-h-he's doing it again! He says that, but I know deep down inside, he really cares about me!

I use Appraise to check how he really feels about me.

☆RISTA'S LOVE APPRAISAL☆

-Your love rating with Seiya:	2 points
-Seiya thinks you're:	a parasitic weed.
-A tidbit of advice:	He feels nothing for you. The relationship is almost unsalvageable. You should think about breaking up soon!

…?! Ahhhhhhhhh! His feelings for me are completely gooooooone! He thinks I'm no better than a parasitic weeeeeed!

In utter shock, I approach Seiya as if walking on pins and needles.

"N-no…! This can't be happening! Everything was so perfect…!"

"Get away from me."

"Think back to all the wonderful days when we got along!"

"It's a dark past that I'm trying to forget. And how many times do I have to tell you to *get away from me*? If you get any closer, you're going to get much more than a fist."

"I'm not going to stop!! You're mine, Seiyaaaaaa!"

I leap to embrace him when…

"Gwfff?!"

I take a blow straight to the cheek! Then, without missing a beat, he buries a knee in my solar plexus.

"Gwah?!"

I take an elbow to the right breast.

"My booooooob?!"

He punched me, kneed me, *and* smashed my boob—the menacing three-hit combo drops me.

"Mn…errr…ahhhh!"

As I lie on the ground in agony, Braht somehow manages to recover and stands by my side.

"Wh-what a monster! He won't even hesitate to hurt one of his own! G-Goddess! Are you okay?!"

It was so violent, even Braht starts to feel sorry for me. But…

Th-this boob pain…! Heh-heh-heh! This sure brings back memories! This actually looks like it fired him up! At the very least, this beats seeing him being a wimp! This is what makes him one in a billion! This is Seiya Ryuuguuin, the surly, ill-mannered, overly cautious Hero who saved Gaeabrande! Heh-heh-heh… Ha-ha-ha-ha!

"Heh-heh… Ha-ha-ha-haaa!"

"…?! How can you laugh after he did that to you?! You're both sick!"

Braht backs away from me. Meanwhile, Seiya glares at the people of Little Light.

"Now…who's next?"

"Aaahhhh!"

The townspeople fall into despair when…

"Hero, that is quite enough."

A young yet firm voice can be heard nearby. Everyone looks in its direction to find Eich, the Earth Mage and creator of the underground settlement. With a slightly downcast gaze, Eich continues.

"Deep down, they understand. They know that this is really not your fault but the Demon Lord's. Even so, everyone has lost friends and family, and the only way they can cope is to take out that frustration on you."

"E-Eich!"

Someone stammers her name. When I look into the crowd, I even see people crying.

"Besides, Hero, you made a vow. Perhaps you don't remember it, but you made a promise to me as well…"

Gazing up at the glowstones glittering in the ceiling, Eich says:

"'I will defeat the Demon Lord and save this world.' However, you lost to the Demon Lord and were killed along with my b-brother…"

The tears fall to the earth. Eich, who had been acting so mature, begins sobbing just like any other girl her age.

"Sniffle…! Colt…! Colt…!!"

"Eich…!"

I, the people of Little Light…everyone helplessly watches as she weeps. Seiya, on the other hand, looks almost appalled.

"He promised to defeat the Demon Lord? What an idiot. He got carried away and let his emotions get the best of him, and look how that turned out. Vows need to be based on carefully constructed plans with perfect and certain chances of victory."

"No, um… That was you who made that vow," Braht asserts timidly.

"Don't look at me. That was me, yet it wasn't. And since I don't know how strong the Demon Lord is, I won't be able to make any rash promises like saying I'll save the world."

Everyone knows the reality of the situation, but being forced to face it only brings gloom. As the heavy atmosphere pervades the settlement, Seiya approaches the sobbing Earth Mage.

"But there is one thing I can promise."

Standing before Eich, Seiya raises his hand in the air.

"S-Seiya?! Don't! She didn't do anything!"

The townspeople start yelling at him as well.

"You better not lay a hand on her!"

"If you want someone to punch, punch me!"

The Hero's hand comes crashing down like a meteor. Eich faintly gasps as she tightly closes her eyes. However...Seiya simply places a hand on her head. While looking down at her with a penetrating gaze, he continues.

"Eich, I am going to make my first real promise to you today."

"A real...promise...?"

With Eich's halting query, a powerful aura of ambition radiates from the Hero's body. The people of Little Light forget their anger as they look at Seiya.

"No matter what happens, I'm going to free this town from Bunogeos's reign."

CHAPTER 8
A New Class

After making his emancipation declaration, Seiya heads straight to Enzo the Baptist, who can change classes. I nervously follow behind.

"Oh, look what the cat dragged in. Interested in changing classes?"

The old man Enzo broadly smiles, missing most of his front teeth.

"Yeah. I have something I need to ask you first, though. Will I be able to change back to my original class after changing to a new one?"

"You sure can."

"You better be telling the truth…unless you don't mind losing an appendage."

Enzo's smile instantly disappears.

"Heh. You're one scary kid. Not saying what appendage I'd be losing makes it even scarier. But I'm telling you the truth. Just come to me, and you can return to your original class."

"I have another question, then. When I change back, do I keep the skills I learned?"

"No. Once you return, you forget whatever moves you picked up. But, well, you can use them again if you go back to that class."

Seiya continues interrogating Enzo about changing classes after that. He seems to be interested, but personally, I'm conflicted. What kind of job would he switch to that'd be better than a Spellblade? It's an advanced class, after all. In Seiya's case, he'd be able to equip two classes if he gave up his Spellblade categorization, but he'd lose powerful moves like Phoenix Drive and Phoenix Thrust…

"These are your choices as of now."

Enzo points to the available classes.

Monk, Lancer, Mage (Wind, Lightning, Earth), Merchant, Seer, Jolly Piper.

Hmm… Looks like he has an aptitude for many different jobs. Oh, hey! There are even throwaways like Seer and Jolly Piper! Ha-ha-ha—ack! This is no time for joking around! He needs to defeat Bunogeos… So how about going with Lancer? He might be able to learn a powerful thrust attack like Phoenix Thrust. For a second, he should probably go with Mage. I wouldn't mind if he stuck with Fire, but Wind and Lightning might not be so bad, either.

But Seiya says to Enzo:

"I'll start with Mage—an Earth Mage."

"What?! Earth magic? You mean just like Eich?"

The unexpected choice takes me by surprise, which catches Seiya's attention.

"Huh? You're here?"

"Of course I am! Are you seriously still mad?! You already hit me, kneed me, and smashed my boob, so I think it's about time you forgive me!"

"Whatever. Just stay out of this."

"But you're choosing earth magic. It's not good for offensive spells. I mean, I'm sure there are spells you can use to break the ground to hurt the enemy, but it's not something you choose over powerful fire spells."

"Just shut up. Earth Mage is going to be my secondary class. My primary class is going to be something else."

Oh! He's going to choose something like a Lancer, which specializes in offensive abilities, and use the earth magic as backup! Well, if that's the case, then…

The instant I expel a relieved sigh, Seiya says to Enzo:

"I want my primary class to be Jolly Piper."

"…?! You've gotta be kidding me! You're gonna play the flute?! You're joking, right?!"

Seiya continues the conversation in spite of my astonishment.

"Jolly Piper as your main job and Earth Mage as your support job, eh?"

"That's it."

"Wait, wait, wait! Hold up! You are *not* picking Jolly Piper! It's not happening! Besides, your stats are going to lower exponentially if you choose that as your main class!"

Seiya's attack and defense are higher than average because he's a Spellblade, which is an advanced class. If he chooses a throwaway job like Jolly Piper, all of his attributes will suffer. And yet…

"You've got it, kid… Class Change!"

Enzo's hand begins to glow, wrapping Seiya in a blinding light. The light eventually fades, revealing Seiya in a bizarre costume reminiscent of a street performer.

"All right, all done. Starting today, you're a Jolly Piper and Earth Mage."

"A-ack! He really changed classes! H-hey, it isn't too late to change back, Seiya. Are you sure you don't still have a touch of amnesia?"

Seiya shoots me a reproachful glance.

"Can you stop talking for one second? Go take a nap or something."

"No! I'm worried about you!"

"I don't need you worrying about me."

"What?! What's wrong with worrying about my party member?!"

"Who ever said you were my party member? I never planned on taking you with me."

"Excuse me?!"

"You're useless, and you'd just slow me down. Now be a good girl and wait here."

"I—I admit it was my fault you didn't get to prepare long enough in the spirit world! But that's exactly why I want to help you!"

I desperately try to convey how passionate I am, but Seiya turns a distant gaze on me.

"Bunogeos can use Chain Destruction. In other words, all monsters in Ixphoria can kill you. I'm not confident I can protect you like I did in Gaeabrande."

"That's fine! I can take care of myself!"

"So you don't care if you die?"

"I'm willing to risk my life!"

After a few moments of silence, Seiya mutters:

"Knock yourself out."

I nod with a solemn expression, but I'm gloating on the inside.

Heh-heh-heh! How do you like that! I'm willing to put everything on the line! I bet my love rating has gone way up now! We're in this together, after all! Come! Let us save the world of Ixphoria with the power of our love!

Brimming with anticipation, I use Appraise on Seiya.

☆RISTA'S LOVE APPRAISAL☆

-Your love rating with Seiya: 1 point

-Seiya thinks you're: a stubborn parasitic weed.

-A tidbit of advice: Even though he told you not to come, you won't listen, which seems to have really annoyed him. He wishes he could just roll you up into a ball and throw you away!

What the…?! Not only did our love rating lower, but now he wants to throw me away?! What kind of garbage is this?!

Seiya begins to walk off as I droop my head in despair. I chase after him until we reach the item salesman sitting behind his mat. Lowering my voice so the shopkeeper doesn't hear, I whisper to Seiya:

"Hey, Seiya… This guy basically only sells farm equipment. None of this is gonna help you on your journey."

"That's not necessarily true."

Seiya picks up an iron cylinder from the mat, snatches the pouch of money Ishtar gave me, and pays.

"I should be able to make a flute out of this with little effort."

"You seriously plan on playing the flute…?"

"I am a Jolly Piper, after all. But I didn't come here only to buy a flute… Hey, shopkeeper. I'll take a thousand glowstones as well."

"You've got it, sir. Thank you very much for your pat— One thousand?! What are you going to do with a thousand?!"

I'm used to Seiya's ridiculous purchases, but the shopkeeper is taken aback. While I'm not surprised, I still realize we don't have enough money and won't be able to carry that many anyway. Plus, I can see where the shopkeeper is coming from. What would he need that many glowstones for? I somehow manage to talk Seiya down to fifty.

Seiya buys a huge sack and stuffs it full of glowstones, but it doesn't end there. He points to something on the mat that looks like jarred pickles.

"I'll take those emergency rations and that canteen of drinking water as well. In fact, give me all of them."

"Um... If you take all of them, we won't have anything to eat or drink..."

"I-I'm so sorry! Just sell us as many as you can, please!"

Seiya places the food and water he bought in another sack before handing it to me. It's like we're preparing to descend into a dungeon or something. After shopping, Seiya mutters:

"I need some equipment. Even though I'm a piper, I should at least have a sword. It's a shame Bunogeos stole the platinum one."

"That's fine, but there aren't any weapon or armor shops here."

"What are you talking about? There are plenty of weapons and armor."

Seiya points at Braht. Noticing Seiya approaching, he yells:

"What do you want?!"

Braht tightly knits his eyebrows when...

Whack!

"Hrblbrbl...?"

Once again, Braht begins foaming at the mouth before collapsing.

"...?! Seiya?! Why did you hit him again?!"

Seiya swipes the sword off the unconscious leader's body, then casually equips it as if he's done nothing wrong.

"Guess I'll take his armor while I'm at it."

He strips Braht of his armor, then passes it to me.

"Perfect. Now I've got a steel sword and some steel armor."

"Y-you're terrible!"

Furthermore, his eyes fall on one of Braht's friends, who was watching in the distance.

"Hmm... I could use a few spares as well."

"Eek?! Please...! No...!"

Seiya chases the man down, beats him unconscious, and robs him of everything he has... Common sense tells me this definitely isn't something a good person would do. But after considering the fact that we have to save the world and need resources to do so, I decide to keep my mouth shut.

W-we don't have any other choice. This is the only way we can get the items we need...

As I try to justify what we're doing, I feel a sharp pain on the top of my head.

"Owwwww!"

Rip, rip, rip! Seiya tears out handfuls of my hair without so much as asking!

"Wh-wh-what the hell are you doing?! Seiyaaaaaa!"

"Stop complaining. It's for synthesizing platinum swords."

"You could have at least said something first!"

"...Well, now that we're stocked up on items and equipment, what should we do next?" I ask while rubbing my head.

"We leave tomorrow morning. Today, we'll stay at the inn and rest. I need to examine my new magic and characteristics."

"Wait! What?! We're leaving tomorrow?! Shouldn't we take our time?!"

I figured Seiya would have wanted to train here for a while!

"Don't worry. I have a plan."

"R-really? Well, if you say so... More importantly, there doesn't seem to be an inn here..."

"We can just make someone host us at their place."

"I don't know... I mean, not many people really like us here."

"I don't care. We're going to find a place."

Seiya surveys the area until he spots a lanky, timid-looking young man. He approaches him.

"Hey, you. What's your name?"

"Huh? C-Caron. Why?"

"Okay, Caron. Provide us with shelter for the night."

"What?! Do you mean my house?! I—I can't! It's too small! Plus, it's dirty!"

"I don't mind. Where is it?"

"I-it's really, really dirty... It's a terrible place to sleep..."

"Caron, if you are really that dissatisfied with your house, then leave."

"…?! Wh-what?!"

"From now on, it's my house."

I wrap an arm around the young man's shoulder as he starts to cry.

"C-Caron, don't worry! It's just for one night! After that, we'll be gone!"

"Mn… *Sniffle*! Does that mean…I can still live in my house…?"

"Of course! I mean, it's your house! You have every right to live there!"

"Thank goodness! I've grown…so attached…to that house! I'm so… happy…!"

And just like that, we force a young man we just met to let us stay the night.

The next morning, we pick up our sacks of belongings and leave Caron's house.

"All right, ready to head out?"

"Y-yep…"

We take our leave of Little Light, but only after causing a lot of trouble for the townspeople. Needless to say, nobody comes to see us off.

CHAPTER 9
Jolly Piper

Glowstones dimly illuminate the long staircase as we climb toward the outside world. But when the floorboard to the old house finally comes into view, Seiya suddenly stops and places his left hand on the dirt wall.

"Hmm? What are you doing?"

A massive cavern thereupon appears behind the wall without even making a sound! I stand back in shock, but Seiya steps inside.

"S-Seiya?! Wait!"

I shortly follow after him. Seiya illuminates the cavern using a glowstone from the item pouch. It's a very mysterious enclosure. Although the narrow cavity can hardly fit us, a new cavern forms whenever Seiya approaches a wall. Moreover, whenever we continue down a new path, the way we came closes off and disappears. It feels more like the space is moving for us, rather than us digging holes and moving the dirt ourselves.

"This is amazing! Is this earth magic?"

In a lowered voice, Seiya explains:

"Cave Along. It's essentially a mobile cavern that allows you to freely walk through soil."

He then slows down his pace.

"We're currently around one meter underground outside the shack."

Right when I'm about to ask him why he randomly decided to use this move, he suddenly stops in his tracks and silently shakes his head. From there, he points up. I gaze at the earthen ceiling faintly illuminated by the glowstone and hear a muffled voice.

"Is the Hero really gonna come out of this shack?"

"Yeah. We've been getting eyewitness reports of humans disappearing near this place for a while now."

I don't even have to think about it. It's beastkin talking. We listen carefully with bated breath.

"But they already thoroughly searched it and didn't find any humans, right?"

"According to Bunogeos, there's a human who can use earth magic, and a few humans are hiding deep underground. The entrance apparently only opens when a human's nearby."

"And that's where the Hero is, too?"

"We've already checked everywhere on the surface. It's the only place left."

The beastkin lets out a vile chuckle.

"I can't wait to rip him in half!"

"Yeah, let's kill us a Hero!"

After listening to their conversation, Seiya stealthily moves forward without saying a word. We walk for a short while until he looks back at me and silently nods. It seems it's okay to talk now.

"S-Seiya! They're looking for us!"

"It's no surprise. We ran away in the middle of battle, so no doubt Bunogeos is fuming. It makes sense he would be doing everything he can to find us."

"But it sounded like they were talking about Eich's earth magic and how the entrance to the settlement works…"

"And…?"

"And it means they've already marked the deserted house, so we can't use it to go back anymore!"

"I expected this to happen. That's why I bought the food and glowstones."

"What?! So we're going to live in caves you make from now on?!"

"Essentially, yes. Just to reiterate, while we may be underground, they're still beastkin. Some of them may even have hearing far superior to humans', so don't make any noise."

"O-okay."

I nervously reply in a whisper, but my heart is racing for an entirely different reason.

So, wait! Does this mean we're gonna be in this dim, narrow space together?! Just the two of us?! N-never mind fixing our love rating! Something even hotter and steamier might be waiting for us in here! Hff! Hff! Hff! Hff!

In the midst of my excitement, Seiya places a hand on the earthen wall.

"What are you doing?"

"I'm checking to see if there are any beastkin nearby."

Seiya then quietly stares at me.

"Rista, you said you wanted to help me, right?"

"Y-yeah, of course! But…"

Out of nowhere, Seiya crouches and grabs my ankles! His face is right next to my crotch!

Wh-what's going on?! What is he going to do to me?! Wait… N-no! Stop! We can't! That would be far too lewd! But…on second thought, I actually wouldn't mind! If anything, I want him to do it! Yes, Seiya! Take me! Rip these panties right off!

But before I even realize it, I'm soaring.

"…Huh?"

The Hero tightly holds on to my ankles with his extraordinary strength as he lifts me into the air like a parent with their newborn. Naturally, my face is getting closer to the earthen ceiling!

Eeeeeek!

But I don't feel the impact I'm expecting. Surprisingly, it's a rather gentle feeling, as if my face were being pushed into water. And then…

When I open my eyes, all I can see is the purple sky and a desolate town! In the distance, I can also see the dog and cat beastkin! *Only my head is on the surface! Ahhhhhh! Wh-what the helllll…?!*

Moments before I freak out, my head slips back through the ground!

"Ahhhhh!"

Despite the fact that I'm shivering in fear, Seiya coldheartedly asks:

"So? What did you see? Were there any beastkin nearby?"

"Th-there weren't any nearby, but I saw two over there… Wait, no! I am *not* a periscope!! What were you gonna do if someone saw me?!"

"You said you wanted to help, right? I made sure the area was clear before sending you out, and I would have pulled you back in right away if I needed to... At any rate, let's carefully head up to the surface."

After Seiya undoes the Cave Along spell, we gradually float to the surface. He quickly looks around, finds a shadowy area, and trots over to it. From there, he watches the beastkin. I can hear them talking.

"I freakin' hate this Hero hunt. I'm so pissed right *meow*. Once I get back home, I'm gonna eat one of my slaves out of spite."

The dog beastkin raises an eyebrow to the cat beastkin's assertion.

"Yo, don't. You know how strict this town is with its 'no eating humans' rule."

"Yeah, yeah. But *fur*-real, though, I heard that Bunogeos is eating humans himself when nobody's watching. It's nothing to worry *mew*rself over. Besides, we're in the middle of searching for the Hero. Nobody'd even notice if a slave or two disappeared."

"You raise a fine point. How about saving half of your slave for me?"

"You're in *fur* a treat. Come on—let's do this."

I whisper to Seiya:

"S-Seiya! They're going to kill one of the slaves!"

"Relax."

Seiya pulls a slender silver object out of his shirt pocket.

"I'm going to play the flute."

"...?! This is no time to be playing the flute! Someone's about to be killed!"

But that's when I notice that the instrument Seiya is using is no ordinary flute. Only the tip and end piece have holes with nothing on the body. Seiya squats and picks up a small handful of dirt. He rolls the soil between his fingers as if he were kneading clay.

"Wh-what are you doing?"

"I'm hardening the soil with my magic and giving it an aerodynamic shape to reduce air resistance."

He creates something narrow and long with a pointed tip in his hands.

I-it reminds me of a bullet from Seiya's world...but I guess it's closer to rifle ammo!

Seiya sticks it on the tip of the flute, then locks a sharp eye on the beastkin a few dozen meters away.

"I lost a lot of abilities when I quit being a Spellblade, but I learned new abilities in exchange. Resilient Lungs, Sustained Fluting—I will integrate all Jolly Piper special abilities into this one blow."

He brings the silver flute to his lips.

"Take this! Burst Air!"

Bang! A dry sound echoes.

…I have no idea what just happened, but when I look in the direction the flute is pointing, I'm speechless. Although he was happily chatting with his friend up until a few seconds ago, the cat beastkin's head is now gone!

"Huh…?"

Noticing his friend's head missing, the dog beastkin foolishly barks:

"H-hey, uh…? Where'd your head g—?"

Bang! Another dry *pop*.

The dog beastkin's head instantly vanishes! Black blood flows from their necks before they simultaneously hit the ground.

While trembling at the horrific sight, I think to myself:

Jolly Piper, my ass!

"S-Seiya!! What the hell is that?! I thought that was supposed to be a flute!"

"Calling it a 'blowpipe' would be more accurate. I combined the flute with your hair last night and synthesized it just like when making platinum swords, thus creating a platinum blowpipe, which has increased durability and improved noise reduction when firing."

"A platinum blowpipe…!"

Without even giving me a second to retort, Seiya walks out of the shadows and approaches the two bodies while keeping an eye on his surroundings.

"What are you doing? Somebody might see you."

"Yes, we shouldn't stay here for long, but I still need to clean up."

"B-back to your old ways, huh?! But I'm pretty sure they're dead!"

"You can't be so sure. Beastkin might have healing capabilities that far exceed human imagination. Only knowing that they lost their heads worries me. I won't be able to relax until they're ash."

"But you can't use Hellfire anymore."

"I know. I'm going to safely and swiftly dispose of their bodies with a new spell."

"What kind of spell is that?"

"Curious, huh? Then allow me to explain."

Seiya suddenly places a hand on my head.

Crumble!

"Huh?!"

My body starts sinking into the ground! Before I know it, I'm staring at Seiya's ankles! Once again, only my head is aboveground!

"What are you doing to me this time?!" I yell out in a rage, unable to move.

Seiya, on the other hand, is calm.

"I was trying to completely bury you alive with my earth magic, but as you can see, your head is still above the surface. I partially blame myself for not mastering earth magic yet, but I'm unfortunately unable to make you sink any more than that."

"How awful can you be?! What's even the point of trying to bury me?!"

"Just shut up and listen. You don't have an especially strong resistance to earth magic, but being a living creature gives you some magic resistance. That's why I can't completely bury you in the soil."

Seiya then touches the headless beastkin.

"Endless Fall!"

The two bodies instantly disappear as if sucked into the ground. U-unlike with me, they completely sink in! …Oh! Dead beastkin have no magic resistance! That's why earth magic can be used to its greatest potential!

"How far did you drop them? Ten meters or so?"

"No, even farther. I don't know how far down the core of this planet is, but I dropped them as far as I could. I'm assuming it's only a few thousand kilometers, so it shouldn't be long before the extremely high temperatures near the center vaporize them."

"…?! You dropped two dead bodies a few thousand kilometers?! Isn't that a little much?!"

"Ideally, seeing them vaporized with my own two eyes would make me feel most at ease, but unfortunately, that's not possible, since I would be vaporized along with them."

Of course you'd be vaporized! How can you even say that with a straight face?!

In a sense, what he just did is even more terrifying than Hellfire. I shudder when…

"Hey! I heard a noise!

"It came from that way!"

"Oh no! Seiya! We have to get out of here! …Wait! My body's still buried in the ground!"

"It's fine. We're going back underground."

Seiya promptly uses Cave Along, and my face instantly slips underground.

"Ahhh!"

I land in a narrow cavern. My brain still hasn't processed what happened, and I feel like I was tossed into a pool of water. Meanwhile, Seiya takes out a glowstone and illuminates the cavity.

"All right, come on. We're changing locations until I find somewhere I can safely snipe the beastkin again."

Trotting after Seiya, I timidly ask:

"Hey, Seiya… What exactly do you plan on doing?"

"I said I was going to free this town from Bunogeos's reign, didn't I? After finding the enemy with Cave Along, I'm going to use Burst Air to snipe them from a safe distance in order to reduce their forces. In other words…"

The Hero's eyes sharpen in the abyss.

"I'm beastkin hunting."

CHAPTER 10
The Miserable Life of a Mole

After taking out two more beastkin with Burst Air, Seiya places a glow-stone in the middle of a narrow underground space with a radius of around 1.5 meters, then sits on the ground. It looks like he's taking a short break.

"Our objective is three hundred beastkin, which means we have two hundred ninety-six to go. Rista, you're going to be keeping count."

"O-okay. Got it."

I don't know exactly how many beastkin are occupying the city of Galvano, but three hundred is a number that none other than Seiya came up with. He must be confident that we'll be able to reclaim the town if we beat that many.

"The goal is fifty a day. Taking into account our food and water supply, I want to finish within a week. Anyway, ready to start back up?"

Following my nod, Seiya places a hand on the earthen wall and concentrates. After checking if there are any enemies in the area, he stands and grabs my ankles. Lifted high into the air, my head pokes out onto the surface, and I search for beastkin. Whenever we discover one, we create some distance, and Seiya snipes them with his blowpipe. Just like that, we kill one beastkin after another without putting ourselves in danger.

I was pissed about being used as a periscope at first, but after really thinking about it, I realize this is the first time Seiya and I are working together as a team. I feel like I'm helping him as his teammate, and I experience that sense of fulfillment every time I discover another beastkin. Eventually, night falls. Seiya places his blowpipe on the ground in the narrow cavern.

"All right, I still have some MP left, but these are beastkin I'm up against. Some of them might even be nocturnal, and Burst Air is less accurate at night, so let's not take any risks and call it a day."

Our first day of hunting comes to an end thanks to Seiya's cautious nature. Even then, we were able to surpass our goal and defeat fifty-one beastkin, which is amazing. After eating some of the rations in the cavern he made with Cave Along, Seiya says:

"Get some rest. We've got a long day tomorrow."

——*I-it's finally happening! We're gonna spend the night snuggling together in this narrow space!*

As my heart begins to race, Seiya gets up and places a hand on the earthen wall.

"Our bodies won't be able to get sufficient rest in such a tight space. I'm going to make the cavern a little bigger."

The cramped cave silently expands until it's around a radius of three meters. After placing a few glowstones in the ceiling, Seiya draws a line on the illuminated floor with his sheath.

"This is my side of the room, and that's yours. Don't even think about setting foot in here without my permission."

"Wh-what the hell?! Rude! You make it sound like I'm gonna force myself on you!"

"It's possible. You randomly throw yourself on me sometimes, after all."

Tch! He saw right through me!

"Listen, if you even attempt to cross this line, I'm undoing Cave Along and leaving you behind."

"But I'll be buried alive if you do that! ...F-fine!"

...This was the start of my miserable life as a mole, far different from the sweet life I imagined.

Day two of my life as a mole.

Seiya violently shakes my body under the dim glowstones, making it impossible to tell if it's even morning yet.

"How long do you plan on sleeping? Come on."

Just like yesterday, I act as a periscope and search for enemies while Seiya relocates us with Cave Along and snipes them.

"Enemy spotted at three o' clock!"

I promptly give Seiya the signal after bringing my head back underground. We've repeated this routine so often, it has become second nature. Before long, our kill count approaches a hundred by the time noon rolls around.

I actually take pride in my role as the periscope now. Life underground is unsanitary and miserable, but I feel fulfilled. Seiya's opinion of me has probably gone up as well due to how seriously I'm taking this. He even leaves me in charge of item management when underground.

But that night after hunting…the Hero tells me something devastating.

"My earth magic leveled up, so I don't need a periscope anymore."

"What?!"

"Watch this. Clear Ceiling!"

Seiya holds his hand toward the ceiling, and it suddenly becomes transparent like glass.

"This new spell works like a magic mirror. They can't see us, but our view of the surface is pretty clear, right? In addition, I learned a move called Ground Penetration. With this, I can use Burst Air without worrying about the earthen ceiling getting in the way. In other words, I can find and snipe the enemy while underground."

"O-oh… W-wonderful…"

Some roles become obsolete and fade away with the changing of the times. In Seiya's world, these would probably be jobs like milkman and elevator operator. My job disappeared with the improvement of Seiya's earth magic.

Day three of my life as a mole.

We're able to annihilate the beastkin thanks to Seiya's new spells Clear Ceiling and Ground Penetration. This is a safer and more time-efficient method compared to using me as a periscope, so our hunt quickly progresses.

Meanwhile, I spend the entire day zoning out. Without a job or a purpose, I just feel empty. Seiya won't even talk to me unless it's necessary, and he ignores me if I try to start a conversation unless it's something important.

The filthy, dim underground life catches up with me, and before I realize it, I'm completely stressed out and in desperate need of a bath.

That night, Seiya suddenly crosses the line and enters my territory. After looking at the item pouch, he frowns at me.

"Rista, what's going on? We should have more food rations than this."

"Oh… Sorry. I ate some."

Yep. I secretly ate some of the food rations, partly due to stress.

"But why? You're a goddess. You won't die without food, so why are you eating more than I am?"

"Just because I won't die doesn't mean I don't get hungry!"

I stick my tongue out and giggle, but Seiya doesn't even crack a smile.

"D-don't worry! We still have plenty of food! We should be okay for another four days at the very least!"

"Don't give me excuses. I said a week, but that was only an estimate. The tides of battle are always changing. We might end up underground far longer than planned, and I'm not comfortable with how few rations we have left."

Seiya then mutters:

"It looks like we'll just have to find a new source of food."

He approaches the earthen wall and strains his eyes until he swiftly shoves his hand into the dirt.

"Hiss!"

Dangling in Seiya's hand is a massive worm baring its fangs. It's around ten centimeters long. He shoves it in my face.

"Check if it's edible."

"Th-there's no way that's edible!"

"Just use Appraise and check."

Grumbling, I use Appraise.

Death worm: It's a worm that lives in the dirt in Ixphoria. They're harmless unless you taunt them. Also, if you're curious whether or not you can eat them…they're edible. Just barely.

E-ew! This is edible?! There is no way I'm eating that!

I shrug in a disappointed manner.

"Sorry. It's completely inedible, unfortunately."

Thereupon, Seiya casts a frigid gaze at me.

"Don't lie to me. The appraisal results say it's edible."

"What?! How did you know?! W-wait...! Don't tell me you can use Appraise, too?!"

"There's nothing you can do that I can't."

"You tricked me, you jerk! You're terrible! I can't believe you!"

"*You're* terrible. What you did was inexcusable. Now eat it."

Eyes stained with bloodlust, Seiya approaches me with the death worm in hand.

"N-no! I'm a goddess! I'd rather die than eat that!"

But Seiya forces the live death worm down my throat!

"Mmmmmm?!"

He opens and closes my jaw with both hands, forcing me to chew the worm! A bitterness nearly impossible to describe spreads throughout my mouth!

"*Blaaargh...!! Bleeehhh...!!*"

As the tears well in my eyes, the Hero coldly says to me:

"You're eating death worms from now on."

...Even when I close my eyes to sleep, all I can see are countless death worms squirming around.

"*Urgggh!* One death worm, two death worms, three death worms..."

The harsh environment slowly chips away at my sanity.

CHAPTER 11
Impatience and Irritation

Day four of my life as a mole.

While life underground is beyond miserable, our beastkin hunting is going better than expected. If my calculations are correct, we've already defeated over two hundred and fifty beastkin. Seiya's Jolly Piper level also went up, apparently, so he can now use the special ability Modest Flute, which further helps him reduce noise when using Burst Air. It increased the range as well, essentially making the blowpipe a sniper rifle with a silencer. Seeing Seiya steadily take out the beastkin without being noticed is like watching an elite assassin.

That's when Seiya lays out the new plan.

"It's about time we go looking for Bunogeos."

...While hunting is progressing well, we still haven't reached our target of three hundred beastkin. I feel like going after Bunogeos now is a little hasty for such a cautious Hero.

"Are you saying you want to find Bunogeos so you can locate the spell stone?"

If we break the spell stone, we'll be able to go back to the spirit world and train. That's probably why Seiya is willing to take the risk. But Seiya merely lets out a "hmph" before briskly walking off into another underground cavern.

"H-hey?! Wait up!"

"Just follow me."

I watch Seiya from behind while thinking to myself:

Is Seiya also sick of living underground? Is that why he's in such a hurry to defeat Bunogeos? Actions that spring from impatience and anxiety oftentimes don't lead to good results.

Even then, I still inwardly shake my head.

No... I need to trust Seiya! He's not the same reckless Hero anymore, so I'm sure he has some sort of plan! Besides, I want to be freed from living as a mole as soon as possible, so I'm not gonna argue.

We leave the desolate residential area where we've been hunting and head for the slave market because we heard a few beastkin talking about how Bunogeos had a mansion nearby. Apparently, he's using a noble family's house as his own. After arriving at the market, Seiya uses Clear Ceiling and begins searching for a building that matches the description. He eventually finds the house. Despite being somewhat run-down, it's still the biggest residence in town, and it sounds exactly like the house the beastkin were talking about when we were eavesdropping. Seiya heads straight for the mansion without even a moment's hesitation.

"A-are you sure we'll be okay? He won't find us, since we're underground, right?"

I'm sure we'll be okay, since Seiya values safety above all, but if Bunogeos were to somehow find us, it'd be over. His stats are far greater than any other beastkin. However, Seiya seems to be brimming with confidence.

"Don't worry. Cave Along is evolving. Not only are the walls down here soundproof, but we're currently three meters underground as well."

"Ohhh! No wonder everything looks farther away with Clear Ceiling."

"Exactly. And if deemed necessary, we can hide up to ten meters under the surface. Normal attacks won't be able to hit us if we're that far underground."

After hearing Seiya's explanation, I continue following him until we're right underneath the mansion itself. Even though we're using Clear Ceiling, all we can see are the residence's dark floors over the earthen ceiling. However, if we listen carefully, we can hear someone pacing while stomping on the floor.

"Damn it!! That cowardly Hero's been sneaking around and killing my meeeeeeen!"

I hear Bunogeos's rage-filled voice. Seiya then takes a seat on the cavern floor and pricks up his ears to listen. Bunogeos is a powerful enemy with stats that rival those of the emperor in Gaeabrande. Fighting him head-on would be suicide for Seiya in his current state. That's probably why he's risking getting caught by going right under Bunogeos's mansion and looking for an opportune opening. When I strain my ears, I hear Bunogeos's wild cry:

"L-Lord Grandleon!"

The Beast Emperor?!

Hearing the name of the monster who rules over the entire continent of Rhadral sends me into a panic, but it sounds like Bunogeos is the only one in the room. He repeats, "Yes. Of course. Yes, my lord..." as if he's talking to himself. He must be using a crystal ball to communicate with Grandleon, who's somewhere else. Incidentally, Grandleon's voice is muffled, so I have no idea what he's saying.

"*Sigh.* That Hero has killed a lot of my men... Huh? How many? Um... It's around—it's a lot. *Sigh...* I promise I'll make sure to know my numbers next time we speak..."

He seems to be at a loss when asked how many beastkin were killed, but his sorrowful tone is short-lived, for his voice suddenly lights up.

"Oh! You're going to send *him*?! What an honor! I have nothing to fear now! Heh. What...?! Are you serious?! Wee-hee-hee! Thank you very much, my lord!"

I whisper to Seiya:

"I'm getting a little concerned. What do you think they're talking about?"

"Keep quiet."

"S-sorry..."

I shut up, not wanting to disturb Seiya while he's concentrating...

"Oink."

I hear a pig squeal by my side. Naturally, Seiya's the only one by my side, though. I think I'm hearing things when...

"Oink. Oink."

It turns out it was Seiya. Wearing his usual dignified expression, he oinks like a pig.

"Oink, oink, oink-oink, oink."

What the…?! What is going on?! Why is he oinking all of a sudden?!

Worried he might still be confused, I use Scan, but I can't see his status, since he seems to be using Fake Out.

H-he just got his cautious personality back, and now he's a pig?! The harsh underground environment must be causing his mind to deteriorate!

I've been pretty down the past few days, but this is no time to be worrying about myself. I'm far more concerned about Seiya's decaying mental state…

Day five of my life as a mole.

We finish hunting early for the day and go back to Bunogeos's mansion to eavesdrop.

"Hey, Seiya. How are you feeling? Have you found Bunogeos's weakness yet?"

I whisper in his ear, but he doesn't reply. He must be getting irritated because he hasn't been able to find any clues as to how to beat Bunogeos. I cut a death worm in half and give it to him.

"You shouldn't push yourself too hard. How about having some death worm to relax? It's actually pretty good once you get used to it."

"I'm not hungry."

"Okay…"

I munch on the death worm all by my lonesome when out of nowhere…

"Weeee-hee-hee-hee."

Seiya laughs like a disgusting pig!

"Wh-wh-wh-what's wrong?! Why are you laughing like a maniac?!"

"It's nothing."

Oh no…! Oh no, no, no! This is seriously bad! He has genuinely lost his mind! I recommend temporarily sneaking back to Little Light when the beastkin aren't looking, but he immediately turns down my suggestion. I don't even want to think about what will happen to me if I say something that rubs him the wrong way. I decide to keep everything I say mild for as long as he's like this.

*   *   *

Day six of my life as a mole.

To no one's surprise, Seiya continues to eavesdrop on Bunogeos underneath the mansion today as well. However, this time, we hear the footsteps of someone other than Bunogeos. It sounds like another beastkin has come to the mansion, and Bunogeos's voice is bubbling with glee.

"Ohhh! Thank you for coming!"

"*Screech!* It was a long flight here, but these were Lord Grandleon's orders, after all!"

"Anyway, let's get down to business! Let's use those powers of yours and find the Hero!"

"No need. He could already be nearby!"

And then…

Skreeeeee!

I hear a faint high-pitched sound, thanks to having a better hearing range than humans. It looks like Seiya was able to hear it as well, though.

"He said he flew here. A bat-type beastkin, perhaps? I'm not familiar with bats, but he used echolocation. He probably found these caverns."

"What?! But we're underground!"

"Echolocation is effective, whether underground or in the water."

"Wh-what?! Then we have to go deeper!"

"No. Even if we descend ten meters, which is Cave Along's threshold, we risk the chance that Bunogeos's attacks will still reach us, burying us alive."

"…?! I thought you said we had nothing to worry about?!"

"I said that normal attacks wouldn't be able to hit us, not Bunogeos's. Anyway, we need to make a move unless we want them taking the initiative."

Seiya promptly undoes Cave Along, sending our bodies up toward the surface. When we arrive at the narrow space between the ground and the bottom of the mansion's flooring, I try to crawl out from under the mansion, but my head bumps into a floorboard and cracks it open.

"*Screech!* See? There they are!"

A frowning bat-like monster looks down at me as my head pokes out from the cracked floor. I'm overcome with despair, but Seiya is already bringing the blowpipe to his lips. As the bat beastkin carelessly stares at the hole in the floor, he is hit with Burst Air at point-blank range. His head explodes, and his body tumbles to the floor. Then Seiya bursts out from under the floor to send the headless body flying before firing Burst Air at Bunogeos. He must have already figured out Bunogeos's location while under the floor. Unfortunately for Bunogeos, the orc doesn't have the reflexes to dodge Seiya's sudden, accurate attack, and Burst Air's bullet hits him right in the head. However...

"Tch! That huuurt! Ya little...!"

Bunogeos places a hand over his forehead while glaring at Seiya. It looks like the attack was only strong enough to leave a small cut!

"Ya little shiiiiiiiiit! You've been hiding under my hooouse?!"

C-crap, crap, crap! This is bad! Burst Air was Seiya's one and only attack move as a Jolly Piper! But it hardly did any damage!

In the extremely spacious, dilapidated room, Bunogeos grabs the ax on his back. He then points his weapon at us as it glows with the sinister aura of Chain Destruction.

"I'm not lettin' ya get away this tiiime!"

Seiya can't use fire magic to create a smokescreen anymore, and if he uses Cave Along to dive underground, Bunogeos will smash the ground and bury him alive!

"Wh-what are we going to do, Seiya?!"

When I glance in Seiya's direction, he's already putting his platinum flute away in his breast pocket! *H-he's lost the will to fight?! Noooooo! We're done foooooor!!*

But at the very next moment, he holds a hand before his face and mutters:

"Class Change...! Jolly Piper / Earth Mage to Earth Spellblade!"

I watch Seiya in astonishment as he is wrapped in a blinding light.

"What...? No way! You can change classes without even asking Enzo in Little Light?!"

"There's no reason that toothless old fart can do it and I can't. I only had to watch him do it once to figure it out."

What he's saying is extremely rude, but this isn't the first time he has done this. He learned Elulu's Fire Arrow and my Appraise ability in the blink of an eye.

The light disappears, and Seiya is no longer a Jolly Piper. His equipment has transformed into that of a Spellblade.

D-did he really change classes? …Oh yeah! Why don't I just use Scan and see for myself? He probably hasn't had enough time to use Fake Out, since he just changed jobs!

I focus mainly on his class while using Scan…

SEIYA RYUUGUUIN

Class: Spellblade
(Earth)

LV: 99 (MAX)

HP: 321,960   **MP: 88,155**

ATK:	DEF:	SPD:	MAG:	GRW:
293,412	287,644	268,875	58,751	999 (MAX)…

I—I saw his stats! He really did change classes! …Wait! What the…?!
"Tch. Stop."

After noticing that I was using Scan, Seiya immediately uses Fake Out, blurring his status.

At any rate, it looks like Seiya was telling the truth. He changed classes on his own. But…that's not what shocked me the most.

H-he's at max level already?! How?! When did that happen?! W-wait… Hold on! That's it! It only makes sense for him to level up like this after sniping so many beastkin! Especially since he started out with the EXP Boost ability as well!

Leveling up after defeating monsters is only natural, but given this Hero has never leveled up like this before, it didn't even cross my mind. Oblivious of my surprise, Seiya calmly brushes back his glossy black hair.

"I hit my target of three hundred after defeating that bat thing. I was able to surveil Bunogeos as well. There's no point staying here any longer."

"Enough rambling! Are ya prepared to fight me or whaaat?!"

"'Prepared'? Hmph…"

Seiya unsheathes his platinum sword. He elegantly swings it a few times as if to refamiliarize himself, then points it at Bunogeos.

"I'm perfectly prepared."

I-it's been so long since I've heard him say that!

Every time Seiya utters that phrase, he crushes his opponent. Nevertheless, it's too early to relax just yet. Bunogeos is a powerful foe. Other than speed, his stats aren't too different from Seiya's, despite being at the max level. In addition, he has special abilities such as Dark God's Blessing and Total Magic Nullification to compliment his weapon that can destroy our souls. Just like when Seiya fought the emperor, I'm sure it's going to be a close match where even the smallest mistake could be the end.

...Seiya makes the first move. Raising his sword aloft, he closes the distance with his incredible speed...but to my surprise, he destroys the table right by Bunogeos's side instead.

"What the...?!"

I watch in bewilderment as particles of glass glitter in the air like rain. Bunogeos cackles.

"Wee-hee-hee! Hate to break it to ya, but that's not the spell stone ya broke. That was just an ordinary crystal ball. Made sure to hide the spell stone somewhere you'd neeever find."

Acting like he was going to attack Bunogeos but striking the spell stone instead... Yep, that's something Seiya would do. But despite being mocked that it wasn't his target, Seiya's expression doesn't change.

"I was just making sure you couldn't contact Grandleon anymore. I figured you'd be begging him for help by the end of the battle."

"Wh-what?!"

As Bunogeos's nose twitches in rage, Seiya scornfully glares at him, flips his sword around, and sheathes it.

"Seiya?! What are you doing?!"

"I'm only going to use my sword to deliver the final blow. Earth magic should be enough until then. By the way, I only leveled up to the maximum for caution's sake. I actually could have defeated this thing on an even lower level."

"Whaaat?! Then why were you spying on Bunogeos for three days straight?!"

While I may be genuinely surprised, Bunogeos's face is burning red with rage.

"Y-y-y-you're gonna wish ya hadn't said thaaaaaat!"

He raises his ax in the air and charges Seiya! But out of nowhere, Bunogeos clumsily collapses with a loud *thud*.

"Hmmmm? Whaaaaaat?!"

I look carefully and notice something tied around the beastkin's ankle.

I-is that earth magic?! It is! That's a magic snake that can be controlled remotely! It's similar to Automatic Phoenix and can only be cast by high wizards! The earth serpent twists its head and tries to sink its teeth into Bunogeos's hip, but...

"Is this a joooke?!"

He slices clean through the elongated serpent's body with his ax, effortlessly turning it into sand.

"Wee-hee-hee! Pathetic!"

Bunogeos grins smugly until, almost instantly, he hears a sound. Cracks spread across the entire floor, followed by dozens of earth serpents squirming out. Earth serpents are even invading from within the walls and windows!

In an unrestrained voice, Seiya says:

"The mansion is already surrounded by hundreds of earth serpents. There is nowhere for you to run, and no one is coming to save you. This place belongs to the snakes now."

Wh-when did he summon this many earth serpents?! ...Oh! Seiya wasn't just hiding underground and stalking Bunogeos these past three days! He was taking his time creating earth serpents! He must have then sent them out to surround the mansion after that!

Countless earth serpents slither across the floor, while even more tear holes through the walls and ceiling, endlessly appearing. Each of them rushes toward Bunogeos as if they're all trying to surround him. The eerie sight sends a chill up my spine. This is something a demon would do! I refuse to believe that a Hero, who's trying to save the world, would do such a thing! Just as the numerous snakes lunge toward Bunogeos...

"Don't you dare underestimate meeeeee! God Chopper!"

The orc freely swings his ax, creating a gust of wind. The earth serpents that are grazed by the blade or brushed by the wind are reduced to sand and blown away.

"Wh-what power...!"

The fact that he was able to obliterate over a dozen earth serpents in the blink of an eye leaves me gaping. Bunogeos, on the other hand, casts a glance at the piles of sand on the floor and smirks.

"Looks like yer magic snakes can't regeneraaate."

Bunogeos places his free hand on his steel breastplate, then tears off his armor.

"What the...?!"

I gasp at the sight of his body. From his chest to his stomach is a massive, open mouth baring an irregular set of fangs!

"I'm gonna eat these snakes with a side of humaaaaaan!"

H-he's gonna swallow us whole?! This can't be happening!

I direct my gaze to Seiya for help.

"What are we going to do, Seiya?! I think he's gonna try to suck us into that mouth!"

"Yeah, I remember him having a skill like that. This is where you come in, Rista."

"Huh?! M-me?! What do you want me to do?!"

"Sink."

"Huh?"

Seiya promptly raises a hand into the air, then...*whack!* He suddenly drops his fist on the top of my head!

"...?! Hawaaaaaah?!"

Crack! Crack! Whack!

The Hero's extraordinary power sends my lower body through the cracked floor and into the ground.

"Wh-wh-what has gotten into you?!" I yell, looking up at Seiya with half my body buried in the dirt.

That's when...

"Dieeeeee! Vacuum Shredder!!"

...the mouth on Bunogeos's body flies open. As expected, the sound of a powerful vacuum rattles my eardrums as the earth serpents are gradually sucked into his mouth! I can even feel my gorgeous blond hair on the verge of abandoning ship!

"Ahhhhhh!"

He's probably going to draw us in, destroy our souls, then swallow us. Bunogeos waits with the Chain Destruction–infused ax in hand.

No, no, no! I'm gonna die!!

I panic, but I'm able to endure Bunogeos's vacuum, since half of my body is underground. And Seiya...has his arms wrapped around my shoulders to keep himself from being sucked in as well.

"Hmm? Wait a second! Do I look like a pole to you?!"

My irritation doesn't last for long, though. After all, in a way, it's like Seiya is holding me in his arms from behind.

H-huh...? Hold on... This isn't half-bad. In fact, it's amazing. Well...it looks like I'm a pole now. I'll stand tall and support you no matter what, Seiya. Because that's what poles do!

I'm on cloud nine until I'm almost immediately drawn back to reality... because there isn't a single earth serpent left!

Bunogeos stops his vacuum attack and shuts the mouth on his stomach before smugly smirking.

"Wee-hee-hee-hee! I turned every last one of yer snakes into duuust!"

H-he's powerful! Too powerful! Seiya needs to stop messing around and unsheathe his sword! But even if Seiya did that, he wouldn't be able to move once the orc starts using Vacuum Shredder again! How are we gonna beat this pig?!

In spite of my panicking, Seiya takes his hands off my shoulders, then faces Bunogeos while leaving himself vulnerable.

"Seiya?! You have to stay behind me! You're gonna be eaten if he uses Vacuum Shredder again!"

"There's no need to worry about that. The battle is already over."

In a detached tone, Seiya continues.

"Bunogeos, you may believe you ate and destroyed all of the earth serpents, but you're wrong. I turned a few live ones into sand to make it look like you destroyed them. I made sure to mix a few in the sand of the ones you killed."

"Hmm? What was thaaat?"

"They're already turning back into snakes inside your stomach as we speak."

"Wh-what…?! N-no…!"

"Your exterior may be protected with Total Magic Nullification, but I'm willing to bet your insides are pretty fragile, hmm?"

Bunogeos's face turns pale as the Hero stares at him with a distant, penetrating gaze.

"Devour the enemy… Transform: Automatic Naga!"

Without delay, Bunogeos's stomach and chest expand as if being pushed by numerous slender bars from the inside, followed by the horrifying sound of flesh bursting apart.

"Gwaaaaaah!"

The earth serpents bore holes in Bunogeos's body.

"Eeeeeek!"

I scream at the horrific sight. Automatic Nagas crawl out from every part of his body with the exception of his arms and legs. Blood spews into the air as they devour his flesh. When the last one crawls out of Bunogeos's stomach, he coughs up black blood from both his normal mouth and the mouth on his stomach. And just like that, his massive body falls forward onto the floor… After a few moments go by, he doesn't even twitch.

"I-is it over?"

"Yeah."

Seiya places a hand on the top of my head—*pop!*—and pulls me out of the ground!

"…?! Hey!! Do I look like a radish to you?!"

I'm annoyed by his crude treatment, but he ignores me. Though after finally shifting emotional gears, I find myself impressed with how he handled Bunogeos.

"I can't believe it. You really defeated Bunogeos without drawing your sword. It wasn't even close. Earth magic is powerful stuff…"

"It outclasses all other magic when it comes to deception. If used efficiently, I may be able to defeat other enemies the same way, regardless of their status."

"Yeah… Yeah! I bet we can even beat Grandleon with earth magic!"

"Don't be rash. Earth magic alone isn't going to cut it any longer. I need something to complement it, which is why we need to return to the spirit world. But to do that, we need to destroy the spell stone."

"Oh yeah! I wonder where it could be. I mean, Bunogeos said he hid it somewhere we'd never find…"

As I frantically scan the room, I catch sight of something that makes me shudder. Bunogeos's massive body is slowly getting up off the ground!

"S-Seiya! He's alive! He's still alive!"

The cautious Hero declared that the battle was already over, so I believed him! But despite having his innards devoured and endlessly hemorrhaging black blood, Bunogeos is still alive! What unbelievable vitality! Seiya and I got cocky… We forgot that this was the SS-ranked world of Ixphoria!

"It's not…over yet…!"

Bunogeos then proceeds to shove a finger into his left eye!

"What the…?!"

I cover my eyes and peek through the opening between my fingers. Bunogeos is pulling his eye out with his finger!

"Wee-hee… Wee-hee-hee-hee! This is the spell stooone! The Demon Lord embedded it in my body! Th-this stone has enough mana to curse the entire town. O-once I eat this, no one will be able to stop meee…!"

Then Bunogeos promptly brings his eye—the spell stone—to his mouth.

"Ya should have killed me when ya had the chaaance! You're gonna wet yerself when ya see this! Second Form: Beast Hazard! Ahhhhhh!"

"S-Seiya!"

Although I'm losing my mind, Seiya doesn't seem concerned.

"Your second form, huh? I'm kind of curious, but I'm not going to watch you transform, and I'm not going to wet myself. If you wanted to defeat me, you should have gouged out your eye and transformed from the start. You would have had a slight chance of winning then. But, well, I made sure to piss you off so that wouldn't happen."

The instant Bunogeos starts to swallow the spell stone…

"Mmm…?!"

The orc's throat suddenly expands until something shoots out his mouth with the stone! The creature then slithers over to Seiya with the spell stone in its mouth.

"Did I not make myself clear the first time? This battle is already over."

Just like Bunogeos, I gasp at the sight. Holding the spell stone in its mouth… is an earth serpent! It suddenly appeared in the orc's mouth and stole the stone!

"Wh-what?! There was still an earth serpent in his body?! Why…?!"

"Bunogeos has a lot of HP. There was still a chance that he'd survive even if the Automatic Nagas in his body delivered a fatal blow. Therefore, I made sure to sneak one more inside him to keep him in check in case he tried to launch one last attack before dying."

Seiya snaps his fingers, signaling the earth serpent to instantly shatter the spell stone in its mouth. Trembling in fear, Bunogeos begins to shrink away.

"Wh-what are you…?! Wh-what *are* you?!"

"The spell stone has been destroyed. Now it's time to deliver the final blow with my sword."

After unsheathing his weapon, Seiya softly exhales. The platinum sword glows as if reacting to his breathing, and the air in the room begins to shake. One warrior doesn't even have a scratch, while the other is on the verge of death. Surely, Bunogeos has already prepared to meet his fate. He screams:

"K-killing me won't save ya! You're done for! Lord Grandleon himself is coming to Galvano tonight, and yer little tricks aren't gonna work on the almighty Beast Emperorrr!"

Seiya grips the platinum sword in both hands and raises it into the air. Then…

"Atomic Spirit Slash!"

The earth version of his magic sword attack from Gaeabrande is reborn in Ixphoria! The blade runs clean through Bunogeos's skull, immediately followed by an explosive roar and a shock wave. The floors are annihilated, and Bunogeos limply falls into the crater left in the ground.

"He appears to be dead, but just in case..."

Seiya relentlessly repeats the attack. Even after eating a few Atomic Spirit Slashes, which are at the max level, Bunogeos's body still remains in its original form. I decide not to get too comfortable this time and use Scan just in case. Despite Bunogeos being dead as a doornail, Seiya continues unleashing earth magic on him. He even uses Endless Fall on the Chain Destruction–infused ax to send it straight to the depths of the underworld.

"Seiya! Grandleon's going to be here soon, right? Shouldn't we run?"

But Seiya simply places a finger on his chin as if thinking, showing absolutely no signs of concern.

"He decided to scout Galvano the day before yesterday while speaking to Bunogeos through the crystal ball. He seems to be pretty cautious, seeing as he already planned to investigate two days ago. But...I expected as much."

Seiya finally instructs me to open a gate to the spirit world. After creating the gate, I timidly open the door.

"Oh, hey! The wall inside the gate is gone! We can finally go back to the spirit world!"

"He said Grandleon would be here tonight. That gives me around another hour. Under the assumption that he gets here early, I need to learn a new move that I could use against him within thirty minutes in the spirit world."

Thirty minutes? Since time moves more slowly in the spirit world, that gives us about two days. Is that really going to be enough? Wait... I should be rejoicing! I get to return to the spirit world! I don't have to eat death worms anymore, and I can finally take a bath!

Passing through the gate, I smile back at Seiya.

"Seiya! Hurray! We don't have to live underground any longer! I thought you were going to completely lose your mind down there!"

"Don't confuse me with yourself."

"Oh, come on! You were oinking like a pig! You were on the verge of madness!"

"I was doing that on purpose. You'll see."

"H-huh...? What does that even mean?"

But only after returning to the spirit world do I finally understand what Seiya meant.

CHAPTER 13
The Goddess of Shape-Shifting

I decide to connect the gate to the spirit world's plaza this time. Leaving the evil, desolate lands of Ixphoria and entering a pure, holy world is breathtaking to say the least.

"We're finally back!"

I stretch out while filling my lungs with the fresh air when…

"Rista!"

I turn in the direction of the familiar voice. Sitting at a garden table with an umbrella in the corner of the plaza is Aria, her eyes wide. She jumps out of her seat and comes rushing over.

"I was so worried!"

We haven't been back to the spirit world for a week in Ixphoria time, which means it has been around two years in the spirit world. All of the deities in the spirit world, including me, are immortal, so the flow of time doesn't really cross our minds. A few years is nothing to us. Even then, Aria is elated to see me, with tears welling in her eyes.

"I can't see Ixphoria through the crystal ball anymore, and I heard the enemies had weapons with Chain Destruction… Anyway, I just couldn't stop thinking about you two!"

"Thanks, Aria! But we're fine!"

I put on a smile, but Aria looks back and forth between Seiya and me dubiously.

"Really? You look a mess."

I lower my eyes and look at myself. My clothes are completely black with mud from living underground for so long. That's when…

"Oh, you're right. It's hard to believe she's a goddess."

"Y-you smell t-terrible, Rista…"

I hear a few more familiar voices. When I look up, I see Cerceus and Adenela…both of whom are pinching their noses as if they'd planned this.

"I—I was living underground, so…!"

But they don't listen to my excuses and begin staring at Seiya. He's just as filthy as I am, and yet…

"Look at Seiya. What a badass."

"Y-yeah, he's s-so dreamy."

"He looks even more refined than when he left…unlike Rista."

"Hey!"

Why am I the only one who gets called smelly and dirty?! We were both living underground! Unbelievable!

Cerceus offers me a cup of steaming coffee to ease my nerves.

"Here, have a drink. It's an espresso."

That's when I notice that Cerceus looks different. He's dressed in a vest and is wearing a bow tie.

"Wh-what's the getup for?"

"Oh, this? Actually, there've been a few changes while you two were gone! I finally opened my dream café! Welcome to Café du Cerceus! Please enjoy yourselves!"

"W-wow… Congratulations…"

As I look around, I notice a few more tables. It appears to be an open-air café. No wonder Aria and Adenela are hanging out in the plaza's corner… *Wait. Wasn't Cerceus the Divine Blade? Why is he running a café now? I—I mean, as long as this is what he wants, then I guess it's okay…*

While sipping on my hot coffee, I am suddenly shown something that looks like a tree branch.

"This is my newest creation! They're called churros, and they're to die for!"

Uh… How about putting it on a plate and trying that again?! Under normal circumstances, I wouldn't even think of touching it, but I'm starving. I basically swipe the churro out of his hand before sinking my teeth into it.

"H-how is it? You like it?"

"It's amazing! It's so, so good!"

"Really?!"

"Yeah! It's even better than death worms!"

"Oh, wonderful! ...Huh? 'Death worms'? I don't know what those are, but I doubt that's a compliment!"

Cerceus seems puzzled, but he clears his throat to switch gears and offers Seiya a plate of churros.

"A-are you hungry? Please have a churro."

But Seiya instantly turns him down with a frigid glare.

"I don't need any of your death churros."

"...! What do you mean 'death' churros?! They're normal, delicious churros!"

Seiya ignores Cerceus's cries and turns his gaze to Aria.

"Aria, I want to train with another deity, as we discussed before. Can I start now?"

"S-sure, I let them know quite a while ago, but..."

"Then let's go."

"S-Seiya?! Hold on! How about changing first?! You're not even gonna take a bath?!"

"I can do that later."

Seiya and Aria start to walk away, leaving Cerceus disappointed that Seiya didn't eat his churros and Adenela disappointed that they couldn't talk more.

"It wouldn't kill us if we took a little break..."

I complain loud enough for Seiya to hear me, but naturally, he ignores me. With Aria in the lead, we climb up a smooth mountain slope, for we're heading to the secluded celestial mountain of the unified spirit world. While it appears majestic from the view at the sanctuary, this is the first time I've ever actually climbed it. I hear deities who wish to train as hermits live here, but...

We walk over the small pebbles for a while until we can see a small log house at the foot of the mountain. Aria knocks on the door.

"Rasti, it's me, Aria. I'm coming in."

I follow Seiya and Aria into the cabin…and my knees almost give way…because there's a cyclops inside!

"What?! Wh-why is there a monster in the spirit world?!"

But the moment the beast grabs a book off the top of the shelf, a bright light illuminates the room. The massive cyclops instantly shrinks until the light fades, revealing a little girl with a book in her hand. While she is robed in mature, kimono-like attire, she's around the same age as Eich in Little Light. The little girl then explains things to me as I gawk.

"The bookshelf is really tall, and I couldn't reach a book at the top, so I changed into a cyclops."

Aria introduces her with a cheerful smile.

"This is the Goddess of Shape-Shifting, Rasti."

"The Goddess of Shape-Shifting…?"

My eyes naturally drift in Seiya's direction for answers, but he acts like I've terribly inconvenienced him as he explains.

"Ixphoria is overrun and ruled by monsters, so I was originally planning on mastering shape-shifting here before starting my journey, since I'd be able to freely get around if I turned into a monster. Too bad a certain some-one ruined that plan."

Seiya stares hard at me as I awkwardly stand in silence.

"I'm talking about you, Rista."

"I—I know that! You don't have to rub it in!"

In a desperate attempt to change the subject, I approach the young girl in front of us, bend at the knees, and smile.

"Um… Nice to meet you, Rasti! I'm Ristarte! You can call me Rista!"

The young girl then furrows her brow.

"Don't talk down to me like that. I'm a higher-ranking goddess than you."

"…Huh?"

"Rista! Rasti has been here for tens of thousands of years!"

"S-seriously?! I-I-I'm so sorry!"

How was I supposed to know?! She looks and sounds like she should be in day care!

"You smell, and you're filthy. What are you, the Goddess of Filth?"

"N-no! I'm the Goddess of Healing!"

As I frantically try to explain…

"Out of the way, Goddess of Filth."

I'm suddenly hit in the butt from behind!

"Aieeeeee?!"

Seiya's kick sends me skidding across the floor. Aria gasps.

"Huh?! I thought you two were close now!"

"A lot...has happened since then...and I've been demoted to parasitic weed..."

Aria is taken aback while I rub my butt, but Seiya just talks to Rasti like nothing happened.

"I have a question. Can you turn invisible with shape-shifting?"

"No. You can only transform into people or monsters that you've seen. And while this goes without saying, your abilities and status remain the same even after you shape-shift."

"Hmph. All right, let's get started."

"Okay. Since you have Hero qualities, learning how to shape-shift in a week is very possible."

"That won't do. I've got ten hours."

Rasti's expression instantly clouds over.

"Don't underestimate shape-shifting. It's not like you're changing clothes. It's a divine skill that requires you to change who you yourself are: your voice, smell, physique, and even presence. It's not something you can learn in one night."

Rasti then raises a slender arm into the air before us.

"Awaken the monsters of your past buried in your subconscious...and chant the spell of shape-shifting."

After chanting a spell, Rasti's arm sparkles before instantly transforming into a colossal cyclops arm.

"You'll need at least three days until you're able to do this. It may look easy, but actually doing it takes a lot of effort."

However...

"Like this?"

Before I know it, Seiya's arm has already changed into a cyclops's.

"H-have you learned how to shape-shift before?"

"No, this is the first time."

"B-but actually changing your voice is difficult! You have to imagine the

monster's voice while chanting this spell… Then your voice will deepen into a cyclops's just like this. After that—"

Rasti's voice suddenly changes as she speaks, but…

"Oh? So, in short, like this?"

Seiya speaks up in an already deep, cyclopean voice.

"Wh-wh-wh-what?!"

…Feeling at ease, Aria and I retire from the hut and smile at each other as we walk.

"It looks like he's going to learn the move in no time!"

"Yeah! He probably doesn't even need the full ten hours!"

Seiya's amazing spongelike brain is nothing surprising to us anymore. It looked like Rasti's eyes were going to pop out of her head in astonishment, though.

"Oh yeah! Rista, you need to go see Great Goddess Ishtar later. She said she wanted to talk to you."

"Huh? I wonder why."

"I don't think it's anything bad, so feel free to take a bath and get cleaned up before you go."

After descending the mountain, I return to the sanctuary and take a hot shower in the bath area. I put on a clean dress, brush my hair, then head over to Ishtar's room…

"Ristarte, I am so glad you're safe."

Wearing a gentle smile, Great Goddess Ishtar is knitting in her chair just like always.

"I apologize for worrying you."

"I heard everything from Adenela. She told me the first enemy from Ixphoria you encountered possessed a weapon with Chain Destruction…"

Her expression slightly tenses.

"There is one more thing that concerns me. When you broke the spell stone, the mist covering Ixphoria briefly cleared, but I couldn't sense Demon Lord Ultimaeus's presence."

"Wh-why not?"

"I don't know. While the current situation is dire, I feel that something even more frightening is about to occur…"

Ishtar then slowly gets out of her chair.

"I believe saving Ixphoria has gone beyond the scope of punishment. Let's go to the heart of the spirit world together. I will ask the deities to reduce your sentence."

I deeply thank Ishtar for her kindness. She is just like a loving mother. But is this really going to work? The heart of the spirit world—I've heard of its existence, but I've never been there. I don't even really know where it is.

Ishtar ends up bringing me to the Chamber of Eternal Stasis, where all of the eternal souls of the gods are stored. Nobody is allowed to enter the room without Ishtar's permission. Ishtar chants a spell, and the door's seal breaks. The moment I set foot in the room, I'm struck with a mysterious feeling.

"This way."

I quietly follow her. Shelves line the walls, storing palely glowing souls. After walking for a while, I find the shelves eventually come to an end, and I'm standing in front of a huge painting. It's a mysterious landscape of a meandering path leading up to a sanctuary on top of a cliff.

"This is the heart of the spirit world."

"Huh?"

Ishtar takes my hand, then begins to walk into the painting!

"Ahhh?!"

We run right into the canvas—or so I thought. I find myself on a meandering path. Standing tall on a cliff in the distance is a sanctuary. We've entered the painting. After walking to the stone staircase before the sanctuary, Ishtar suddenly comes to a stop and kneels, so I imitate what she's doing and kneel as well.

"Three pillars of the heart of the spirit world—God of Creation, Brahma; God of Logic and Reason, Nemesiel; and Goddess of Time, Chronoa—I, Ishtar of the highest order in the unified spirit world, have come with a request."

Before long, I hear a dignified voice coming from the back of the sanctuary.

"What is it, Ishtar?"

"Nemesiel, God of Logic and Reason, I come to speak with you about this goddess, Ristarte, in regard to her punishment to save the SS-ranked world of Ixphoria…"

Ishtar explains how the enemies of Ixphoria possess weapons with Chain Destruction that can destroy the souls of gods. She earnestly pleads with them, since Seiya and I could lose our souls if we continue our journey. However…

"Ishtar, the judgment is final. It cannot be altered. Ristarte and Seiya Ryuuguuin must bring salvation to Ixphoria."

Ishtar calmly replies to his stern tone.

"Then, at the very least, could you allow Ristarte to use her divine powers?"

"No, it wouldn't be punishment if we allowed that."

Her request is immediately shot down, but…

"Nemesiel, don't you think that's a little too much?"

I hear a goddess's voice coming from the sanctuary.

"As the parents of the gods, it's our duty to protect our children. While we cannot change the destination, we need to make a little compromise if the enemies have weapons that can kill gods."

"Goddess of Time, Chronoa, are you contesting the judgment that I, the God of Logic and Reason, have made?"

"I'll answer your question with a question, Nemesiel. Do you not care if our children die?"

"I never said that."

"Your words were no different—"

A neutral voice suddenly interjects moments before an argument breaks out.

"That's enough, you two."

Both Nemesiel and Chronoa fall completely silent. Ishtar then whispers in my ear:

"That's the ruler of the heart of the spirit world, Brahma, the God of Creation."

Th-that's the voice of the highest-ranking god—Brahma?!

Hearing the voice of the Father of all Deities turns me into a nervous wreck!

Wh-what is He going to say?! Is He going to take my side?! Or is He going to agree with Nemesiel?!

Brahma's voice echoes throughout the heart of the spirit world.

"Nemesiel, Chronoa, listen well. Without the use of Order, Ristarte's healing abilities are actually rather miserable and no better than healing herbs."

…?! Brahmaaaaaa?!

The supreme deity's words almost make me cry, and Chronoa and Nemesiel begin whispering to each other.

"Did you hear that? 'No better than healing herbs'?"

"Even though she's a goddess?"

Nemesiel asks Brahma, "Are her powers truly that insignificant?"

"Indeed, they are most pathetic."

…?! Did the supreme being just call my powers pathetic?!

After a few moments go by, Nemesiel says:

"Very well. We will allow Ristarte to use her pathetic—*ahem*—her healing powers, but she is not allowed to use Order."

After returning from the heart of the spirit world, Ishtar places a hand on my shoulder and quietly nods. There are so many things I want to say, but I manage to suppress my feelings. I just need to be thankful that I can use my healing abilities.

CHAPTER 14
The Woes of a Mermaid

I thank Ishtar and begin to leave the Chamber of Eternal Stasis when...

"Ristarte, take this with you."

I suddenly hear a voice in my head.

"This data from the past may help you."

I recognize that it's the voice of the Goddess of Time, Chronoa, the moment a sheet of paper softly flutters down from above.

"Chronoa...?"

I mutter her name after picking up the paper, but there is no response. Nevertheless, when I lower my gaze to see what's written, I'm stunned.

DEMON LORD ULTIMAEUS

LV: 99 (MAX)

HP: 1,092,174   MP: 354,788

ATK:	DEF:	SPD:	MAG:	GRW: 999
817,772	806,584	789,834	265,473	(MAX)

"I-it's Demon Lord Ultimaeus's status!!"

Ishtar nods back at me after I scream.

"The Goddess of Time prepared that just for you."

"But is this even okay?! Should I even be looking at the last boss's status?!"

"I believe that data is from one year ago when Ultimaeus defeated Seiya's party and received the Dark God's Blessing. She must have thought that showing you past data wouldn't be an issue."

I run my eyes over the data once more. The Demon Lord's special abilities and skills aren't listed, but his stats are extraordinary. I'm at a loss for words, having never seen attributes as terrifying as these. Ishtar is staring at me seriously as well.

"While the battle against the Demon Lord is still a long way off, I have a hard time believing a human Hero can defeat an enemy with attributes like this. Saving Ixphoria is going to be harder than I imagined."

Noticing the tension in my expression, Ishtar grins from ear to ear just like she always does.

"A dangerous force is approaching, yes? Please tell Seiya Ryuuguuin to return to the spirit world at once after taking care of it. I wish to make another proposal to the deities of the heart of the spirit world..."

After saying good-bye to Ishtar, I put together some rice balls and simple snacks in a lunch box and head for the hut in the secluded celestial mountains. But when I open the door, I almost drop the lunch I made...because standing before me is none other than Bunogeos! While I'm sure it's nothing more than shape-shifting, the overpowering, frightening aura from his body sends a shiver down my spine.

"Um...Seiya? That's you...isn't it?"

"Yeah."

H-his voice sounds just like Bunogeos's, too! I can't tell them apart! That's when I finally realize: Seiya's planning on disguising himself as Bunogeos! No wonder he spied on Bunogeos for three days in a row, despite being confident that he could beat him! That explains why he was oinking, too! He wasn't going mad. He was practicing!

There's a radiant light, and Bunogeos transforms back into Seiya.

"Seiya?! You mastered shape-shifting already?!"

"Yeah. It looks like I finished earlier than expected."

"Wait... Where's Rasti?"

"She's sitting over there."

Rasti, who isn't a big person to begin with, is curled up in a ball in the corner of the room.

"R-Rasti?!"

"...Leave me alone."

I don't even need to ask what happened. Her confidence must have taken a hit after Seiya learned the shape-shifting technique so quickly. I'd rather not have her take her anger out on me, so I ignore her.

"Oh yeah! Seiya! I can use my healing magic again! Ishtar asked the deities in the heart of the spirit world to lighten our sentence!"

"Hmph."

Seiya grunts as if he couldn't care less.

Y-yeah, yeah! You can stop pretending because I know you're ecstatic deep down inside!

I decide to bring out Appraise for the first time in a while.

☆RISTA'S LOVE APPRAISAL☆

-Your love rating with Seiya:	**5 points**
-Seiya thinks you're:	**a walking healing herb.**
-A tidbit of advice:	**He views you as a walking healing herb; that's only slightly better than nothing!**

...Yes!! I've been promoted from parasitic weed to walking healing herb! He thinks I'm better than nothing, and our love rating has gone up four whole points! Yaaay...

I limply fall to my knees at Rasti's side.

"...What's up with you?"

"I'm just...extremely depressed... That's all..."

But I can't let myself mope around all day. I have something I need to give to Seiya.

"Hey, Seiya! The Goddess of Time, Chronoa, gave this to me! It's past data on Demon Lord Ultimaeus!"

"Information on the Demon Lord? Is it reliable?"

"Of course! She's a goddess from the heart of the spirit world!"

Seiya swipes the paper out of my hands and lowers his gaze. After a few moments pass, he mutters with a straight face:

"His attack and defense are higher than the Demon Lord of Gaeabrande's."

Ahhh! He's even stronger than Gaeabrande's final boss—the Demon Lord Seiya had to risk his life and use Valkyrie's ultimate attack, Gate of Valhalla, twice against in order to defeat!

It's not like I'm surprised, but actually putting it into words is devastating. Do we really even stand a chance in the face of such a powerful foe?

Rasti, who had been just as depressed, suddenly stands back up and takes a peek at the paper as well. She shudders.

"U-unbelievable... That thing's even more powerful than your run-of-the-mill deity. Are you two going to be okay?"

"I—I don't know..."

Seiya then further adds fuel to the flames of despair.

"You said this was past data, correct? It's highly likely that the Demon Lord has become even more powerful by now."

"But, Seiya...! The Demon Lord's already at max level. How could he—?"

"I'm already at the maximum level, too, and I'm still trying to find a way to surpass those limits. In other words, the enemy is probably thinking the same thing."

"N-now that you mention it, Great Goddess Ishtar said she couldn't sense the Demon Lord's presence! Do you think that means...?!"

"It's reasonable to assume he's accumulating power to break the level cap barrier."

I can see only darkness in our future. I feel listless. The room is dead silent. As if to change the mood, Seiya speaks up in a loud voice.

"At any rate, we need to focus on getting past Grandleon's inspection for now. I'd prefer to go alone under normal circumstances, but as saving Ixphoria is also part of your punishment, I have no choice but to bring you with me. Therefore..."

Seiya turns his penetrating gaze on me.

"You're going to need to turn into a monster."

"M-me?! But I can't even shape-shift!"

"You don't have to worry about that. He even mastered my ultimate move: Transform Target. With that, he can turn whoever he wants into whatever he wants."

"I'm turning you into a mermaid."

…Huh? A m-mermaid…? Seriously?! I'm a little fired up now! B-but I feel like just turning me into a mermaid isn't going to be enough…

The bright light enveloping my body eventually fades. I quickly examine myself in the full-length mirror Rasti brought over…and my jaw drops.

…A head like a tuna.

…Rugged scales covering my body.

…A putrid, fishy smell flowing from every pore.

I was turned into a bipedal, upright fish-person.

"…?! What the hell?! This isn't a mermaid! I'm supposed to be human on *top* and fish on the *bottom*!"

"The fish-type beastkin I saw in Ixphoria looked like this, so we have no other choice."

"What's the point of even making me a fish-person in the first place?!"

"According to my research, fish-type beastkin have lower IQs than other beastkin and essentially only flap their lips, since they can't talk. You're less likely to have your cover blown when you can't say anything stupid. That's what makes the fish perfect for you."

"Seiyaaaaaa! Turn me back right now!"

"This isn't a game. You need to take your role seriously."

"No! I am a goddess! I'd rather die than—"

"…Rista."

Seiya heaves a sigh as I throw a tantrum in my fish body.

"Could you make yourself useful just this once?"

"…?!"

It's not like Seiya to ask for favors. He must be getting frustrated with me.

"F-fine… I'll do it…"

"Great. Then let's start training."

Seiya then begins lecturing me on how to act more fish-person-like. Despite my completely resembling one thanks to his shape-shifting ability, the enemy might get suspicious if I behave strangely.

"Listen carefully. I don't want you speaking in human tongue in Ixphoria unless I give you permission. Whenever you talk, just flap your lips and make fish noises like *uwoh uwoh.*

"Now I'm going to tell you how we're going to communicate. You're going to flap your lips twice for 'yes' and three times for 'no.' Now, if the enemy starts catching on, I want you to flap your gills instead.

"No. You need to bob more like a fish-person.

"Do not even get near other fish-type beastkin. If any of them happens to talk to you, do not say a word.

"You still don't pass for a fish-type beastkin. Throw away the old you. You're a fish."

I pour my heart and soul into the role as Seiya guides me along. Rasti rolls on the floor, roaring in laughter as I bob around the hut like a fish-person. She even says "it smells like fish in here" to make fun of me. Regardless, I keep my chin up and dedicate myself to practicing.

Meanwhile, Seiya seems to be making use of his downtime by raising the ground outside the hut and refining his earth magic. When I ask him about it, he replies:

"I'm preparing for the remote chance that Grandleon sees through our disguises. If I had more time, I would have liked to talk to the earth deity to train, but there's no time for that now. It will just have to wait until next time."

After my conversation with Seiya, I go back inside the hut and return to practicing walking like a fish-person. I make sure not to forget to smack my lips like a fish and say *uwoh uwoh,* either.

Around an hour has gone by. Halfway through practice, Rasti's laughter turned into genuine praise.

"Wow, Rista! No one will be able to tell you apart from a real fish-person now! There isn't even a hint of goddess in you left!"

"Uwoh, uwoh, uwoh!"

"…?! Rista?! What's wrong?!"

"Oh…sorry. I forgot how to speak for a second there."

That's when Seiya comes walking back into the hut.

"Hmm... It looks like you've gotten the hang of it. All right, it's about time we head back."

Still disguised as a fish-type beastkin, I create a gate to Ixphoria. Seiya shape-shifts back into Bunogeos as well.

"Our objective is to convince Grandleon that Bunogeos defeated the Hero. However..."

The orc Hero's gaze sharpens.

"If the opportunity arises, I will kill Grandleon and take his form. Be prepared."

"O-okay!"

Before walking through the gate, I ask Seiya:

"Seiya... Are you perfectly prepared?"

"That all depends on you."

...*Fair enough.*

CHAPTER 15
A Hero's Miscalculation

I connect the gate to the inside of a hut nearby Bunogeos's mansion just as Seiya requested. Disguised as Bunogeos, Seiya promptly opens the portal, but instead of going inside, he pulls something slender out of his breast pocket. It falls from his hand, then slithers through the gate.

"Was that an earth serpent?"

"Yeah. It's an Automatic Naga dedicated to scouting. Our eyes are linked."

Seiya closes his eyes and doesn't say a word for a few moments until...

"Okay. There aren't any beastkin in or around the hut. Let's go."

Only after ensuring the coast is clear do we finally make the passage. After the gate disappears, Seiya peeks out the window of the dim hut, then reminds me:

"Rista, do not speak in human tongue without my permission. Got it?"

I smack my lips, making a fishlike sound, and nod. Seiya then does something completely unlike his usual cautious self. He boldly opens the door, then begins leisurely striding down the streets of Galvano. His heavy gait is just like Bunogeos. I bob after him, mimicking a fish-person as best as I can. Before long, two dog-type beastkin notice Seiya and approach us.

"Lord Bunogeos! There you are!"

W-we're gonna be okay, right?! They can't see through our disguises, right?!

My heart hammers against my chest, but Seiya doesn't seem to be even slightly startled.

"Yep. I killed the Hero, but he wounded meee, so I was takin' care of iiit."

He drawls just like Bunogeos while rubbing his stomach. Taking a closer look, I notice scars and cuts all over Seiyageos's body. There's even blood coming out of his left eye where the spell stone was. Seiya, being as cautious as he is, must have thought it would have been bizarre for Bunogeos to win the fight unscathed. The dog-type beastkin continue talking to him as if nothing is different about him at all.

"So is Lord Grandleon not heeere yet?"

"Seems that way."

"Okaaay. Well, I guess I'll get things prepared to welcome hiiim. Hey, if you see Lord Grandleon, then tell him to meet me at my mansiooon."

"Yes, sir."

Seiya begins to walk away, leaving the dog-type beastkin behind as they bow. I bob after him, acting like I'm helping.

…Phew. *They had no idea. Shape-shifting is amazing!*

Even after encountering a few more beastkin, nobody suspects us, and we make it to Bunogeos's mansion. After searching every inch of the building, Seiya closes his eyes in the middle of the room. He's probably using his scout earth serpent to remotely search the area. Before long, he approaches me and whispers in my ear:

"Okay, you can speak in a whisper."

He places his hands on my shoulders and pulls me in. It's the perfect romantic situation, aside from the fact that he's an orc and I'm a walking tuna. On second thought, there's nothing romantic about this at all.

"It looks like we still have some time before Grandleon arrives. I'm going to place some earth serpents around the mansion while we can. That way, we can attack whenever necessary… Rista, I want you to clean up the room a little. Cleaning up the place too much would seem suspicious, so make sure it still looks like there was a battle here."

I start tidying up as Seiya heads outside. A good bit of time goes by until he returns with a young man and woman in shackles. Seiyageos tethers the frightened slaves in the corner of the room like pets.

H-he even brought human slaves! I can't believe how thoroughly he's preparing for this!

"Rista, these slaves— Wait."

Seiya suddenly freezes before looking at me and nodding.

Huh?! I-is he coming?! Is Grandleon...?!

We've already proven that our disguises are flawless, but even then, my racing heart won't slow down. My intuition as a goddess is ringing the alarm bell. A few seconds go by until...*stomp, stomp, stomp!* The room shakes. It's even louder than horses' hooves clattering against the ground. When I look out the shattered window, I see a carriage being led by two dragons with a colossal goatlike beastkin sitting in the front, steering it. Resting his chin on his palm, a lion ensconces himself in a chair with a backrest as his golden mane flutters in the wind. He wears jet-black armor over his muscular body. While not equipped with a sword, he has knifelike black claws on both hands. In one, he holds what appears to be a burned human arm, which he brings toward his mouth.

A-ack! He's eating a human arm...! That's the Beast Emperor Grandleon?!

I can feel his intimidating aura even from this far away. It's sinister, unlike anything we've faced yet in Ixphoria. Watching the Beast Emperor's entrance by my side...

"Mn...!"

Seiya suddenly strains his voice.

"His stats...! They're...!"

It sounds like he's using Scan. At any rate, what kind of stats does this monster have for Seiya to be so surprised? I use Scan and cast a gaze at Grandleon...

BEAST EMPEROR GRANDLEON

LV: 99 (MAX)

HP: 1,200,044   MP: 0

ATK:	DEF:	SPD:	MAG:	GRW:
856,121	819,637	807,711	58,754	999 (MAX)

Resistance: Fire, Wind, Water, Lightning, Ice, Earth, Holy, Dark, Poison, Paralysis, Sleep, Curse, Instant Death, Status Ailments

Special Abilities: Dark God's Blessing (LV: MAX)

Skills: Jet-Black Nail

Personality: Wicked

"His attack power…is over 850,000?! What the—?!"

I shake Seiyageos's shoulder with my trembling hand.

"Th-th-this has to be some kind of mistake! He's using Fake Out, right?! He's falsifying his stats, right?!"

"Keep your voice down. What we're looking at are his real stats."

"B-but…! His attack and defense are higher than Demon Lord Ultimaeus's!!"

"Relax. Just stick to the original plan and focus on making it through Grandleon's inspection. Got it?"

Seiya pierces me with his gaze.

"I don't have time to explain, but no matter what happens, just keep quiet. Got it? No matter what happens. If you don't do that, we're dead."

"O-o-okay. G-got it."

I tell him I've got it, but I'm already panicking on the inside! One of the Demon Lord's henchmen has stats that surpass his own! Is something as unusual as this even possible?!

The footsteps get closer to the room, but I still can't calm myself down. Without being able to resolve my feelings, I see the door to the room slowly open. Beast Emperor Grandleon appears. He quickly surveys the room, then says:

"…This place is a mess. The Hero broke into your house, huh?"

His deep voice rumbles around the room as he studies it.

After looking at Seiyageos, he turns his gaze to the beastkin behind him—me. My heart skips a beat, but he swiftly returns his attention to Seiyageos. I guess that means it's not that unusual for the ruler of this city to have a beastkin follow him around for help.

"Bunogeos, you look injured. You okay?"

"Yeah. I—I was able to defeat the Hero…but he was more of a pain than I expected…"

"You defeated him? Well, I suppose there would be no way a mere human could defeat you."

But Seiyageos staggers and slams a hand against the wall. He groans in pain.

"Hey, are you sure you're okay?"

"W-wee-hee-hee. I-I'll live."

"He really did a number on you, huh? I hate to do this while you're injured, but I need to finish inspecting the place. It'll be over soon, though."

...I listen to the conversation, impressed with Seiya's performance.

H-he's good! Acting like he's injured will make it even harder for Grandleon to see through his disguise! Even if he behaves differently than Bunogeos would, he can just blame it on the injury!

"Now, as for the reason why I'm here..."

Grandleon decided to come inspect Galvano two days ago when Seiya was assassinating beastkin with Burst Air. In other words, he was probably already planning on helping Bunogeos defeat the Hero. But since the current story is that Bunogeos scraped out a victory over the Hero, what was it Grandleon still needed to inspect?

The next thing the Beast Emperor says sends a chill down my spine.

"I'm gonna be straightforward with you, Bunogeos. I need to make sure you're really Bunogeos."

Wh-wh-what did he just say?!

"The tawny-haired demon told me that the Hero might defeat you and turn into you."

I-it's that "tawny-haired demon" again! Th-this is bad! This is real bad! They knew exactly what we were going to do!

"So I hate to do this to you, but I'm gonna need to check a few things to make sure you're the real Bunogeos. I'll be out of your hair after that."

Grandleon slowly approaches Seiya with a menacing look until he's close enough that Seiya could feel him breathing. Then...there's silence. The few dozen seconds that go by feel like an eternity to me.

"Your scent, aura, and stats...are all Bunogeos's."

"O-of course they arrre."

As Seiyageos puts on a fake smile, Grandleon questions him further.

"Where's the Hero's body?"

"I accidentally pulverized him into a pulp. I wanted to capture him alive, but..."

"He was a strong opponent, so it's understandable...but are you telling me the truth? This is *you* we're talking about. Are you sure you didn't just eat him?"

"I—I would never… Wee-hee-hee-hee…"

"Tch. Next question. Do you remember when we last communicated through the crystal ball? Let's hear your answer."

"H-huh? My answerrr?"

"I told you to look into it. I want to know exactly how many. I don't need to explain myself any further, do I?"

As Seiya keeps silent, Grandleon stands over him with a piercing glare. But even then…I remain calm! Grandleon is asking for a number—the number of beastkin killed by the Hero! We already figured that much out while we were eavesdropping under the mansion! Yep. All those days living as a mole were for this moment! I can't believe Seiya was planning on becoming Bunogeos long before he defeated him! What a genius!

"Hey, what's wrong? I told you to check, didn't I?"

"Y-yes… You want to know…how many beastkin were…killed by the Hero, right?"

"I do. Now answer me, Bunogeos."

I immediately start panicking, noticing Grandleon losing his patience.

Wh-what's wrong, Seiya?! Don't tell me you forgot! We killed exactly three hundred! Three hundred! That's all you have to say to dispel his suspicions!

"Why aren't you saying anything? Answer me!"

"Th-that's, um…"

Sweat profusely pours down Bunogeos's cheeks while Grandleon's fiendish aura grows.

"Answer me, you filthy pig! If you don't…I'll kill you!"

Wh-wh-what?! Why isn't he answering?! My breathing grows unsteady as I lose my presence of mind. But eventually, Grandleon slightly relaxes his fierce expression.

"I knew you wouldn't know your numbers…"

Huh?! Wh-what's going on?!

"That's so like you, Bunogeos."

"F-forgive me…"

O-oh! He didn't tell him even though he knew the answer because he figured Bunogeos wouldn't know! Wh-what a genius! He's too good!

"Well…it looks like you're the real deal…"

"O-of course I am…"

"Yeah… But that filthy tawny-haired demon told me he got some noise a few days ago when he was watching the Hero through the crystal ball."

A few days ago? That was probably when Seiya's personality went back from "reckless" to "cautious"! Does that mean Seiya predicted the enemy was watching him and used Fake Out to create static to blur the crystal ball? B-but even then…!

"That noise still hasn't cleared up, though. And according to the tawny-haired demon, that means the Hero could still be alive. He told me to be inquisitive because the Hero might be really convincing."

Grandleon slams his fist against the table in an annoyed manner, and his unbelievable power instantly turns it into dust.

"That filthy demon…! I'm sick of this! There's an easier way to tell humans and monsters apart!"

Grandleon points at the trembling girl in the corner of the room.

"Bunogeos, this is your final test. Kill that woman!"

The woman instantly screams. Even Seiyageos squeals a bit.

"A-are you sure? Killing humans is prohibited in this t—"

"Kill her. I'll let it slide this one time."

Sweat begins pouring out of my body.

Wh-what?! I don't care how dire the situation is! We can't kill a human! The slaves Seiya brought for added authenticity ended up working against him!

"Killing her should be no problem for you… That is…unless you're really the Hero."

Grandleon places a hand on Seiyageos's shoulder.

"O-okay…"

Seiyageos grabs the ax on his back.

It's actually a platinum sword that's been transformed! It looks like he has no other choice! He's going to act like he's going to kill that woman, then unleash a surprise attack on Grandleon! After that, we just need to get out of here somehow…

But my prediction isn't even close! Seiyageos approaches the slaves, then mercilessly swings his ax at the woman before she can even say anything! The powerful blow creates an explosion that shatters the floor, turning it, along with the woman, into powder and creating a massive crater in the ground!

I freeze at the horrific sight as if paralyzed.

This can't be happening! Seiya...killed her?!

Seiyageos then calmly states:

"Wish I could've eaten her insteaaad... Oops! D-did I say something? Wee-hee-hee! Just kidding!"

"Now, that's the Bunogeos I know."

They chat in amusement, but I can't stop trembling. *S-Seiya would never kill an innocent person! He just made it look like he did! That's gotta be it! But...! But...!*

The moment his ax struck that woman is burned into my mind. I saw her limbs get chopped off moments before her body was swallowed by the crater...

As if I've lost control of my body, I involuntarily approach Seiya from behind.

"S-Seiy—"

Before I can even finish saying his name, Seiyageos turns around and grabs me by the arm. He then opens his eyes wide, silently signaling to me: *Shut up! Don't say a word!*

Grandleon casts me a dubious gaze.

"Hey, what's with the fish?"

"O-oh... It helps me take care of little things."

"Did I just hear it talk?"

Grandleon begins moving toward me but suddenly stops and shakes his head with a frown.

"Ack. It smells like old fish."

I decide to scratch my head and make fishlike noises.

"U-uwoh, uwoh."

"Tch. I can never figure out what these fish-people are thinking."

Grandleon faces Bunogeos once more.

"Sorry for all that, while you're still injured. The inspection is over. I'm returning to Termine."

After exchanging a few more words with Seiyageos, Grandleon turns on his heel to leave. I see Seiya bow, so I follow suit and bow as well.

It isn't long before I hear the door close. When I lift my head again, Grandleon is nowhere to be found. I try to talk to Seiya, but he silently shakes his head and closes his eyes. Understanding that he's busy, I wait in silence until he's done. Soon enough, he gives me a nod. I guess he used his Automatic Naga to make sure Grandleon was gone.

"S-Seiya! D-did you j-just k-k-kill that—?"

I finally begin articulating what's on my mind when Seiya suddenly grabs me by the collar.

"Eek!"

Simultaneously, there's a sudden radiant light that changes us back to normal. The Hero…is staring at me with the eyes of a hawk.

"I told you to keep quiet no matter what happened."

"B-but…!"

"The only reason you didn't blow your cover was because you got lucky. If he'd fixed his attention on you, it would have been over."

Seiya violently shoves me away, and I fall to the floor.

"B-but…! S-Seiya, you…!"

Seiya approaches the male slave in the corner of the room and raises a hand over his head.

"Huh…?!"

The light fades to reveal that the man was nothing more than a doll made of clay.

"I combined earth magic with shape-shifting. I thought Grandleon might make me kill a human to prove myself, so I prepared those two clay dolls and placed them in the room."

"I—I had no idea you could do that!"

"Not only can they do simple movements, but they can also speak a little as well. Furthermore, I used Fake Out to make it look like they had the stats of average people, just in case someone used Scan on them. Of course, I used Fake Out on both of us as well."

"You thought that far ahead…?!"

"Yes. But it doesn't matter how much I prepare if you can't keep your mouth shut."

"S-sorry…"

After clicking his tongue, Seiya mumbles as if speaking to himself.

"Encountering enemies with stats that rival the Demon Lord's was to be expected, but I honestly never anticipated running into one this early on, let alone an enemy with stats that surpass the Demon Lord's. I need to make some major adjustments to the plan…"

It's not often that Seiya is surprised. His tone is slightly gruff as well. Nevertheless, his frustration is understandable. Not only did an enemy with unbelievable stats appear, but I almost got us killed to boot. If Grandleon had seen through my disguise, we'd be dead right now…

The mood in the room is heavy, to say the least, and all I want to do is run away.

CHAPTER 16
A Goddess's Declaration

Anyway, we somehow managed to avoid disaster. After creating a gate to the spirit world, I timidly tell Seiya that Ishtar wants to see him, but he doesn't say a word. He creates a Bunogeos doll using earth magic and shape-shifting, then places it in Bunogeos's bed before pulling the covers over it. I'm guessing he's trying to buy some time while we're in the spirit world.

"By the way...are you not going to tell the people of Little Light that you defeated Bunogeos?"

But he ignores me and heads for the gate.

"H-hey?! Seiya?! Are you even listening?!"

"The people of Little Light will be slaughtered if Grandleon discovers their existence. They're safer living underground, not knowing anything."

Seiya sputters without even looking at me. And just like that, we return to the unified spirit world together, awkward tension and all.

I connect the gate to the hall before Ishtar's room. When we arrive, Seiya bursts right in without even knocking.

"Hey, Grandma, did a god from the heart of the spirit world really give us that data on the Demon Lord?"

Seiya almost gives me a heart attack. He doesn't even greet the Great Goddess as he immediately presses her for answers.

"Yes, it was a gift from the Goddess of Time, Chronoa."

As usual, Ishtar doesn't snap at Seiya. Instead, she kindly listens to the Hero's complaints while nodding—that is, until she hears about the Beast Emperor Grandleon's stats exceeding the Demon Lord Ultimaeus's. She suddenly wears a solemn expression.

"Then please avoid engaging directly with that enemy—Grandleon. With strength in excess of 850,000...his attributes rival that of the Goddess of War, Adenela, after unleashing her full goddess potential with Order. I am going to be brutally honest with you. It is impossible for a human to defeat Grandleon."

I gulp audibly and shiver. The highest-ranking deity of the unified spirit world clearly just declared that beating Grandleon was impossible.

"Th-then what should we do?!"

"There is a way to defeat him. Grandleon's phenomenal strength is surely the result of receiving the powerful blessing of a Dark God. You should be able to weaken him if you can stop the supply of power."

Ishtar then turns her gaze to Seiya.

"Under normal circumstances, I would have waited until your battle against the Demon Lord, but...it seems we have no other choice. Seiya Ryuuguuin, I am going to teach you the Hexagram Ritual of Retribution. I have already received permission from the deities at the heart of the spirit world."

Taken aback, I mutter:

"The Hexagram Ritual of Retribution?!"

Both Seiya and Ishtar turn to me.

"Oh? Ristarte, have you heard of it?"

"Nope! Not at all! What is it?!"

...An awkward silence fills the air. A few seconds go by before Seiya says with a straight face:

"Rista, all you're doing is taking up space. You have five seconds to get out of here."

"O-okay... Sure."

After closing the door, I grit my teeth in silence.

What's his problem?! So what if I don't know?!

* * *

"…The Hexagram Ritual of Retribution… I don't know the details, but I hear it's a well-kept secret technique used by deities to destroy powerful Dark God–class enemies."

I ended up heading to Aria's room. After listening to her explanation, I let out a deep sigh, and she sends me a worried glance.

"Rista? Are you okay?"

"Yeah… It's just…things have been really rough lately…"

"You must have been through a lot. Drink this. It'll make you feel better."

I finish off the tea she hands me with a side of kindness, then put my mouth on autopilot and let the complaints pour out.

"…And you know what? I did the best I could! I even ate death worms and turned into a fish-thing while acting like an idiot! I'm a goddess, damn it! But he treats me like I'm dead weight!"

"But you would have been killed if Grandleon saw through your disguises, right? I don't think Seiya overreacted…"

"You don't?! I don't even know anymore! Is that really the man I was in love with in a past life?!"

Aria, on the other hand, calmly sips her tea before looking my way.

"Hey, Rista… People don't remember their past lives when they're reborn. Goddesses are no different. Do you know why?"

"Huh? That's, uh…"

As I find myself stuck for an answer, Aria firmly says:

"In order to forget it all and live a new life. You can't allow yourself to dwell on the past."

"Y-yeah…"

…What Aria's saying makes total sense, but I can't deny that Seiya still means a lot to me.

I decide to head back to Ishtar's room after retiring from Aria's. Of course, I'm going because I want to check up on Seiya.

"Excuse me. May I come in?"

I open the door…but Seiya is no longer inside.

"What the…?! Did Seiya learn how to do it already?!"

Ishtar smiles.

"He has always been a sponge for information, and memorizing the ritual's procedures isn't a difficult process to begin with. Putting the ritual into practice is the difficult part."

"S-so where's Seiya now?"

"He's a very cautious boy. He probably wasn't comfortable only knowing the secret ritual. He said he wanted to learn new skills and went to the rooftop to see Valkyrie."

That last nugget of info gives me a bad feeling in my gut, so I thank Ishtar and hurry to the rooftop.

When I open the door to the sanctuary's rooftop, there are two moons—a crescent moon and a full moon—side by side and glittering in the sky. Bathing in the moonlight, Goddess of Destruction Valkyrie and Seiya are locked in what appears to be a passionate embrace!

"Hooooold up! What the hell is going on here?! Is this really happening again?!"

My gut was right. I scream at what feels like déjà vu, but even then, they continue to embrace as if in their own little world. The goddess, whose only article of clothing is the chains wrapped around her body, whispers:

"Seiya, I always believed you had what it took to return to me, safe and sound."

"I was only able to save Gaeabrande thanks to your techniques of destruction, Valkyrie."

The distance between their faces continues to dwindle until they're close enough to feel the heat of each other's breath!

Wh-why?! Last time they embraced, it was just to grant him an aura of destruction! They were never actually intimate!

"By the way, I remembered Shattered Break even though I forgot the other divine techniques. Why do you think that is?"

"The Valkyrja techniques are a symbol of our bond. There is no way you could ever completely forget them. It won't be long before they all start coming back to you."

"I see… Valkyrie, I'm searching for a way to surpass my maxed-out stats.

Incidentally, when I used Scan on you, I noticed you had a special ability called Status Limit Break. Do you know something that could help me?"

"Unfortunately, that's something I was born with as the Goddess of Destruction. It's not something I can teach."

"I see…"

As Seiya stares into her eyes, Valkyrie averts her gaze in a slightly awkward manner.

"There is someone in the unified spirit world who knows how to break past your status limit, but Ishtar can't say who it is, and I can't exactly tell you, either."

S-someone like that exists, but she can't tell him who?! Why?! Is the method that dangerous?!

"Seiya, go to the Divine Forest. There, you will find a clue."

…Feeling invisible, I decide to make my presence known and slide in between them before yelling:

"Seiya! Great Goddess Ishtar told me you learned the secret ritual, so why are you risking your life on something so dangerous?! We already have a way to defeat Grandleon now!"

"Because if things don't go as planned, I don't want to be thinking, *I wish I had done that.* By then, it would be too late. You don't go all out during battle. You do that during practice."

Valkyrie crosses her arms and nods in agreement.

"Exactly. You really know your stuff."

She then rubs her slender finger down his cheek with rapt attention.

"If only *I* were the goddess assigned to you…"

"Yeah. Saving Ixphoria probably would have been easy with you by my side, Valkyrie."

"H-h-hey?!"

As I begin trembling, enduring the humiliation, Valkyrie presses her body nearer to Seiya's once more.

"Seiya, don't use Gate of Valhalla ever again. I'd be so lonely without you…"

"Okay. I'll avoid using it if possible."

They bring their faces even closer together, looking like they're about to kiss…

"Ahhhhhh!! Stoooooop!"

Unable to take it any longer, I forcibly peel them off each other.

"Wh-what do you think you're doing, Ristarte?!"

Tears roll down my cheeks just like they did the last time this happened.

"*Sniffle…!* I would've preferred you lost to the Demon Lord in Gaea-brande if I'd known things would end up like this!!"

"H-how can you even say that?! You're supposed to be his goddess!"

"*Sniffle!* I-it's not my fault he—*waaah!*"

"Ristarte…"

Valkyrie puts on a serious expression…and yet, at the very next moment…

"Ha-ha-ha-ha! You're a total mess when you cry! And you call yourself a goddess?!"

She clutches her stomach while cackling.

"Hey…! Seriously?!"

Bawling, I flail at Valkyrie, but the strongest deity in the spirit world doesn't even try to dodge my cat slap. She just looks fed up.

"*Sigh.* Get it together, Ristarte. You're not a human anymore…"

Although I'm still sobbing, I follow Seiya to the Divine Forest. It's a long way from the sanctuary's rooftop to the woods, and after some time, my sadness turns to pain. And then…

Sigh… *What am I doing? I'm acting so stupid…*

My pain eventually turns to anger and frustration.

Yeah! Valkyrie's right! Aria and even Seiya already pointed it out! I'm not Princess Tiana anymore! I'm a goddess, and Seiya is a human! No matter what happens, we'll never be together!

The moonlight peeks above the Divine Forest, faintly lighting up the entrance. After wiping my face with the hem of my dress, I yell out to Seiya from behind:

"Seiya Ryuuguuin!"

He listlessly looks back at me.

"What?"

"I am a goddess! And you are the Hero I summoned! Nothing more, nothing less!"

"…And…? Why are you stating the obvious?"

"I'm saying this for me—to remind myself!"

I puff out my chest and declare:

"We're going to save Ixphoria! But I'm going to need your extraordinary talent, Seiya Ryuuguuin!"

Seiya stares at me like I'm an idiot.

"Hmph."

He then starts walking into the forest. I follow him once again, but this time in high spirits.

"…So, Mitis, do you know anything about Status Limit Break?"

"Indeed, there is a way to accomplish such a thing."

The alluring Goddess of Archery's lips curl when she hears Seiya's question.

"Then tell me. What is it?"

"Tee-hee. I can teach you, but there's something I need to know beforehand." Mitis coos.

"…Why am I tied to this tree?"

After finding Mitis, Seiya wasted no time approaching her from behind and knocking her out with a karate chop to the neck. Then he proceeded to tie her tightly to a big tree nearby.

"Because you're a nymphomaniac. I didn't want to have to worry about fighting off a naked goddess, so I decided to take precautions."

"I see."

Not only does Mitis not argue, she even seems satisfied with his answer. Tied to a tree and wearing a serious expression, she says:

"Deep within the forest…in the depths hidden even from Great Goddess Ishtar's second sight…exists an entity that may help you break your limit."

"Oh? The depths of the forest, huh?"

Seiya thereupon swiftly turns around, leaving Mitis behind. Taken aback, I ask, "Huh? You're not gonna untie her? She told you what you wanted to know…"

Concerned, I look back at Mitis, only to find her quivering and blushing.

"Oh…! You're going to leave me tied up for a bit of neglect play…! How deliciously stimulating!"

Yep… I'm not sure why I even asked. It's not like she'd die if we just left her there forever. We turn our backs on Mitis and continue into the depths of the Divine Forest.

While walking in silence for a while, I suddenly notice the trees around us are eerily distorted. The moonlight is blocked out by the forest, making it hard to see. I know this is supposed to be a holy forest in the spirit world, but it's starting to feel as if we've wandered into a forest of the underworld.

I'm about to latch onto Seiya's arm out of fear, but I stop myself. I repeat *I am a goddess! Seiya is a human!* in my mind as I clench my fists and press on. Seiya then suddenly comes to a halt.

"Hmm… Looks like this is the place."

After finally pushing through the ghastly trees, I see an old well in the middle of a field.

"What in the world is a well doing here? …Wait! Is this…?!"

…It happened soon after I was reborn as a goddess. Aria told the young, wayward me, *"Rista, if you don't do what I tell you, I'm going to throw you down the Well of No Return in the forest."*

I got so scared, I cried, so she said, *"All you have to do is listen to me, okay?"* After that, she gently rubbed my head.

The Well of No Return…! I thought that was a fairy tale Aria made up to scold me, but it's real…!

I shake Seiya by the shoulders.

"S-Seiya! We can't be here! Aria used to tell me that getting near that well makes you lose your mind!"

"Looks like you've got nothing to worry about."

"…?! …Huh…? Hey! What's that supposed to mean?!"

Seiya presses forward. He has never shown any sign of caution when it comes to training.

"You want to save Ixphoria, right? I won't be able to break my limit without taking some risks."

"S-sure, I get that, but…!"

There's a rope ladder leading into the well. Seiya tugs on it to make sure it's safe before climbing down. Although hesitant, I follow after him. When I reach the bottom, I find myself in a dim, open space.

"This is the inside of the well? It's more spacious than I imagined…"

I can see the opening to a cavern in the distance. It looks kind of like a modern-day tunnel made out of concrete.

"S-Seiya, wait."

I chase after him, but the moment I set foot in the tunnel…I hear a loud voice.

"Get down!"

Something flying out of the tunnel suddenly rams right into me!

"Gwah?!"

The impact sends me straight to the ground.

"Wh-wh-what the…?!"

I lift my head and look back to find someone on top of me dressed in a filthy camouflage uniform. In addition, I feel two soft things touching my back…which makes me guess… *It's a woman…? B-but why would she even be here?*

Thud! Thud! Roll!

The woman, who has loose, disheveled hair similar to Adenela's, gets off me and starts rolling on the ground.

"The enemy's explosion magic is about to go off! Spread out!"

She screams while looking ahead. I follow her gaze, but there's nobody there.

"The battle of the unified spirit world, Armagezeeda, isn't over yet!"

"Arma-what…? Wh-what is she rambling about?!"

Instantly, the woman in camouflage lunges on top of me with her eyes wide open.

"Eek?!"

"You don't know about the war?! Are you a new goddess or something?!"

"I—I don't know anything about a war! I'm sorry! Forgive me for being a new goddess!"

Out of nowhere, she throws her fist into the ground.

"During the first war of Armagezeeda, my squad fought under the command of Mersais, the God of Tyranny, but we were almost completely wiped out after battling the pro-Ishtar Goddess of Destruction, Valkyrie! Mersais lost because of Valkyrie's techniques of destruction, and before Goddess of War Adenela's Dual Unlimited Eternal Blade, I…! Mn…!"

Rage burns her face, but she almost immediately softens her expression.

"But…! After much refinement, I was able to perfect my ultimate attack, Berserk: Phase Three! Adenela will be no match for me now!"

The creepy woman is all smiles, contrary to her behavior a few seconds ago. I manage to speak up and ask:

"Wh-what—who are you?!"

"Oh… I still haven't introduced myself, have I? My apologies…"

The woman then turns her unfocused gaze in my direction.

"I'm Zet, the Goddess of Warfare."

CHAPTER 17
Goddess of Warfare

The goddess in camouflage scratches her head, messing up her already disheveled hair.

Z-Zet, the Goddess of Warfare…! So she knows how to use Status Limit Break? We have to— Huh…? Where'd she go?

I look down to find her crawling flat on her stomach.

"*Hff! Hff!* I've gotta prepare—*hff! Hff!*—for the second war of Armage-zeeda!"

Wh-what the…?! She's just as—no, she's even weirder than Adenela! I should probably be careful how I act around her!

But Seiya glares at her and says:

"Hey, you. Yeah, you—the weird, creepy goddess."

"…?! You're not even gonna sugarcoat it?!"

How can you say something like that to someone you've just met?! Do you not realize how weird you are, too?!

"I'm already at max level, and I can't get any stronger. Do you know how I can break this limit?"

"…Affirmative."

Zet stands upright, then swiftly brings her face right to Seiya's.

"In order to defy the boundaries of humanity, you must give up being human! If you become a berserker, your stats will double, with the exception of magic!"

Th-they'll double?! I-it sounds too good to be true! B-but even if it is, there's no way she would teach him such an amazing ability so easily!

But Zet smirks at Seiya.

"I've got some free time, so I can teach you if you want!"

"...?! Seriously?! You're gonna help us that easily?!"

"I've been trapped in this well for so long. I'm bored. Even if you can leave, I can't because of the force field Ishtar created."

"Let me ask you a question before we begin. Has there ever been a human who mastered this technique?"

"Hmm... Well...there was one."

"How dangerous is mastering said technique?"

"Hmm... Well...you won't die."

Th-this really is too good to be true! His stats will double?! Yeah right!

I call Seiya over and secretly whisper in his ear:

"H-hey, uh... There's no guarantee you'll be okay, is there? Maybe we should try something else."

"According to Ishtar, the Hexagram Ritual of Retribution can only be used once, on a single predetermined target. I need some other way to defeat Grandleon in case the ritual fails."

"But just because this goddess is gonna teach you how to do it, that doesn't mean you'll be able to master it!"

"Valkyrie wouldn't have led me to her if she didn't believe I could do it. It's worth a shot."

There he goes bringing Valkyrie up again. She must really put a lot of faith in the cautious Hero...

Seiya faces Zet, then demands:

"All right. Teach me this Berserk: Phrase Three that can apparently defeat Adenela."

Zet's nose twitches when she hears that name. It seems pretty clear to me that there's some friction between the two of them.

"Phase Three, which quadruples stats, would be impossible for a human to learn. Even Phase Two, which triples stats, wouldn't be possible. You will be learning Berserk: Phase One."

Zet then walks into the dark tunnel and waves Seiya inside. After following her into the abyss, he turns around one last time and looks at me.

"Rista, you better not tell anyone I'm training here."

…I walk through the dark forest alone and head back to the sanctuary.

Berserk—is it really necessary for Seiya to risk his life in order to learn this move? Would the Hexagram Ritual of Retribution not be enough?

But Seiya himself came to this decision. Besides, the training already started, so there's no point in debating it anymore.

That's when all of a sudden…

"This way…"

I hear someone calling out to me in the night.

"Over here… This way…"

"Eeeeeek!"

Terrified, I cover my ears and run as quickly as I can. After returning to the sanctuary, I think about it some more and come to the conclusion that it must have been Mitis, still tied to the tree.

…I should probably untie her tomorrow.

The next day, I pack some lunch and make my way to the Well of No Return. After climbing down the rope ladder, I see Zet crawling flat on her stomach before the tunnel.

"U-um… Where's Seiya?"

"Oh, Seiya Ryuuguuin? He's currently in the Human Modification Lab… I mean, the Chamber of Concentration."

"…?! Wait! What was the first thing you just said?!"

"Chamber of Concentration."

Concerned, I try to head into the tunnel, but Zet spreads her arms out wide and stops me.

"Any farther, and you would be getting in the way of his training."

I reluctantly hand Zet the lunch I made for Seiya and leave.

Two days later, after making lunch for Seiya, I pass by the café on my way to the forest when Aria calls out to me. Cerceus and Adenela are with her as well.

"Hey, Rista. Who's Seiya training with this time?"

"Huh?! Oh, u-um… H-he's learning a really amazing move from a really wild god!"

Adenela's eyes suddenly light up.

"Wh-why are you b-being so abstract? Wh-where is S-Seiya right now?"

"H-he's having private time in his room!"

Cerceus rolls his eyes.

"What's that supposed to mean? You make it sound like he's on the pot."

"Yup, that sounds about right! Anyway, we're really busy, so I've gotta get going! Bye!"

Cold sweat drips down my neck as I basically sprint out of there.

Th-that was a close one! I need to make sure to stay away from that café for now.

…I can't meet with Seiya at the Well of No Return today, either. Sporting a headband, Zet is practicing her thrusts with a bamboo spear.

"Revo-lution! Revo-lution! Dawn is fast approaching!"

Seeing Zet like this worries me almost to death, but the lunch box I brought him yesterday is lying empty in front of the tunnel. It looks like Seiya's eating, so I feel a little better now.

I don't see Seiya the next day, either. I wait in front of the tunnel for some time, but as it doesn't seem like he's coming out, I reluctantly decide to go home. However, after climbing out of the well, I realize that I brought Seiya's chopsticks with me, so I rush back into the well… That's when I see the unthinkable.

"*Munch, munch! Nom. Nom, nom, nom!* These rations are delicious!"

Zet is eating Seiya's lunch with her bare hands!

"H-hey?! What do you think you're doing?!"

"Oops! How rude of me! But Seiya Ryuuguuin is in the middle of training! I figured it would be better if I ate this instead of letting it spoil!"

"…?! Wait, wait, wait! Have you been eating the lunches I made this entire time?! Does that mean that Seiya hasn't come out of the tunnel for three days?!"

Unable to sit around and wait any longer, I rush into the tunnel. I make my way to the back, where I run into a dead end with a glass door. On the door is a plate that says HUMAN MODIFICATION LAB. Right as I approach…

"*GROOOOOOAR!!*"

"Ahhh!"

Something rams into the door with a beast-like roar. On the other side of the glass is a monster with deep-red fur, baring its fangs. *Wait... That isn't a monster. He's wearing clothes, and judging by his physique...*

"Seiya?!"

"Oh, wow. It seems like he's just about ready. He grew into one beautiful berserker."

I hear Zet's voice, then turn around and sharply glare at her.

"Wh-what the hell did you do to him?!"

"I changed him into a berserker just like he wanted. Use Scan and check Seiya Ryuuguuin's new status."

SEIYA RYUUGUUIN

Class: Spell-blade (Earth)	Condition: Berserk			
LV: 99 (MAX)				
HP: 643,920	**MP: 88,155**			
ATK: 586,824	**DEF:** 575,288	**SPD:** 537,750	**MAG:** 58,751	**GRW:** 999 (MAX)...

"See? His stats have doubled, right?"

"I don't care! Look at Seiya! Is he even conscious?!"

"Of course not. He has no control or consciousness. Seiya Ryuuguuin is no longer anything more than my obedient doll."

"Wh-what?!"

Zet takes a key and puts it in the door's keyhole with a smirk.

"You are a foolish goddess. Did you not think to question why Ishtar prohibits this method, despite how easy it is to double your stats? It's because no mind can endure the mental contamination of transforming into a berserker. Even if someone did somehow manage to endure it, they would be mentally broken. But, well, I said he wouldn't die, so I was telling the truth."

I'm speechless. The door opens...

"Grrrrr…!"

And Berserker Seiya slowly trundles out. The aura radiating from his body isn't malice…but insanity!

"Seiya Ryuuguuin has transformed into a fighting machine! Now use that power to break through the barrier Ishtar created and free me from this well! Let the second war of Armagezeeda begin!!"

Wh-what the…?! No wonder the Goddess of Warfare was locked away in a well! We should have never asked her for help!

I abandon myself to grief while Zet roars with laughter.

"Grrr…"

But the berserker simply continues growling without moving.

"H-huh? Go break the barrier! Hurry!"

"Grrr… I refuse."

A moment of silence passes before Zet screams:

"He refused while growling?! Does that mean he's still maintaining some of his humanity?!"

"Grrr… Revert."

Almost immediately, his hair changes back to its normal color, his fangs disappear, and the aura of madness fades. I watch in amazement while Zet points her trembling finger at Seiya.

"Th-this can't be happening! You were supposed to turn into a berserker who lives only for fighting!"

I scratch my cheek while listening to Zet's complaints.

"Well…Seiya's always been like this, so…"

Ever since we first met, it's always been about training, training, training. I think back to how Cerceus once called Seiya a super-berserker, despite being human.

"H-he's only ever been interested in fighting? Th-that's impossible! Humans like romance, games, food, sleep—there are so many different things they enjoy! Don't you have anything else you like?"

"…What are you talking about?"

"Whaaaaaat?!"

Seiya leaves Zet to her bewilderment and turns his gaze on me.

"Come on, Rista. We're done here."

"O-okay!"

We walk through the tunnel and head for the ladder, but just as I reach for the rope, Zet comes rushing after us.

"What do you want?!"

"I-it's not what you think! As someone who also lives for battle, I wanted to give Seiya Ryuuguuin a warning…"

She adopts a serious expression.

"Seiya Ryuuguuin, just keep this in mind: You will not be able to use any magic or skills while berserking. Don't even think about trying any higher phases, either, especially Phase Three. It will destroy your brain. I, the Goddess of Warfare, am the only one who can use it."

"Hmph."

When Seiya gives a snort of disgust, Zet's face changes colors.

"You're thinking, *I can do it*, aren't you? I admit that it wouldn't be impossible for you to pull off Phase Two! However…! There are heights that humans were not meant to reach. If a human uses Phase Three, their mind will be forever lost to madness! The scars of the berserker will be carved into your very soul and will remain even after you return to your original world! I am telling you this because I respect your way of life."

"…I'll keep that in mind."

"I mean it. Don't even try."

Zet's lips broadly curl upward.

"Now go, Seiya Ryuuguuin! Use Berserk and fight until there's nothing left in that world!"

"That's the plan."

"Seiya? No. You can't do that… We need to *save* the world…"

Even after climbing out of the well and walking through the forest, I can still hear Zet talking nonsense in the background.

"Ah, how I yearn for the day we meet again! Next time, we will wish each other luck in the Dimensional Vortex! Until then, take care…"

Back at the sanctuary's cafeteria, I smile at Seiya as he bites into his third loaf of bread.

"I bet you wish you did that before going to Gaeabrande now, huh? It probably would have made saving the planet much easier!"

"No. I almost lost consciousness a few times in the tunnel due to the ominous aura. I was only able to endure the mental contamination because I wore the aura of destruction and have already experienced the aftermath of using Gate of Valhalla twice. Valkyrie must have guided me to Zet, the Goddess of Warfare, because she knew I was ready."

"O-oh… That must have been really rough…"

"I need to train a little more until I have complete control over Berserk."

Seiya thereupon heads to the café where Adenela is drinking coffee, grabs her by the back of the neck like a kitten, and drags her away.

"Adenela, it's time to train."

"O-okay! S-sounds good!"

I start to follow them to the Summoning Chamber when Aria suddenly pats me on the shoulder.

"Rista, Great Goddess Ishtar wants to see you."

"Huh?!"

D-does she know that we met with Zet? W-we're not in trouble, are we? Her powers aren't supposed to be able to reach the depths of the forest, so…

"…You asked for Zet's help."

The first thing that comes out of her mouth almost gives me a heart attack, but…

"Regardless of the Hexagram Ritual of Retribution's outcome, he wanted to gain the power to defeat Grandleon… He's as cautious as ever, isn't he?"

Ishtar doesn't seem to be mad in the least.

"But, Ristarte, allow me to repeat myself just so you don't forget. Do not engage in direct combat with Grandleon. Even after using Zet's forbidden technique, Seiya Ryuuguuin's attributes still fall far behind his."

"O-okay! I understand!"

"But if he weakens Grandleon first with the Hexagram Ritual of Retribution, then his chances of defeating the enemy will greatly increase."

Ishtar smiles for a moment, but her face soon slightly tenses.

"You will not be able to return to the spirit world while you are in Grandleon's base, just like in Galvano. You should be able to use gates within Termine to travel, but that may allow the enemy to detect you. Therefore, only open a gate in an emergency."

"Okay!"

"One last thing—Termine Kingdom was your home in your past life. While I know it may be a painful memory, I am sure you will be able to conduct yourself as a righteous, caring goddess."

I bow to Ishtar once more and remove myself from her room.

A "painful memory," huh? Aria was worried about me as well, but I actually don't have any of Princess Tiana's memories, so I don't think there's anything to worry about...

When I arrive at the Summoning Chamber, the door is already open, and Seiya is glistening with sweat outside the room.

"Hmm? Seiya, are you done already?"

"Yeah. I already finished fighting Adenela at her best. She was tough. That's all I needed to know."

"What?! Don't tell me you used Berserk against her?! Especially after you told me to keep it a secret!"

"I just didn't want anyone bothering me during training. It doesn't matter anymore, since I've learned the move."

Adenela unexpectedly pokes her head out into the hall.

"R-Rista, c-come here."

The door is tightly shut, leaving only us two in the Summoning Chamber. Adenela suddenly sends me a scornful gaze.

"Y-you let Seiya l-learn Zet's Berserker technique, d-didn't you?"

"I-I-I'm sorry!"

I bow my head, but Adenela only lets out a deep sigh.

"Um... So how was he? Was Seiya stronger?"

"Yeah, h-he was unbelievably strong. Th-there will probably n-never be another h-human like him."

"...?! Does that mean he was able to prevail against Dual Unlimited Eternal Blade?! Wow! Seiya really is amazing!"

I scream in admiration, but her expression clouds over.

"N-no, i-it took S-Seiya everything he had j-just to protect himself from D-Divine Sword: Soaring Falcon."

"...!"

"R-Rista, Seiya is strong, b-but he's still human. I-if this G-Grandleon monster really has s-stats close to mine at f-full power..."

The cruel words hit me unexpectedly.

"Th-then Seiya won't be able to w-win, even if he u-uses a higher Berserk Phase."

When I walk out of the room, leaving Adenela behind, Seiya asks me:

"Are you done talking?"

"Y-yeah."

"Then let's go."

"Seiya, are you sure you're ready?"

A few moments of silence pass until Seiya speaks up with his usual air of confidence.

"I'm perfectly prepared."

...Words that used to fill me with confidence now feel empty after hearing what Adenela said.

Does Seiya even know that Adenela was going easy on him? This is Seiya we're talking about, though. I'm sure he knows. When he said he was perfectly prepared, I'm sure he meant he was going to make sure the Hexagram Ritual of Retribution gets the job done.

——But if by any chance the ritual fails...what then? A-ah! What am I thinking?! Of course it's going to work!

And just like that, I create a gate to Ixphoria before my head can fill with negative thoughts.

CHAPTER 18
The Former Kingdom of Termine

Before walking through the gate, Seiya gives me a brief rundown of what we're going to do in Ixphoria next.

"First, we're going to scout Termine Kingdom. Cave Along would be safest, but there is only so much information you can collect underground. That's why, although risky, we're going to shape-shift into beastkin and walk the streets."

Seiya transforms into a dog-type beastkin, since they're relatively common and won't stand out. I, on the other hand, get turned into a fish-person—as expected. Compared to Seiya's sharp Doberman-like appearance, my entire body is completely orange, like that of a goldfish. At least it beats having a tuna head...I guess.

"Incidentally, the Bunogeos puppet I left in Galvano is designed to say, 'Do you wanna dieee?' if anyone tries talking to him. That should buy us a decent amount of time, but defeating Grandleon in three to four days before anyone notices would be ideal."

Seiya stops speaking, then sends an earth serpent through the gate. Only after making sure our destination is safe do we finally depart. We arrive in the wastelands around Termine Kingdom and start our journey toward the castle in the distance. The castle gradually comes into view the closer we get. A massive wall surrounds the town encircling the castle. Nevertheless, it's falling apart all over, making it virtually useless.

The moment I step into town, I am overcome with a sickening sensation. This must be the Dark God's power. I guess that means we won't be able to return to the spirit world as long as we're in Termine. Seiya, assuming the form of a dog-type beastkin, gives me a look that clearly means, *From here on out, you are not to speak any human language.* I silently nod in response.

Seiya and I walk down the ruined city's filthy street. Not much remains of the houses around us, but beastkin seem to be living in them. It looks like there are even beastkin using the human-made buildings to do business, just like in Galvano.

Out of nowhere, an offensive stench assaults my nose and makes me sick to my stomach. I look in the direction of the smell when…

Mn…!

I instinctively want to scream. A burned, headless human corpse is hanging from a chain connected to the edge of the roof.

"Yummy, yummy humans! Best human meat in Termine!"

A lizard beastkin fans the dead body with a paper fan. Next to him are dried human arms, legs, and organs lined up. It looks like a scene straight out of hell. I'd rather be in Galvano in spite of the slavery. This place is far, far worse. In Termine, humans are regarded solely as food. I look away, but Seiya approaches the shop.

"How much?"

…?! You've gotta be kidding me! Is he really gonna buy that?!

I'm taken aback, but it looks like he's just trying to gather information, rather than actually buy anything. While asking the price, Seiya naturally learns that they still use the same currency the humans used to use in Termine. Their conversation progresses even more.

"Oh? So you two came all the way from Galvano, huh?"

"Yeah, we traveled here because we heard you could freely eat humans. They're more expensive than I thought, though."

"Humans are costly. If you want an all-you-can-eat setup, then your best bet would be joining the Beast Emperor's unit."

"'The Beast Emperor's unit'?"

"The elite soldiers who work directly under Lord Grandleon. They're guaranteed a good life, if you know what I mean. They're even allowed to go inside the palace. They say you can receive an even higher level of Dark God's Blessing if you pray at the Dark God's temple in the palace."

"Oh? You don't say. So how do I enlist?"

"They run trials every day at the plaza. All you gotta do is defeat your opponent and prove your strength."

I thought that Seiya would head straight for the plaza, but he walks into the shop next door instead. Inside, the bearlike shopkeeper is eerily arranging skulls to sell. It looks like an item shop. The shopkeeper smirks when he sees Dog-Seiya.

"Yo. How about a Dark God's Amulet for the road? It's the shop's best-selling product. Just holding it will grant you a minor Dark God's Blessing."

Strange letters are carved into the black stone slab, which Seiya stares at with great interest until he eventually pulls out his money pouch.

"I'll take a few."

"Heh! Pleasure doin' business with ya! How many ya want?"

I swallow my breath.

S-Seiya! You know we're in enemy territory, right?! Someone's gonna get suspicious if you try to buy a thousand!

Seiya nods as if he can feel my eyes burning a hole in him.

It looks like he's figured out what I was trying to say! Thank goodness!

"I don't mean to be a cheapskate, but…I'll just take thirty for now."

…?! That's the opposite of being cheap! I'm sure this was Seiya doing his best to lower the amount, but that's still too many! … Wh-what's going to happen?! Surely beastkin and humans perceive things in different ways! But maybe it'll be fine!

The bear-type beastkin frowns.

"You're not being cheap at all! In fact, nobody buys that many! 'I'll just take thirty for now'? Ha-ha-ha!"

Ahhhhhh! So it was too many!

The shopkeeper's loud voice could even be heard from outside, causing beastkin passing by to stop in their tracks and stare at us.

Ack! So much for trying to not stand out!

"Very well. I'll take five, then."

The bystanders make a short fuss, but Seiya ends up purchasing five. His next stop is the weapon shop next door. Right as he walks in, a frog-headed beastkin wastes no time before recommending a creepy sword with a reddish-black blade.

"Welcome, *ribbit*. Could I interest you in a sword that sucks the life force out of humans? Perfect for when you're in the mood for some dried human, *ribbit*."

Wh-what's up with that suspicious-looking sword?! I can't think of a single thing we could even use it for! There's no way Seiya's gonna—

"I'll take it."

Seiya whips out his money pouch.

Is he seriously buying more stuff?! What's he gonna do with all this junk?!

"Shopkeeper, I apologize in advance for being so cheap, but…I'll just take five for now."

"*Ribbit?!* H-how is purchasing five being cheap?! More importantly, what are you going to do with five of the same sword, *ribbit*?!"

A commotion ensues. Every beastkin, both inside and outside the shop, stares at Seiya. I grab him by the arm and drag him away until we reach an empty street. I thereupon point to the ground in silence. Seiya seems to get what I want to say, so he sends out an earth serpent to make sure there's no one else around just in case. Then he uses Cave Along to send us underground. Under the dim light of the glowstone, I unleash my pent-up rage on Seiya.

"Everyone's suspicious of you now! They're probably even going to start recognizing you!"

"It's fine."

Seiya then shape-shifts from a Doberman to a Siberian husky–like beastkin. In addition, he changes me from an orange goldfish into a darker-colored goldfish.

"O-okay, fine! You can shape-shift! That still doesn't explain why you need all that junk!"

I scream while pointing to the amulets that radiate pure malice, as well as the ominous sword.

"I want to purchase every item and weapon in town if possible. They might come in handy later."

"Maybe if this were a normal town and we were on a normal journey! But we're in a city full of beastkin! Those weird items and weapons are useless! A-and could you not use shape-shift on me when we're underground?! I hate looking like this!"

"But nobody's looking. *Sigh*. Women are such a pain in the ass sometimes."

Seiya mutters to himself but undoes the spell. A bright light envelops my body before reverting me to my original goddess self. I pull out my pocket mirror and check my face.

Heh! Oh my... I am so much more beautiful than a fish! ...Wait. That almost sounds like I'm dissing myself!!

"Anyway, Seiya, you have a plan, right?"

"Of course. I'm going to perform the Hexagram Ritual of Retribution to defeat Grandleon. I've already conducted a simulation."

He begins telling me his plan in a disinterested tone.

"First, I'm going to pass the trial and join the Beast Emperor's squad. From there, I'll sneak into the palace. There, I'll place the six barrier stones that Ishtar gave me around the Dark God's temple, which is the origin of the Dark God's power. After that, I'll get ahold of some of Grandleon's essence, since he's the recipient of said power. Some fur should do the trick. Once preparations are complete, I'll perform the Blade Dance of Retribution for three hours within a five-hundred-meter radius of Grandleon. This comes with a condition, though. No one can see me perform the sword dance. Once the blade dance is over, the ritual is complete, thus weakening Grandleon."

Seiya makes it sound like a walk in the park, but the plan has many components and sounds like a pain in the ass. Especially the last part...

"Um... The Blade Dance of Retribution, was it? Won't that be hard? I mean, you have to do it near Grandleon for a long time without anyone seeing you..."

"Ishtar said it was the biggest hurdle. Apparently, the ritual will fail the instant I'm seen, and I'll never be able to use it to defeat Grandleon again. Having said that, I can use Cave Along. It shouldn't be a problem if I go underground beneath the palace and secretly perform the dance."

"O-oh, okay! That makes sense!"

"…The only problem…is you."

Seiya casts a distant gaze at me.

"I'd normally want you quietly sleeping somewhere while I work…but Aria and Ishtar won't stop reminding me how saving Ixphoria is part of your punishment. So unfortunately, I have to bring you along."

"Well, excuuuse me!"

Seiya suddenly reaches out to me, and I scream.

"Ah?!"

I brace myself for a punch, but he doesn't do anything. Instead, something crawls out of the wall, then slithers up my leg and into my dress at lightning speed!

"Eeeeeek!"

The dreadful sensation of it brushing across my skin makes me shriek.

"Wh-wh-what did you do to me?!"

"I hid a few earth serpents in your clothes. After this, we're going to the plaza to take the trial. All you need to do is stand still, and the earth serpents will defeat your opponent."

"O-okay… Wh-whatever you say…"

When I look down my top, there are countless serpents wrapped around my chest and waist. My skin crawls, and I look away.

"We might get split up after the trial, but the earth serpents should protect you."

Uh-huh… It looks like Seiya's actually thinking about me after all. Maybe he really does c—

Seiya suddenly shoots me a stern glare.

"They'll be keeping an eye on you as well. They've been given orders to bite your jugular if you try speaking in human tongue."

"What the…?! You're awful! You don't have to do that! I won't talk!"

Paying no heed to my rage, Seiya calmly declares:

"You're of secondary importance—I mean, if we can even consider you important. The ritual is the priority because it's our safest, surest method to defeat Grandleon."

"Hmph! Whatever! Just don't mess things up!"

"…Who do you think you're talking to?"

Confidence radiates from Seiya's body as he crosses his arms. Although I'm lashing out at him, I feel relieved to see him like that.

As always, it looks like he's perfectly prepared. But I guess I shouldn't be surprised. This Hero is the master of working undercover and in secret. What in the world was I so worried about?

Before I even realize it, the fear I felt in the spirit world has subsided.

CHAPTER 19
Enlistment

After shape-shifting back into dog and fish beastkin, we reemerge on the surface while no one is around, then head to the city plaza. As we get closer, I see a crowd of beastkin excitedly raising their fists into the air while shouting.

Only when we cut through the mob and make our way to the center do I finally get a clear view of what is there. Four pegs are hammered into the ground and connected by rope, creating a squared-off space. It looks like this is where they're holding the trials. The beastkin around us seem to be spectators, which makes the enlistment trial look more like a martial arts competition than a test. Before a peg stands a beastkin with a crow head yelling:

"*Ka-kaaa!* Who is the next challenger?"

Seiya raises his hand to the crow-like beastkin.

"We'll give it a shot—the fish and me."

"You've got it! Let the trial begin!"

A massive tiger-type beastkin suddenly appears and lumbers toward the peg diagonal from us. I guess that's our opponent. Something doesn't seem right, though. In the beastkin's hand is a chain attached to someone behind him with a hemp sack over their head. Obviously, I can't see their face, but they have an iron ball clamped to their ankle. The tiger beastkin shoves them into the ring, then removes the mask.

What?! But…!

I gasp. It's a human. He appears to be in his late thirties or early forties. Judging by his height and physique, he seems to be an elite warrior, but his eyes are sunken in, and his skin is pale. His unkempt, frizzy hair grows freely. Under his ragged clothes, I can see stitches all around his arms and legs. In addition…

What's that putrid smell?!

"…He's undead."

Seiya mutters by my side.

"Ka-ka-ka!"

The crow beastkin cackles before continuing.

"They say he used to be a famous general in Termine. Heh. Nothing more than an undying toy now, though."

H-how horrible! They turned the Termine general into an undead…!

"Humans are either food or toys."

The crow laughs in amusement once more before shoving Seiya forward.

"Go get 'em! You defeat that, and you're in! Hello, Beast Emperor's squad!"

The crowd instantly goes wild. Everyone eagerly waits for Seiya, disguised as a dog beastkin, to get into the ring. Seiya, though, shakes his head.

"I said I would give it a shot, but I never said I was ready to fight. Consider me a spectator for now."

"O-okay, then how about the merfolk?"

"No, this one's just going to watch for now as well. We'll go later."

…The crowd gives us a few boos, but Seiya doesn't seem to mind. He plops himself down by a peg and gets into position to watch, so I timidly take a seat next to him. During that time, a new challenger volunteers—a grayish-brown sewer rat–like beastkin. Unlike Seiya, he climbs over the rope without hesitation and enters the ring in high spirits.

I use Scan on the sewer rat beastkin. To my surprise, both his attack and defense are over 50,000, which is relatively high compared to the beastkin in Galvano, who were around 30,000 on average.

"Let the trial for enlistment begin!"

On the heels of the crow's declaration…

"Squeaaak!"

The sewer rat beastkin bares his fangs with a smug grin, then lunges toward the undead. He cuts halfway through his opponent's neck, spraying black blood into the air. The match is over...or so I thought.

"You're mine now," the undead says in a deep voice, despite suffering a wound that would have been fatal to a living creature.

Before I know it, the undead's right hand is clenching the sewer rat's face. *Crunch.* It sounds like a fresh apple being crushed. The faceless rat then listlessly falls to the ground.

H-he's strong! That undead is unbelievably strong!

The former general gazes into the sky, then utters:

"For the Kingdom of Termine...and for her...I will kill as many beastkin as I can!"

His eyes are brimming with determination even in death. I decide to use Scan on the undead in the ring.

GENERAL JONDE

Condition: Undead

LV: 59

HP: 172,234   **MP: 0**

ATK: 119,874   **DEF: 98,111**   **SPD: 282**   **MAG: 0**   **GRW: 698**

Resistance: Poison, Dark

Special Abilities: Corpse Regeneration (LV: 3)

Skills: Death Squeeze

Personality: Loyal

...Th-those are some impressive stats! No wonder the rat lost!

Noticing my surprise, the crow by my side remarks:

"He may be a toy, but you can't underestimate him. The Beast Emperor's men are the best of the best, so naturally, the trial isn't going to be easy. Failing…is synonymous with death."

When I look back at the ring, the missing part of the undead's neck is already regenerating. Undead creatures with high stats gain the ability Corpse Regeneration. While he can't regenerate body parts in the middle of battle, his body will eventually repair itself like this over time.

The crow takes a peek at Seiya's expression.

"What's wrong? Scared?"

"No. I still plan on taking the trial."

"*Ka-ka-kaaa!* That's the spirit! Now get in there!"

The crow lifts up the rope to the ring for Seiya, but he doesn't even budge.

"…Hey, what are you doing? You're going to fight, right?"

"No, I'm going to watch some more."

"S-still?! You made me think you were ready to fight!"

"That's sounds like a 'you' problem. I'm not ready yet."

I—I totally thought he was ready to go, too! B-but that's fine! It's probably in our best interest to watch some more!

Seiya and I continue spectating. The second challenger is a snake beastkin. He freely extends his head and tries to wrap himself around the undead general to squeeze him to death, but his head ends up getting crushed just like the rat beastkin's.

The crow beastkin says:

"Undead are naturally slow, and the iron ball around his ankle reduces his speed to almost nothing. But if he manages to catch you, it's over. Finding out how to not get caught is the key to the trial."

"Yeah. Looks that way."

The crow beastkin lifts up the rope and invites Seiya into the ring, but he shakes his head once again.

"Not yet."

"…! How long are you going to just sit there and watch?! Are you here to fight or not?!"

The upset crow shrieks in frustration, but even then, Seiya doesn't budge.

H-he might be strong, but Seiya's stats are way higher! He'd easily win! This Hero never changes!

…After the former general crushes the third challenger's goat head to pieces, Seiya finally stirs and gets up.

"All right. I'm ready."

"R-really? Are you really going to do it? I'm starting to feel like you're just messing with me…"

After much waiting, Dog-Seiya steps into the ring of the undead general.

"Yes! Let the match begin!"

Immediately, Seiya swiftly closes the distance and swings his right arm, slashing the undead with a claw that is most likely his platinum sword after shape-shifting. The former general's chest tears open. Since undead are slow, Seiya could probably get two or three more hits in, but he promptly leaps back after a single attack. The undead thereupon loses his balance as he tries to grab on to Seiya. Seiya then approaches his opponent again and strikes once before promptly moving away. He does it again…and again. The undead's body is gradually chopped away at and worn down until…

"Y-you mangy cur…!"

The general yells out in frustration.

"Hmph. A simple hit-and-run tactic is most effective against enemies like you."

"Tch! Don't you dare underestimate me!"

The general desperately tries to grab on to Seiya, but it's like watching a man fight a toddler. It's not even close.

"You're wasting your time. I've seen everything you have to offer."

Seiya's words are dripping with confidence, but it's no surprise.

I'd be more surprised if he wasn't prepared after watching for so long…

The undead wears himself out until he drops to his knees. Seiya slowly approaches after making sure his opponent can't fight any longer.

"'For the Kingdom of Termine'? Hmph. No matter how many beastkin an undead like you kill, nothing will change."

Then, out of nowhere…

Ptui!

Seiya spits on the general.

"D-damn you!! Ahhhhhh!"

He explodes with rage but can no longer freely move his body. He still needs a good bit of time before he can regenerate. Seiya kicks the general into the air, then glares down at him with eyes as cold as ice.

"Pathetic. You're not even good at dying."

It was already clear to everyone who the winner was. The crowd erupts in cheers, but the general continues staring at Seiya contemptuously. I, on the other hand, am…shaking inside! *How ruthless! I know you have to be heartless if you're going to pretend to be a beastkin, but this is sick!*

After seeing Seiya's match, the crow beastkin enthusiastically pats him on the shoulder.

"You're amazing! Not only did you dominate, you were brutal, as well! I'm going to recommend you to Lord Grandleon myself!"

Whoa! It's gonna be so much easier getting some of Grandleon's fur for the ritual now! Things are going exactly as planned!

I'm elated…that is, until the crow turns his gaze on me.

"You're up next, fishy!"

"*Uwoh…*"

Switching places with Seiya, I step into the ring. Standing a few meters ahead is the general. Smoke rises from his body as it regenerates.

"Die, beastkin…!!"

…?! Seiya must have really pissed him off! I'm scared, but…

"*Ka-ka-kaaa!* Let the match begin!"

The general has completely regenerated, and the test has started!

"I'm going to tear you apart!!"

The undead general glares at me like a demon!

I-I'm gonna be okay, right?! Seiya said the earth serpents would do something, so all I need to do is stand still, right?!

Enraged, the undead general charges at me.

"You're going to be someone's dinner when I'm done with you!"

Eeeeeek?! Am I really gonna be okay?! If I don't move, he'll tear me apart!

Mere moments pass before he gets close enough to grab me…

Plop.

I hear something drop by my feet.

Huh?

I look down to find a giant fish flopping under me.

I-is this the earth serpent that Seiya hid in my clothes?! He turned it into a fish with shape-shifting?!

Plop. Plop. Plop.

Fish gradually begin falling from my crotch, and the spectators scream at the sight!

"Wh-what the…?! She's popping out babies!"

"I thought fish laid *eggs* when they gave birth!"

"Hold up. Why the hell is she giving birth during the trial?!"

"I think I'm gonna puke!"

What's going on?! This is so embarrassing!!

But in spite of my embarrassment, countless fish continue falling from my crotch before swiftly squirming toward the undead! They latch onto his legs and, wasting no time, start chomping.

"Ahhhhhh?!"

He probably doesn't feel any pain, since he's undead. Regardless, his legs are quickly devoured as if he were in a pond full of piranhas. Taken aback, the general screams:

"Damn you, fish! Damn youuuuu!"

It isn't long before his legs are completely gone, and he falls to the ground.

"He can't move! He can't fight anymore!"

"Did you see that?! She didn't even get her hands dirty!"

"She won with the baby fish she popped out!"

The spectators then turn their gazes at me with expectant eyes.

Uh…?

I glance at Seiya, and he subtly nods back. So I…

"Uwohhhhhh!"

I raise my fists in the air, then unleash a cry of victory. I am showered with applause and cheers from the crowd.

And to tell the truth…it feels kind of good.

CHAPTER 20
The Fool's Tower

I bob after Seiya as the crow beastkin guides him to the palace. Once we get close enough, I notice the palace is still in ruins from the Demon Lord army's attack. We pass by beastkin equipped with armor at the gate and walk through an unkempt garden.

I used to live here when I was human…right?

I survey the garden overrun with weeds, but naturally, I can't remember a thing. Even standing before the grand palace evokes nothing. Ishtar and Aria were so worried about me, so I was expecting that my soul would react and I would start crying my eyes out. Instead, I feel disappointed. At the same time, though, I'm relieved. If by some chance my memories did come back and I got sentimental, it would have interfered with the mission. I would have slowed Seiya down or gotten in the way.

I think that to myself as Seiya goes into the palace with the crow. Flustered, I try to hurry after him, but…

"Hey, you go this way."

Before I realize it, a horse beastkin appears behind me and starts leading me by the arm.

Huh?! I'm not going to the palace?!

"Uwoh! Uwoh, uwoh!"

Fish-people can't talk, so I start pointing back and forth between the palace and me. Realizing what I'm trying to gesture, the horse beastkin neighs before stating:

"Yes, you passed the test."

"Uwoh!"

I nod as if to say, *Of course I did!*

"You are now a member of the Beast Emperor's special unit."

"Uwoh!"

"You're strong."

"Uwoh!"

"But…you smell. A lot."

"Uwoh?!"

"Lord Grandleon hates stinky fish-people, so I'm sorry, but I can't allow you in the palace."

Hey…?! What the hell?!

"But still, you are a powerful warrior, and you passed the trial. Therefore, I have an important mission for you."

The horse beastkin then points at a tower standing in the distance.

"That's the Fool's Tower. I want you to accompany me to the top."

I walk into the tower and look straight up to find a spiral staircase swirling to the top. The tower is just as tall as it looked from the outside. I'm guessing it was originally used as a guard tower to protect the palace from invaders.

"You're free to use this place as your home from now on."

He guides me to a small room in the corner of the first floor. When I open the door, the first thing I notice is there's enough space for one person to relax. There's a desk, a chair, and a simple bed as well.

After that, the horse beastkin begins climbing the spiral staircase. He doesn't talk, but I follow him. Unlike me, he has really good stamina due to being a beastkin, and my legs feel like two brittle twigs by the time we reach the top. The highest floor is nothing more than an open-air room with a handrail, but in the center is a wooden door to another square room. I'm guessing it's somewhere the guards can rest while taking turns keeping watch. The horse beastkin takes a key out of his pocket, sticks it into the doorknob's keyhole, and asks:

"Do you know why they call this the Fool's Tower?"

"Uwoh?"

"Because there's a fool here—a fool who feels no pain."

When he opens the door, there's an old woman crouching in the dim, narrow room. Her hands are shackled, and there's an iron ball chained around her ankle. She's dressed like a criminal, wearing only rags, but there's a hint of dignity hidden behind her weary expression.

"This is the former queen of Termine Kingdom, Carmilla."

Queen?! Sh-she's still alive?! I figured they'd already killed the entire royal family!

…She might be younger than I thought, but she's malnourished. Hanging over her wrinkles are locks of white hair. Queen Carmilla looks to be in her sixties to me.

"She is the only human in the palace who Lord Grandleon spared, annoyingly enough. I wish she'd just jump off the top of the tower and kill herself already."

After listening to the horse's complaints, the queen sputters:

"I will not kill myself. I am a priestess, after all."

She's emaciated, but judging by her words, her spirit is far from broken. Ignoring the horse beastkin, she shows me a pedestal where needles, searing irons, and other horrendous tools rest.

"We've tried every kind of torture, but nothing seems to hurt her."

The horse then places a hand on my shoulder.

"Listen carefully. Your job is to hurt this woman. Once she shows pain, you let me know. I'm sure Lord Grandleon will be thrilled."

I-I'm in charge of torture?! I can't think of anything more revolting!

Oblivious to my internal struggle, the horse beastkin speaks with an amused tone.

"Just try whatever you can think of. But whatever you do, don't kill her. And make sure to feed her once a day."

After a quick explanation of my tasks, the horse beastkin turns on his heel, opens the door, and leaves. Only the former queen of Termine Kingdom and I, a fish-person, are left in the small room.

Th-this person…was my mother?!

I stare hard at her but still can't remember a thing. The memories of the mind and soul are separate. It's something I can't remember no matter how hard I try.

"…What are you looking at, fish?"

That's when I notice that the queen is staring at me with furrowed brows. She heavily drags herself over to me, even though she has an iron ball chained to her ankle.

"It looks like you want to say something to me."

"U-uwoh!"

I shake my head, but the queen frowns even more.

"Oh my. You smell. You smell terrible. I see… So this is how you're going to torture me."

…?! No…!

"You can't even speak. You just make noises. What a truly disgusting beastkin."

The queen stares at me while pinching her nose.

"Come on. Stop standing there and bring me my food. I'm hungry."

"Uwoh?"

F-food? Where is it? Uh…

Out of nowhere, she yells menacingly:

"It's in your room on the first floor! Now hurry up, or I'm going to eat you!"

"Uwohhh?!"

I rush out of the room as if I was running away.

Sh-she's tough! And that's how she is even after being tortured! She's completely different from what I always pictured a mother to be!

After returning to the chamber I was assigned on the first floor, I notice a piece of bread on the desk.

This is all she gets? No wonder she's hungry. I'm actually getting kind of hungry, too, now that I think about it…

I suddenly notice a basket with a cloth over it next to the bread.

Oh! This must be for me!

But when I remove the cloth, I gasp.

…It's two blackened human arms.

Ahhhhhh! I can't eat this! …Wait. Does this mean I have to go without food for the next few days?! B-but…

Disheartened, I take a seat on the bed and let out a deep sigh.

Sigh… I got split up from Seiya, to boot. I probably would have been better off waiting underground if I knew it was going to be this bad... Why did I have to be so stubborn? ...P-pull yourself together, Rista! You're a goddess, not a sloth! This is your chance to show that you're useful to Seiya's journey! Yeah! There are a lot of things I can do! ...Like exploring the area and remembering where things are or searching for rare items on the ground!

But in mid-thought...

Plop.

A fish drops out of my crotch and onto the floor.

"*Uwoh?!*"

I'm taken aback, but the fish returns to sand and begins to scatter into letters.

I'm going to remind you just in case. Don't do anything stupid. Just stay put.

...I stare at Seiya's earth magic message, as if all the panic had been sucked out of me.

So he sent me this message because he thinks I'm going to mess things up, huh? Well, excuuuse me! Looks like you prepared for everything, huh?!

Before long, the message fades, and a new one appears.

Meet me in the palace garden today. That is all.

The sand packs back together, creating a fish...which jumps right up my leg!

"Ahhhhh!"

The bizarre sensation naturally causes me to scream.

O-oh crap! I'm glad no one else is here! B-but where did that fish disappear to? It didn't go anywhere...weird, right?

I pat the area around my crotch as I search for it.

Plop.

Another fish falls to the floor.

Hey?! Why are there even more fish here?! Wh-what does this one want?!

The fish looks at me, then opens its mouth wide.

"*Bleh.*"

And out of nowhere, it spits up a fruit resembling an apple!

Huh? What in the world...? Ohhh! Seiya must have prepared this for me in case I was given food I couldn't eat! I thank the cautious Hero for his thoughtfulness...

"*Bleh.*"

After seeing the fish then cough up a fruit resembling an orange, I roll my eyes.

W-was there nothing Seiya could have done about…the presentation?

Without wasting any time, the fish devours the basket of human arms to make it look like I ate them.

I grab the bread, head up the spiral staircase, and open the door to the room at the top of the tower.

"You sure took your time."

The queen sounds irritated.

"*U-uwoh…*"

I promptly offer the queen the bread. Although she takes it with a dubious stare, she swiftly sinks her teeth into it, devouring it in seconds.

"Hmph. So what's next? Going to start torturing me? Maybe stick some needles in my fingers? Or perhaps press an iron against my stomach? Either way…you'll be wasting your time…for as you know, I don't feel pain."

The queen gives a cynical smirk. But hearing about the torture draws my eyes to her arm instead. Etched in her flesh are burns, cuts, and bruises. I can only imagine the countless scars hidden underneath her clothes. It's heartbreaking.

She acts tough, but I wonder what awful things she must have gone through. Grandleon is wicked. Most people would probably wish they were dead rather than be tortured by him.

…I have no memories of when I was a human, but I feel sorry for the old woman in front of me. It's my divine nature as a goddess reacting.

"Wh-what does this fish think it's doing? Don't tell me you're sympathizing with me? A filthy beastkin like you?"

It appears I was unconsciously rubbing the queen's hand. She knocks my arm away, then averts her gaze in a slightly awkward manner.

"…You're one strange beastkin."

I have a minor epiphany and pat my stomach a few times until a fish drops down from my crotch. But the queen backs away in astonishment.

"What is wrong with you?! Suddenly giving birth in front of me…?!"

"*Bleh.*"

But the fish on the floor regurgitates an orange, which I offer to the queen.

"*Uwoh! Uwoh!*"

"Y-you're giving this to me? ...Is this even edible...?"

I peel the orange and eat a slice to show her it isn't poisonous before handing it back.

"*Uwoh! Uwoh!*"

After timidly eating the orange...

"...You really are one strange beastkin."

The queen faintly smirks and lowers her guard. Her expression changes to that of a noble queen. But all of a sudden, there's a scream that can be heard all the way at the top of the tall tower. The queen's expression tenses, and I jump.

Wh-what was that? It sounded like someone screaming...!

The queen slowly approaches the barred window.

"Another execution..."

She speaks in an indifferent manner void of all emotion.

"Grandleon locked me in this room with a clear view of the execution stage. That monster is doing everything he can to drive me into a corner. He wants to break me."

Queen Carmilla lets out a dry chuckle.

"But he's wasting his time. All my tears have dried up."

Night has fallen, so I head over to the palace garden just like Seiya told me to in the message. But when I arrive, there isn't a soul in sight. I look around, but I don't see a dog-type beastkin anywhere. *Maybe I'm early?* I walk over to the bushes in the corner of the garden when...

Whoosh! The ground suddenly gives way, and I fall into a pit.

"*Uwohhh?!*"

After falling to the ground, I glance up to find Seiya in human form looking down at me. We're inside a cavern made with Cave Along.

"Good. You even screamed '*uwoh*' when you fell. I'm impressed. You're able to stay in character even when the unexpected happens."

"Would it have killed you to be a little gentler?!"

After Seiya changes me back into a goddess, I ask:

"So...? How's the mission coming along?"

"I investigated the palace between sparring sessions with the other beast-kin, but the actual preparations start tomorrow. More importantly…"

Seiya casts a penetrating gaze at me.

"I hear there's a high-profile criminal locked up in the tower you were assigned."

What the…?! He heard about that already?!

Right before I confess that the prisoner is my mother…

"I don't know who they are, and I don't even want to know. But, Rista, listen to me. Do not get involved with them more than you need to. You could blow your cover. Anyway, just stay put."

"Yeah, yeah. I read the message you sent me. I won't do anything, so give it a rest already."

"I have a little proverb for you: No news of Rista doing anything is good news. Keep that in mind."

"You just added a few words to an existing proverb! I can't believe you! How rude!"

"You're like a child, so I have to repeat myself, or I'll worry."

Seiya then glares at me with distant eyes.

"Be that as it may, this is Grandleon's lair. I don't want to arouse any suspicion, so the next time we meet will be the last. Meet me again in three days. Same time, same place. I will proceed with the ritual with certainty and perfection until its final stage. That is all."

The conversation ends like a business meeting. After shape-shifting back into beastkin and sending the earth serpents back to the surface to scout, we separately return to the garden. After parting ways with Seiya, I go back to my room in the tower alone and lie down in bed.

Sigh… *Seiya doesn't seem to be worried about me one bit. Even in Gaeabrande he looked out for me a little, but… Ack! I have to stop thinking about it! I am a goddess and Seiya is the Hero I summoned! Nothing more, nothing less!*

And just like that, I go to bed on a new note, only thinking about the success of the Hexagram Ritual of Retribution.

CHAPTER 21
The Treasonous Beast

The next day, the horse beastkin shows up at my room in the tower.

"Have you tried torturing her yet?"

"*Uwoh.*"

"So? How'd it go?"

"*Uwohhh.*"

The beastkin seems to understand when he sees my slouched shoulders.

"Don't let it get to you. Nobody's been able to make her suffer."

After he leaves my room, I make my way to the top of the tower and head into Queen Carmilla's cell. But when I offer her an apple, she quizzically tilts her head.

"…You're not going to torture me today, either?"

"*Uwoh!*"

I put on a cheerful smile…or at least I try to. I have no idea if it actually looks like a smile, since I'm a fish-person.

"What could this fish possibly be scheming…?"

And yet, she bites into the apple before even checking for poison. She seems a lot more relaxed around me now compared to yesterday. As much as it aggravates me, I'm going to do as I was told and "stay put." It would probably be in my best interest to just pretend I'm torturing the queen here until Seiya finishes the Hexagram Ritual of Retribution and defeats Grandleon.

"So, um…is there more?"

"*Uwoh?*"

"You know…more fruit?"

Hearing her bashfully ask makes me so happy, I pull out an orange and another apple from the shape-shifting fish's mouth. But when I try to hand her the fruit…

"*Uwoh?!*"

I stumble over the chair leg and fall. To add insult to injury, I even hit my head on the table when I try to get back up.

"What are you doing? You're quite the clumsy fish."

The queen picks up the rolling fruit, roaring with laughter for the first time.

"Ha-ha-ha! You remind me of my daughter!"

Whaaaaaat?! A fish-person reminds her of her daughter?! B-but, well, I guess you could say her intuition is dead-on in a way!

"She was clumsy just like you. The only thing she was ever good at was healing magic, and she was hardly qualified to be the princess. But…she was always prepared with a quick-witted comeback. She was sharp in that way. The retainers and townspeople used to call her Princess Razor Blade."

…Did everyone used to make fun of me?!

But the queen continues in a slightly melancholic tone:

"But that Princess Razor Blade went with the Hero to defeat the Demon Lord…and never came back. They say they lost to the Demon Lord and she died…"

"*Uwoh…*"

I glance at the queen's face, expecting her to be on the verge of tears. But to my surprise, one corner of her mouth curls into a smirk.

"But I don't believe that at all! She had the devil's luck! I bet she's still out there somewhere living a carefree life in the country!"

She cheerfully laughs once more.

Well…she got it half-right…

At any rate, I'm just happy to see her doing so well. I decide to give her a shoulder massage after she finishes her fruit. She doesn't want me to at first, but she eventually gives in. I finish by giving her a full-body massage in bed until she falls asleep. After pulling the covers over her, I head back down to my room. And now that I'm alone, I can't help but think about Seiya.

Seiya is okay…right? This is Seiya we're talking about. Everything is going as planned. I'm sure of it.

The following day, I find myself fidgeting when I think about Seiya, but worrying isn't going to change anything. I need to focus on my tasks. With that in mind, I grab today's food ration and ascend the spiral staircase. After unlocking the door, I walk into the queen's room and hand her some bread and fruit. When she's done with her meal, she asks the same question again.

"…Are you going to torture me today?"

I shake my head and wave the idea away.

"Uwoh, uwoh."

"I see."

The queen seems to have opened up to me. She even tells me:

"This ability to feel no pain isn't something I was born with. For some reason, I just stopped feeling pain when the Demon Lord conquered the world. Torture bores me, even. To tell you the truth, I feel like this was a gift from the gods."

…Ixphoria fell into the clutches of evil only a year ago, and yet, Termine has already been thrown into such a state. Other than the queen, the rest of the royal family is dead. The retainers are toys, and the townspeople are food. I can't even imagine how hellish this year must have been.

She sees it as a gift from the gods, but it was probably caused by some sort of emotional trauma. Perhaps the agony she suffered was so great that her sense of pain dulled. Even then, she speaks in such high spirits, contrary to her frail body.

"I bet this is the gods' way of telling me not to give in to the torture—not to give up."

But out of nowhere…

"And what lousy gods they turned out to be."

I suddenly hear a deep voice. We jump in surprise and look in the direction of the voice.

Th-this can't be happening!

Standing tall by the door is Grandleon himself!

"Those gods of yours didn't give you the power to defeat the Demon

Lord but gave you the strength to withstand torture? What kind of worthless gods are those? Well, it's not like they even exist."

"Grandleon…!"

The queen's face changes color as she glares at the king of the beasts.

H-how long has he been there?! I didn't even sense his presence!

A wicked aura thereupon begins filling the room. It looks like he can freely control his aura and cloak his presence. Grandleon begins to approach me but almost immediately stops with a slight frown. It's just like the horse beastkin said. He seems to hate the smell of fish-people.

"Hey, fish, I'm sure you've been told, but you better not eat that old hag until I give you the okay."

"U-uwoh."

"I've decided not to kill her until I see her miserable, tear-stained face."

"Hmph. So you'll put me out of my misery if I pretend to cry?"

Grandleon grabs the queen by the lapel as if enraged by the smug look on her face. The monster then easily lifts her into the air.

"Silence, filth. That attitude of yours really pisses me off. You're nothing but skin and bones, yet you still won't beg for your life."

He callously lets her go, allowing her to fall straight onto the hard floor.

"Fish, make her cry for me. If you can do that, I'll reconsider how I view your people. I'll allow you in the palace, put you in my combat unit, and keep you by my side."

"Uwoh…"

"I'll be back to check on her again."

Grandleon leaves the room.

I-is he really gone?

I cautiously peek outside the door a few times to make sure just like Seiya would, but he's nowhere in sight. Relieved, I turn back around, only for the queen to hand me a needle.

"Come on. You heard the boss. It's about time you start taking this torture seriously. You're going to be putting yourself in danger if you don't."

"Uwoh! Uwoh!"

But even then, I shake my head. The queen is surprised, as to be expected.

"Grandleon gave you orders! How can you still refuse?!"

She seems almost fed up as she brings her face closer to mine.

"You show a lot of promise, so let me fill you in. Grandleon may have made it sound nice, but whatever you do, do not join the Beast Emperor's combat unit. You would only be shortening your life. "

"Uwoh?"

"Even though the Demon Lord conquered the world, Grandleon is still gathering elite warriors for his special forces. Why do you think that is? It's because he's ambitious. He plans on killing the Demon Lord Ultimaeus and becoming the true emperor of the world himself."

What?! I—I can't believe what I'm hearing!

"I can tell. Grandleon has the power to make it happen. You could say... he has the makings of a ruler. Ultimaeus thought he was creating a talented subordinate, but what he created was a wicked monster."

I'm suddenly overcome with anxiety. The palace's combat unit is the squad that Seiya's in.

I-is Seiya going to be okay?!

Not only are Grandleon's stats unbelievably high, but he has something that's immeasurable as well. Just as Queen Carmilla said, he seems to have a certain power that rivals that of the Demon Lord Ultimaeus himself.

The day finally comes. Seiya and I promised to meet today. Seiya should have the final phase of the ritual prepared by the time we meet tonight. I end up heading to the garden slightly early. As always, the garden is virtually empty as I head to the bushes in the back.

Whoosh! I fall into a hole created with Cave Along.

"...Rista. You're early."

I'm relieved to see that nothing has changed about him.

"Seiya! Thank goodness! I was worried something happened to you!"

"What are you talking about? I placed the six barrier stones around the Dark God's temple. I was able to get some of Grandleon's fur without being caught as well. Everything is going perfectly. All I have to do now is hide underground beneath the palace and perform the Celestial Sword Dance for the next three hours. Once I do that, the Hexagram Ritual of Retribution will be complete, thus weakening Grandleon."

"O-oh... But, Seiya...! Grandleon can control his aura and cloak his presence! I know the blade dance is all you have left to do, but don't let your guard down no matter what."

"You don't need to tell me that. I've already factored that into the equation. Everything is fine."

Seiya then looks at me like I'm stupid.

"As always, the only thing we have to worry about is you, Rista."

"M-me?!"

"Yeah, you. To perform the blade dance, I'm going to use Cave Along to position myself ten meters underground. Now, normally, I wouldn't have to worry about a thing...but unfortunately, there's you."

"Wh-what's that supposed to mean?"

"Ishtar said you wouldn't be able to create a gate to return to the spirit world due to the evil energy here. However, you can create a gate to travel within Termine. In other words, you can create a gate to intrude upon my underground cavern."

Seiya glares at me like a hawk.

"The reason I called you here at this critical moment was to remind you one more time not to do anything stupid at the last minute and ruin everything."

"Hey!"

"I will only say this once more: The Hexagram Ritual of Retribution is the one and only way to kill Grandleon with absolute certainty. But if someone sees me perform the ritual, the holy energy will instantly diffuse. Furthermore, we will never be able to use the move on the same enemy again. Failure is not an option."

"For the last time, I get it!"

"One last thing..."

"There's more?! This is getting annoying!"

"I will be prioritizing the ritual over everything else this time. That is all."

"Oh, you don't say! By the way, there's something I've been meaning to ask you! The fish in my body can't see, right?! Just the thought of you watching every move I make pisses me off!"

"Their eyes are simply for appearance only. I have no interest in what you do in privacy. However..."

The instant Seiya snaps his fingers…

Plop, plop, plop, plop, plop, plop, plop, plop, plop, plop, plop.

…around fifteen fish fall out of my crotch.

"…! How many fish did you put in here?!"

"If they bother you, I'll take them back. Even you should be able to survive for three hours without me. But, well, I left one fish for protection just in case."

"You can have them all back!"

"No, I'm leaving that one. It's not for you. It's for me."

After leaving Seiya's moving cavern, I briskly walk out of the palace garden without even looking back at him. I stomp up the tower stairs with fury in my step.

Ugh! He really pisses me off! The hell is his problem?! He even puts me down at a time like this! I'm not going to get in his way!

All I had to do was wait three hours and the ritual would have worked…

CHAPTER 22
Mother

I storm up the spiral staircase until I reach the queen's room. She gets one small loaf of bread a day. I feel sorry for her, so I started giving her fruit for dinner as well. With an apple in hand, I slowly open the door to find the queen lying in bed.

"Uwoh? Uwoh?"

I call out to her, but she's in a deep sleep. After placing the fruit on the table, I take the queen's hand.

Just a little longer... Just a little longer until that rude Hero finishes the ritual. Termine will finally be saved, and you'll be able to get out of this tower...

That's when I notice.

Huh? What's this?

The queen is holding something in her right hand. Curious, I gently open the sleeping queen's hand and grab what she was clutching. It's a small doll of a young girl who appears to be a handmaid. It's probably old, judging by the wear and filth. But even if it wasn't dirty, I would never say it was beautiful craftsmanship, not even as flattery. The face and hair are sloppily done to say the least. But for some reason, I turn it around, look at the back...and my eyes open wide.

To Mom   Love, Tiana

*   *   *

Those words are stitched into the back with black thread.

W-wait... When I was a human, did I...?!

The doll in my hand suddenly disappears.

"Look at the old hag, sleeping like a baby. I've never seen her like this."

"Uwoh?!"

The deep voice sends a chill down my spine. I turn around to find the massive king of the beastkin—Grandleon—behind me, holding the doll I'd been examining.

"Sorry. Didn't mean to scare you. There was just something bothering me. When the hag was looking at you yesterday...that wasn't how she looks at beastkin. And now this. You're here, and she's sound asleep."

The queen suddenly awakens to the sounds of our voices. But one look at Grandleon and her expression stiffens. She braces herself, but...

"Ah...!"

She suddenly shrieks and stares at her right hand. The doll she was holding is now in Grandleon's grasp.

"What? Is this yours, hag? Where have you been hiding it? Under your bed?"

"That's none of your business! Just give it back!"

The usually detached queen is now red in the face and screaming. Grandleon realizes this isn't normal and takes an even harder look at the doll.

"Something special about this doll?"

Grandleon then checks out the back.

"Tiana... That was your daughter's name, wasn't it? Which means... Oh. This was a gift from your daughter."

"G-give that back...!"

The queen walks all the way up to Grandleon and stretches her arm as far as she can to retrieve the doll from the massive beast.

"Give that back! Right now!"

"Shut your wrinkled old mouth!"

With a roar, he pushes the queen with his free hand. That alone sends her flying back and onto the floor.

"Uwoh!"

I promptly rush over to the queen. I help her sit up and rub her back, but the queen's eyes are locked on Grandleon, as if I don't even exist.

"Please... Give it back..."

Grandleon listens to her pitiful pleas, then spits on the floor.

"Is your dead daughter's toy that important to you?"

"Tiana... Tiana isn't dead!"

"Huh? You hit your head and forget or something? Ultimaeus split your daughter open, and she died a miserable death. Just like this..."

The queen violently trembles as Grandleon squeezes the doll in his hand.

"Stop...! Enough...!"

But in the very next moment, the fibers begin popping as the doll is split in half at the waist. Grandleon then offhandedly tosses the broken doll on the floor.

"Tiana...!"

The queen's voice strains.

...I clench my teeth while watching Grandleon's violence. I want to do something, but I'm powerless. I would just get knocked to the ground like the queen. So I try to hold her up while embracing her from behind.

"Mn...! Tiana... Tiana...!"

That's when...

Drip.

Something falls on the arm I have around her shoulder.

What?! N-no...! She's...!

Tears endlessly flow down the queen's cheeks.

"Hey, hey, hey! Look at that! She cried... The old hag cried! It took an entire year, but she cried! Is this raggedy doll really that important to her?"

I'm just as bewildered as Grandleon. Was the doll what kept her going? The doll I gave her in a past life? B-but why is that doll so...?

I look down at the pitiful, torn-in-half doll by my feet, and my desire to know naturally activates Appraise.

A doll that a young Princess Tiana made for her mother. [Warning] Do you wish to know the details?

W-warning?! What the...?!

I hesitate for a moment, but of course I want to know the details if I can. I wish to know more in my head when I suddenly start feeling dizzy.

*   *   *

…I abruptly find myself in a gray world like a black-and-white movie. Luxurious furniture decorates the unfamiliar bedroom.

"Mom! Mom!"

A girl around five years old rushes past me in a white dress. Standing before the young girl is Queen Carmilla in a dress as well. Her once wrinkled face is now completely smooth.

"Tiana! No running inside! It's bad manners!"

Scolded, the little girl lowers her rueful face.

"But…I really wanted to show you this, Mom…"

"What's that?"

"A doll… I made it."

Queen Carmilla reaches for the doll when she notices Tiana's hand covered in scratches.

"Your hand is a mess. You're too clumsy to be playing with sewing needles."

"But, Mom, you've been so busy with work that we hardly have time to see each other, right?"

Princess Tiana cheerfully smiles.

"So pretend this is me and keep it with you wherever you go!"

The young princess playfully moves the doll's arms and legs.

"Look! That way, we'll always be together! Even when I'm far away, I'll always be with you, Mom!"

"*Sigh…* You little…"

After accepting the doll, the queen pats young me on the head, then smiles.

"Thank you. I'll take good care of it."

I blink, and the gray world disappears. Once again, I stand before the monolithic Grandleon. The monster glares at the queen as I hold her up.

"Did seeing your dead daughter's toy break upset you that much? *Tch.* I'll never understand humans."

Grandleon approaches the queen, then grabs a handful of her hair and brings his wicked, lion-esque face toward hers.

"But I'm glad! I've waited so long to taste your anguish! Everyone you love is dead! Your daughter, the king, your retainers, and your people—everyone who has ever meant anything to you—they're all dead! Listen here, you old bat. There is no hope for this world anymore!"

He lets go of her hair, and she crumples to her knees.

"Feels good to get that load off my chest. It's been too long. Termine has finally succumbed to the beastkin."

With an air of utmost satisfaction, Grandleon says:

"Now let's get you over to the execution site so we can lop off that head of yours."

W-wait! What?!

"U-uwoh! Uwoh, uwoh, uwoh!"

Unable to sit back and watch any longer, I stand before Grandleon, blocking his path to the execution site. To my surprise, though, he places a hand on my shoulder in a friendly manner.

"Oh, don't worry. I haven't forgotten about you. I'm impressed. You were working on getting this old hag to open her heart up to you first, huh? Then you dragged out her weakness. You lulled her into a false sense of security, then bam! Found her weakness. You're good. From now on, think of this palace as your home."

N-no! That's not what I was trying to do…!

Grandleon shoves me out of the way to get by. Perhaps misinterpreting that as an attack, the earth serpent disguised as a fish appears and bares its fangs. But Grandleon simply laughs.

"You'll get your reward later. But first, I need to execute this bag of bones."

Ignoring me, he violently grabs the queen by the arm and drags her to the door. The fish that Seiya left for me will protect only me. Once it figured out that Grandleon had no intention of harming me, it returned to my body.

O-oh no! The queen's going to be killed if I don't do something! I have to stop him!

I open the door to go after them and look down the seemingly endless spiral staircase, but Grandleon is already gone.

What the…?! How did he go down the staircase so quickly?!

I rush down the stairs in a panic, but I'm so flustered that I trip and fall down them.

Ugh! Wh-why did this have to happen?! Why now?! It's only been an hour since I met with Seiya! He hasn't even finished half of the Celestial Sword Dance!

After finally making my way out of the tower, I look around, but Grandleon and the queen are still nowhere to be found.

The execution site! When I looked at it from the tower…it was this way!

My hunch proves right because, when I rush to my destination, I hear some beastkin talking while heading the same way.

"I heard they're gonna finally execute that queen."

"What? That old hag's still alive?"

I'm in a hurry, but there are too many beastkin in the way, so I can't get by.

"Uwoh! Uwoh, uwoh!"

The beastkin in front of me look back as if they're annoyed by my screaming.

"What's wrong with this fish?"

"Don't make us eat you."

They can give me dirty looks and taunt me all they want. I cut past them and solely focus on moving forward. After miserably running around for a while, I finally see Grandleon's back. He's making one of his men carry the queen while he leisurely walks ahead.

Th-thank goodness I caught up!

But the very next moment, I stop myself.

Wh-what am I doing?! I run over, catch up with them…then what?! Am I out of my mind?! There's nothing I can do to stop Grandleon!

Lowering my gaze, I notice that I'm standing on gravel. Among the rubble stands a row of crosses for crucifixion, and there's a guillotine nearby as well. Grandleon has already arrived at the execution site.

There's no longer anything I can do! Seiya…!

But Seiya's voice echoes inside my head.

"I will be prioritizing the ritual over everything else this time."

I—I can't…! Am I going to drag Seiya down again?! I can't ask him for help no matter what! Besides, Ishtar told us to avoid direct confrontation with Grandleon!

I'm immediately swallowed up by regret.

All of this… This is all my fault! If I hadn't taken the doll out of her hand, then Grandleon would have probably never noticed it! Seiya was right. This would have never happened if I had just kept my distance! I got too close to the queen!

It's too late for regret, yet I can't help but blame myself. But the only one who can do something about my ceaseless remorse is the Hero.

B-but…maybe Seiya will know what to do? Yeah…! Even if he has to fight Grandleon head-on, his overly cautious nature will once again guide him to victory!

"Seiya won't be able to w-win."

Adenela's words suddenly pop into my head. Even if Seiya somehow uses Zet's Berserk: Phase Two, which is supposedly an impossible task for humans, he would still apparently be no match for Grandleon. Going to Seiya for help like this would be meaningless. The Hexagram Ritual of Retribution is an absolute requirement to defeat Grandleon and save Termine. Which means… Which means…

I'm sorry, Queen Carmilla! Please forgive me! I can't save you…!

The beastkin drags the queen along like luggage, her eyes vacant. Up ahead is the guillotine, standing tall with its blackened blade stained with blood. When I look at the queen's exhausted, hopeless profile, I can still imagine her sweet smile from when I gave her that doll.

Mom…!

The instant I enter the cavern, I hear an ear-piercing crackle as the light inside the cavern violently flickers in the blink of an eye. The divine atmosphere filling the space must have dispersed like mist. Seiya pauses mid-dance, then runs the platinum sword into the ground.

"…Rista, do you realize what you've done?"

Seiya snaps his fingers, returning me to my original form, then casts a reproachful gaze at me.

"All the work I put into defeating Grandleon—it was all for nothing."

"U-um… B-but the queen…is about to be executed…by Grandleon…"

Seiya doesn't say a word. Not knowing what kind of face to make or how to say it, I force a pathetic smile on my face.

"Ha-ha…ha-ha-ha… Y-you're sick of me, aren't you? You're wondering how long I'm going to keep dragging you down. I know… Even after I made up my mind that our relationship is nothing more than goddess and Hero, I'm still here… But…I don't know what to do…"

I approach Seiya, desperate for help, and place my head against his chest.

"Hate me all you want. I don't care if you punch me or kick me. But please... I beg you... Save the queen..."

What am I even saying? There is no way Seiya can defeat Grandleon now that I ruined the ritual. Asking him to save the queen is beyond selfish. It's reckless. But...still...

"Even though my memories are long gone...even though I'm no longer human...she's my mother...!"

The tears endlessly drip off my cheeks.

"Please... Please save my mother! I beg of you...!"

I beg the human Hero as if I were praying to a god. A few moments of silence go by until...

"You're a goddess, and I'm the Hero you summoned. Nothing more, nothing less. I vaguely remember you saying that in the spirit world."

I tremble when I hear his sarcastic tone.

"I'm sorry! I'm so sorry...!"

The moment I apologize, Seiya grabs me by the shoulders and sternly pushes me away.

"Mn...! Sniffle...!"

No words are needed to convey his rejection. As he pushes my body away, I feel as if my spirit is far away from him as well. It hurts so much that I can't hold back the tears.

But...I was wrong.

I hear the sound of metal clinking against metal. When I slowly look up with my tear-stained eyes, I see Seiya equipping his sheathed platinum sword.

"You're right."

"Seiya...?"

"How I feel about you is irrelevant. If the goddess who summoned me wants to save the queen...then that's what I'll do."

After letting out a deep sigh, Seiya cracks his knuckles.

"Besides, I'll never be able to defeat the Demon Lord if I don't have what it takes to defeat the Beast Emperor on my own."

Seiya looks at me with sharp eyes brimming with determination.

"Let's go, Rista. It's time to save the queen and defeat Grandleon."

CHAPTER 23
Beast Hazard

As I bawl my eyes out, Seiya asks:

"How much time do we have left?"

While wiping my tears on the sleeve of my dress, I struggle to get the words out.

"Mom—Queen Carmilla…is at the guillotine at the execution site right now…surrounded by Grandleon and many other beastkin…"

Seiya quietly nods, then asks me to create a gate that opens near the execution site. Before leaving, he turns me back into a merfolk as well.

"I'll distract them while you save the queen."

After placing a hand on the gate to make sure the area is safe, he opens the door.

"Mode: Berserk…!"

A dark-red aura shoots out of Seiya's body. His glossy black hair instantly turns red as fangs peek out from the corners of his mouth.

H-he's turning into a berserker already?! I thought he'd shape-shift into a dog beastkin and sneak into the crowd!

I rush after Seiya as he disappears through the gate, then look around.

The execution site is a few dozen meters ahead. In the distance, I can see a throng of beastkin crowding around the queen standing nearby the guillotine. The supposedly cautious Hero rests his unsheathed sword on his shoulder before powerfully charging forward. Eventually, a single beastkin notices Seiya approaching.

"Huh? What's going on…?"

The beastkin's eyes turn from the queen to Seiya.

"Is that…a human?"

"Where'd he come from?"

The moment the beastkin expresses his curiosity, a red trail zigzags through each one of them. By the time Seiya passes the beastkin, their bodies have already been separated at the waist! A few second pass when…

"E-eeeeeek!"

"Ahhhhhh!"

A few nearby beastkin shriek, but their torsos promptly fall to the ground as well. It's chaos, quite fitting for a berserker. He then relentlessly cuts down each beastkin in his way. Executing the queen is put on the back burner because the site has been thrown into chaos. Even the beastkin in charge of the guillotine seems to have escaped before anyone noticed. Feeling that this is my chance, I head over to the queen while disguised as a fish. Only when she sees me does she finally seem to return to her senses.

"Y-you're…? Did you come to rescue me…?"

"Uwoh!"

I take the queen to a safe location away from the guillotine. Even if someone sees me, they'll probably assume I'm a guard who's making sure the queen doesn't run away. After finding a place with no beastkin in sight, the queen finally notices Seiya. She stares hard as he slays the beast-kin like a demon. Her eyes abruptly open wide as she shakes.

"Is that…the Hero…? Yes… Yes…! He's alive…!"

Her voice is filled with hope. I give her a nod.

I was able to get the queen back thanks to Seiya! My best option would be to take her as far away from here as possible, but…!

Crunch. I hear something massive stomp the gravel.

"…Looks like someone's enjoying themselves in my courtyard."

Behind the mountain of bodies Seiya created is Grandleon, staring at the Hero.

"You killed a few dozen of my elite unit in the blink of an eye. I'm impressed, human."

He seems completely calm, despite the fact that his men were slaughtered.

His imposing presence is exactly what I'd expect from the king of the beastkin.

I use Scan on Grandleon to double-check his stats.

BEAST EMPEROR GRANDLEON

LV: 99 (MAX)

HP: 1,200,044   MP: 0

ATK:	DEF:	SPD:	MAG:	GRW:
856,121	819,637	807,711	58,754	999 (MAX)

Resistance: Fire, Wind, Water, Lightning, Ice, Earth, Holy, Dark, Poison, Paralysis, Sleep, Curse, Instant Death, Status Ailments

Special Abilities: Dark God's Blessing (LV: MAX)

Skills: Jet-Black Nail

Personality: Wicked

Seeing his attributes, which rival a high-ranking deity of the spirit world, again sends a shiver up my spine. Phase One of Berserk doubled Seiya's stats, which means he has around 500,000 speed. His amazing agility even surpasses that of Beel Bub, the extraordinarily quick fly monster in Gaeabrande. But even then...Grandleon's speed substantially exceeds Seiya's. In fact...there's a difference of 300,000!

Seiya probably won't even be able to perceive Grandleon at that speed! There's no way we're going to be able to escape that easily! What should I do?!

I decide to secretly use my goddess powers for now and use Scan while watching Seiya and Grandleon.

"Was there still a human this powerful hiding in Rhadral? Nah, that's not possible. You're the Hero who was summoned, aren't you?"

Seiya doesn't answer and stays in a fighting stance, so Grandleon slightly softens his tone.

"Hey, now. Lower your guard a little. We're just talking right now. You're the Hero who was summoned to this world, right? Right?"

Seiya slowly opens his mouth.

"…Yeah."

"Then I guess that means you killed Bunogeos, which also means you're the one I talked to in Galvano… *Tch*. The tawny-haired demon was right after all."

Grandleon then smiles as if somewhat amused.

"Anyway, you did a really good job playing the part. Really had me fooled."

"I learned how to shape-shift in the spirit world from the Goddess of Shape-Shifting herself. Nobody would be able to tell me apart from the real thing."

"Heh. You don't say."

Grandleon lets out a suppressed laugh before spreading his arms out wide as if he has no intention of fighting.

"I'm a simple beast. Power is everything to me. What do you say? We share a mutual interest. Let's kill Demon Lord Ultimaeus together, you and me."

Wh-what the…?! Is he serious?! No…there's no way he'd do that! But maybe Seiya could pretend to cooperate, and then we could escape when Grandleon's distracted!

But I'm the one who was distracted. Before I realize it, Grandleon has disappeared! As if having teleported, standing in front of Seiya with his right arm in the air is the Beast Emperor.

"Jet-Black Nail!"

He roars with a deep voice while swinging his Chain Destruction–infused claws. The powerful roar shakes the execution site.

Seiya…!

Grandleon's attack splits the ground open…but Seiya is nowhere in sight. *Clink!* Out of nowhere, Seiya appears behind Grandleon. His sword clashes against Grandleon's long claws as he strikes.

"Hmph. You dodged my attack, then tried to attack me yourself?"

H-he dodged that?! And he even counterattacked! Grandleon's stats are clearly higher, so how in the world did he do that?!

I look at Seiya and gasp. The dark crimson aura around his body increases, and even his eyes are red!

Th-this transformation…! I-it's not just my imagination! That's Berserk: Phase Two!

Phase One doubles your stats, but Phase Two triples them! In other words, Seiya's attack is currently slightly higher than Grandleon's! I tremble with joy.

I knew he could do it! This Hero has mastered numerous skills that were said to be impossible! They said he would never be able to use Seven-Shot Shining Arrow or any techniques of destruction, but look at him now! He mastered Phase Two as well!

But then I notice another change in Seiya. His eyes change back to their original color, and his aura is no different than it was a few moments ago.

What?! Wh-what's going on?!

"If that was a fluke, then you better start saying your prayers. Here I come."

Grandleon closes in on Seiya once more and raises his right arm into the air, but Seiya's eyes instantly change color, and he evades another attack. However, this time, Grandleon follows with a second. Twisting his body, he lashes out his left hand with claws extended. Seiya, on the other hand, is ready for it and ducks. The Jet-Black Nail slices off a few strands of hair, but Seiya backs away as if it was nothing.

"You dodged again… It looks like that first one wasn't a fluke after all."

Grandleon is taken aback. But there's something I realize while focusing on Seiya.

H-his eyes changed back to their original color…! Ah…! Seiya… Seiya hasn't mastered Phase Two yet! He must be using it for seconds at a time!

He's using Phase Two every time Grandleon attacks! Then he returns to Phase One after he dodges! It's instantaneous! After learning the truth, I feel my breathing become unsteady. However, there's still a chance we could win if Grandleon doesn't notice.

But the monster, who's plotting to defeat Demon Lord Ultimaeus himself, smugly grins.

"I can't see your stats 'cause of your Fake Out ability, but I can see your aura fluctuate. It looks like your stats are suddenly increasing before every attack. Am I right? Then afterward, your aura suddenly fades again. In other words, you're only able to surpass me for an extremely short amount of time…"

Grandleon slowly moves his hands in a circle as if he was a kenpo practitioner.

"So I'm gonna use Jet-Black Nail on you until you break!"

Th-this is bad! He saw right through us! What is Seiya going to do?! While in Berserk Mode, not only can he not use his skills, but he can't use fire or earth magic, either! If Seiya wants to distract Grandleon with magic and run away, he needs to get out of Berserk Mode first! B-but he'll be killed the moment he goes back to his normal stats!

Before I can even process the situation, Grandleon is already closing in on Seiya! He immediately starts his combo using Jet-Black Nail! Seiya uses Phase Two, dodging and blocking the attacks…but it isn't long before the color of his eyes and aura fade! The Beast Emperor smirks.

"Die."

But Grandleon's body shakes, causing him to lose balance and miss his attack. Seiya promptly backsteps until he's a safe distance from him.

"What the…?"

Grandleon mutters curiously. An earth serpent is curled around one of his legs. He clicks his tongue before slicing the earth serpent to pieces as if brushing dirt off his body. The earth serpent turns to sand while falling to the ground.

"Don't think your pathetic tricks will work on me again."

Grandleon glares at Seiya, but the ground before the Hero begins to crack and protrude. Out of nowhere, over a dozen earth serpents crawl out of the ground!

Earth magic?! But I thought he couldn't use magic while in Berserk Mode!

But when I see the number of earth serpents gathering to protect Seiya, it hits me.

Ohhh! Those are the fish Seiya took from me! He turned them back into earth serpents!

"It doesn't matter how many of those you have. It won't change a thing. I'll just tear them apart."

Grandleon lunges at Seiya! He's so quick that the earth serpents can't even react in time, but Seiya uses Phase Two and dodges the attack! In the blink of an eye, he counters with the platinum sword, but…

"Oof. That was a close one."

Grandleon blocks the strike with his sinister black claws. Seiya's eye color changes back to normal, so the Beast Emperor capitalizes on the moment and follows up with another attack. But the earth serpents lunge at Grandleon in unison, as if sensing their master is in danger.

"*Tch!* Enough of your games!"

He slices through the dozen or so earth serpents one after another with Jet-Black Nail reducing them to sand! Grandleon then instantly rushes forward to attack Seiya!

All of the earth serpents were destroyed! Seiya…!

But Grandleon suddenly stops, resentfully clicking his tongue.

"There are more of those?!"

The ground beneath Seiya's feet protrudes once more, revealing the faces of even more earth serpents! This time there are thirty—fifty—no, at least a hundred of them! *Wh-what's going on?!*

The swarm of earth serpents charges Grandleon from every direction. With a placid tone, Seiya explains.

"I was planning on fighting you from the beginning, so I hid earth serpents underground all over Termine ahead of time. Now I'm just gathering them here."

S-so that's what's going on! But, like…just how many earth serpents did he make?! I mean, he was almost done with the ritual! Just how cautious is this guy?!

But they are nothing more than a distraction. They stand no chance before Grandleon, who destroys them one by one using Jet-Black Nail. Seiya uses Phase Two and tries to create some safe distance between himself and the enemy while Grandleon is dealing with the earth serpents, but the Beast Emperor isn't so forgiving. He chases after Seiya while simultaneously dealing with the fodder. He destroys twenty-four, then thirty-four, and so on. Every attack speeds up my already racing heart.

"…What? Is that it?"

The ground doesn't swell below Seiya this time. Grandleon's eyes light up as if he can already taste victory…then he suddenly charges Seiya! The Hero promptly uses Phase Two, dodging the first attack along with the second. Instantaneously, he thrusts his sword at Grandleon's heart with all his might, but the beast just barely manages to get out of the way in time! Then…the monster throws a third attack at Seiya.

Phase Two is about to end…! This is it…!

But to my astonishment, Seiya's eyes are still red! He parries the attack with his sword before bending his body backward to dodge the incoming left-hand slash. From an untenable position, he swings the platinum sword and grazes Grandleon's nose! This time, it's the Beast Emperor who moves away and creates some distance.

He's still in Phase Two?! How?!

Grandleon appears just as confused as I am.

"Hey... What's the deal? Were you just pretending you could only do that in short bursts to trick me? No... You can't fool these eyes. It took everything you had to barely maintain that power up until a few moments ago."

Seiya twists his neck while cracking his knuckles.

"Using Phase Two puts a lot of strain on the body and mind, so going straight into it would have mentally and physically destroyed me. Therefore, I gradually made adjustments while weaving into it during our fight. However..."

A powerful aura radiates from Seiya's body as he locks his red eyes onto Grandleon.

"I have seen all you have to offer."

Hearing Seiya utter those words, the same thing he said back to the emperor in Gaeabrande, gives me chills.

H–he's a genius! He mastered Berserk: Phase Two during his battle against an unbelievably powerful enemy!

"I won't be holding back anymore."

Seiya unsheathes another platinum sword at his waist. Dual-wielding two blades, he holds one sword aloft and the other waist-high.

"Don't you dare underestimate me, human scum!"

An explosive roar echoes as the two warriors clash. Seiya doesn't use the dual-wielding version of Eternal Blade, nor does he use any skills or abilities. He simply attacks Grandleon relentlessly with both swords. Nevertheless, his speed and power are extraordinary. Hidden within each strike is enough power to make the heavens weep. The claws and blades interweave, creating a shock wave that ruffles my hair despite being so far away.

Grandleon cannot defend quickly enough against Seiya's brutal attacks. His cheek splits open, bleeding black blood. The jet-black armor protecting Grandleon's body cracks as he is slowly pushed back.

Wow! Seiya's talents really are one in a billion! He can do this! He can win without the Hexagram Ritual of Retribution! But then, why did Adenela say he couldn't beat Grandleon?! Ishtar was also really adamant about avoiding one-on-one battle like this as well…

My worries soon become reality. Although forcing Grandleon to retreat, Seiya wears a pained expression. The Beast Emperor, on the other hand, seems overly confident for some reason.

"What's wrong? You seem to be in a rush. You're a cautious man, so I know what you're thinking. Your face practically screams 'I need to kill him before he gets serious.'"

What?! G-Grandleon isn't even serious yet?!

As Seiya breathes heavily during his continuous attacks, Grandleon calmly says:

"Your gut instinct was right. But even then, there's nothing you can do about it. Unlike Bunogeos, I power up automatically after taking enough damage from my opponent without countering. It doesn't matter how cautious or prepared you are."

Seiya immediately slows his attack, but Grandleon scoffs.

"It's already too late, Hero."

Out of nowhere, Grandleon is swallowed by a black radiance.

"Beast Hazard!"

His body discharges an overwhelming jet-black aura, knocking Seiya away! The aura's light eventually fades, revealing a transformed Beast Emperor. On his back are massive bat-like wings. His tail appears to have warped into a sinister snake with a mind of its own. In his new form, greatly resembling a chimera, Grandleon stands tall. A pale light radiates from his body like electricity. He promptly adopts a stance to charge Seiya. Sensing danger, the Hero hastily tries to create some distance, but…

"Volt…!"

Like a pale flash of lightning, Grandleon soars past Seiya so quickly that it looks as if they switched positions for a moment.

…Seiya listlessly falls to his knees. The Hero, who remained calm even when the emperor of Roseguard cut off one of his arms, is clutching his stomach, his face twisted in agony.

CHAPTER 24
In This Cruel World

Sparks flicker from the Beast Emperor's body as he looks down at Seiya doubled over.

"My attack power just surpassed one million, significantly exceeding that of Demon Lord Ultimaeus."

Grandleon's status reflects in my eyes as I use Scan.

BEAST EMPEROR GRANDLEON

Condition: Thunder Beast

LV: 99 (MAX)

**HP: 955,989/
1,200,044**   **MP: 0**

ATK:	DEF:	SPD:	MAG:	GRW:
1,023,987	998,596	938,855	58,754	999 (MAX)

Resistance: Fire, Wind, Water, Lightning, Ice, Earth, Holy, Dark, Poison, Paralysis, Sleep, Curse, Instant Death, Status Ailments

Special Abilities: Dark God's Blessing (LV: MAX), Flight (LV: MAX)

Skills: Jet-Black Nail, Volt, Volt: Sky Strike

Personality: Wicked

Saying the situation is hopeless would be putting it lightly. Gaeabrande was nothing compared to this. No human could ever defeat such a monster.

Just then…

"Y-you're…?"

By my side, Queen Carmilla points at me with a trembling hand. That's when I notice…I am no longer a fish-person.

"Who are you?!"

Desperately fighting the feelings welling in my heart, I tell the queen only what she needs to know.

"I-I'm Ristarte. I'm a goddess who came to save this world. Due to unavoidable circumstances, I had to transform into a fish-person."

"I see…"

The queen nods with a solemn expression.

"You're the goddess of fish…yes?"

"…?! No!! A-anyway, I'll fill you in on the details later!"

Just as I start to return my attention to the battle, it hits me. The hairs on the back of my neck stand up.

W-wait… Why was the shape-shifting spell broken?!

Magic that uses power in nature—earth magic, for example—relies on the energy of the soil itself in addition to the caster's magic. That's why the earth serpents could move even without Seiya's magic. However, shape-shifting works solely because of Seiya's magic. Which means…

Seiya has taken an unbelievable amount of damage!

I stare at Seiya breathing heavily with a hand on his stomach. Just as I expected, blood is pouring out of his torn-open abdomen.

"Seiya…!"

I get ready to rush over to heal him, but…

"Stay back."

Seiya tells me to stop as if he knows my intentions. Grandleon turns his gaze on me as well.

"Huh? Who's that girl...? Oh... That must be the goddess from another dimension who came with the Hero."

The Beast Emperor mutters as if he isn't interested in the least.

"I'll kill her later with the hag. You're up first, though."

Grandleon poises himself to use Volt against Seiya, but the Hero manages to get back to his feet to take a defensive stance.

"I despise humans. The Demon Lord created me after he turned this world into a land of ruin. So I bet I was killed by a human in a past life."

Thereupon, another bolt of lightning shoots past Seiya, and I hear the sound of flesh tearing open. Smoke rises in the distance, and Grandleon stands perfectly still. Seiya must have been unable to completely dodge Volt. His left cheek splits open as if he was cut with a knife. The Beast Emperor licks Seiya's blood off his claws before repositioning himself to use Volt. Another pale trail of lightning shoots forward. This time, I hear metal clinking. It looks like Seiya is able to block the attack, but it sends the platinum sword in his left hand flying into the air. Seiya unsteadily drags himself to where the platinum sword lands, but Grandleon is already standing tall before it. As Seiya defenselessly reaches for the blade, the Beast Emperor swings his claws as if he's about to chop off Seiya's arm... but he suddenly stops.

"...Did you think I wouldn't notice?"

Bam. Grandleon buries his foot in Seiya's stomach, kicking him into the air. When Seiya hits the ground, blood aggressively spews out of his stomach wound.

"I noticed the moment I saw you. Your left arm is engulfed in a strange aura."

I gasp when I hear those words.

W-was he trying to use Counter Break, like he did against the emperor in Gaeabrande?! That means he must have cast it on his arm before using Berserk just in case he got backed into a corner! He was gambling his own arm to cut off one of Grandleon's...!

"So that was the last ace up your sleeve, huh? It's too bad."

The monster saw right through the cautious Hero's plan. Grandleon laughs robustly while restlessly kicking Seiya in the stomach.

"You ran out of luck when you ran into me. I'm going to kill you. Then I'm going to kill Ultimaeus! I will rule all humans and beastkin in the world!"

Tears well in my eyes as I watch Seiya get kicked and stomped on like a sandbag.

This extraordinary Hero...such a talented man...doesn't even stand a chance! He would have easily won if he completed the ritual...! But because of me...! Because I...!

Grandleon delivers a kick that sends Seiya several meters into the air.

"Seiya...!"

I can't watch any longer. I don't care if he kills me. I decide to rush over to Seiya. After placing a hand on his stomach, I get ready to use my healing magic when...

"You don't have to heal me."

Seiya spits out the words in agony. Has he realized that healing him won't change the outcome of the battle? No... He probably just doesn't want my help, since this is my fault.

"I'm sorry...! I'm so, so sorry...!"

All I can do is apologize, but Seiya slowly tells me:

"Rista... You were right. If I'd wasted any more time on the ritual, someone dear to you would have died..."

I—I can't believe Seiya is saying this! S-stop! Don't talk like you're about to die!

But Seiya uses his platinum sword as a cane and slowly pulls himself to his feet.

"This pain...saved me from losing my mind. I should be able to use it now."

Although riddled with wounds, he has strength in his eyes. I can feel it in my bones when I hear his voice filled with determination.

He's planning on using Berserk: Phase Three! Phase Three will quadruple his stats! They would even exceed Grandleon's! It's all or nothing if he wants to defeat Grandleon! But... But...!

"There are heights that humans were not meant to reach. If a human uses Phase Three, their mind will be forever lost to madness! The scars of the

berserker will be carved into your very soul and will remain even after you return to your original world!"

The Goddess of Warfare insistently warned us not to use Phase Three. I've got a really bad feeling about this! I get the feeling this isn't going to be something you can overcome with raw talent and mental strength! Grandleon quietly watches us in the distance until...

"Finished saying your good-byes? Don't worry. I'll kill her shortly after I kill you."

Grandleon gives a muffled laugh.

"Wait... Should I kill her first?"

He suddenly faces me!

"Volt!"

A pale bolt of lightning streaks toward me. Sensing death on the horizon, I instinctively shut my eyes when I hear a loud clash. I slowly open my eyes...only to see an unexpected sight. Grandleon has fallen to one knee! Black blood drips from his mouth and chin.

"Human...!"

His face contorted with rage, Grandleon glares at the Hero. I look over at Seiya and can't believe what I see, either. His aura earlier couldn't even compare to how powerful it is now! Even his skin has turned red, and his fingers are turning crimson as well!

The Hero breathlessly observes:

"It looks like...it worked..."

"I-is that... Is that Phase Three?!"

But Seiya shakes his head.

"Even if I manage to defeat Grandleon...I still have to worry about the Dark Lord. This isn't the time to be taking risks..."

"Th-then what happened to you?!"

"If the full potential of Berserk is an insurmountable wall...then there's no need to get to the top. I just need to...climb the wall...halfway..."

Seiya slowly mutters:

"Berserk: Phase 2.5..."

Phase 2.5?! Phase Two triples your stats, which means Phase 2.5...multiplies your stats by 2.5?! Does that mean he is able to match Grandleon's stats by adjusting the phase between Two and Three?!

"Well technically…it's more like Phase 2.491…"

Th-that's oddly specific, but okay…! Anyway…that's amazing! He was able to adjust it to the decimal point?!

Grandleon spits a mixture of saliva and blood onto the ground.

"So that's the real ace up your sleeve, huh? Nothing has changed, though. You're going to die."

With that, Grandleon charges Seiya using Volt. Engulfed in a dark-crimson aura, Seiya rushes toward the Beast Emperor in turn. The two collide! After a powerful blast, I see Grandleon blocking Seiya's dual blades with his claws. Grandleon smirks but is gradually pushed back as if Seiya is overpowering him!

"What is this power…?! There's no way a mere human could be this strong…!"

"I gave up being human for the moment."

"I've had enough of your crap! Who the hell do you think I am?"

Enraged, Grandleon raises an arm high into the air before swinging his claws through the platinum sword in Seiya's right hand, shattering it into pieces!

"Looks like your weapons can't keep up with your strength."

He was right. Platinum swords are strong, but they aren't fit for duels against Demon Lord–class monsters. Plus, the sword has gradually worn down over the course of their fierce battle.

This can't be happening! And after finally raising his stats to match Grandleon's…!

I fall into a pit of despair…but the ground under Seiya suddenly swells! Out slithers an earth serpent carrying a sheathed sword in its mouth!

"…?! There are still earth serpents underground?!"

"Yeah, I made a spare earth serpent and a spare platinum sword."

Seiya takes the platinum sword and unsheathes it, but…

"My left sword is pretty beat-up, too. I'll switch it out just in case."

As he softly steps on the ground, it suddenly bulges once more, revealing another earth serpent with another sheathed sword!

"A spare earth serpent for my spare, and a spare platinum sword for my spare."

H-how many spares does he have?!

Indifferent to how astonished I am by his thorough preparation, Seiya gets into stance with his two new swords. Grandleon clenches his teeth.

"You're a joke... What are you, a magician?"

Grandleon slowly moves his arms in a circle.

"I'm not gonna hold back any longer! I'm gonna infuse both arms with Volt and tear you apart with Jet-Black Nail!"

Seiya, on the other hand, slowly exhales before muttering:

"Berserk: Phase 2.6...!"

H-he's getting even closer to Phase Three! Is he going to be okay?! There's no way he can maintain that for long...!

But that's when I notice it... Grandleon is clenching his teeth while struggling to breathe!

Oh! Grandleon can't remain in Beast Hazard Mode for long, either! Th-that means regardless of who wins...this match is about to come to an end!

...The dark-crimson aura of chaos faces the pale aura of lightning. The Hero slowly points his swords at Grandleon.

"From this moment on, the continent of Rhadral will be free from your rule."

"Don't get too cocky, human...!" Grandleon roars. "Humans are toys! Humans are food! Rhadral belongs to the beastkin!"

"All of that ends today."

"We'll see about that!"

With the power of Volt, the Beast Emperor swipes his claws at Seiya. The Hero parries the first strike, but the following combo comes in at blinding speed. Nevertheless, Seiya blocks each strike with his dual swords while driving them away!

However...there's a creak! Grandleon throws all his might into his attack, shattering the fresh platinum sword in Seiya's right hand like glass! Grandleon smirks, but a trail of black blood runs down his cheek. Paying no attention to his broken blade, Seiya thrusts with his other sword, skewering Grandleon's cheek! The king of the beasts growls deeply but resumes his relentless onslaught, determined not to let the now-defenseless Hero escape with his life. Seiya's at a disadvantage, but the ground swells below him, revealing another earth serpent with a sheathed sword. Dodging Grandleon's attack with his upper body, Seiya kicks the sheathed sword into the air. As the weapon spins overhead, the centrifugal force pulls the sword out of its sheath before Seiya grabs it with his free hand.

"A spare for the spare of the earlier spare."

Seiya thereupon switches to the offensive. He can't use any abilities while in Berserk Mode, but through sheer natural talent alone, he weaves together countless sword techniques from each and every direction. Scars begin to carve into Grandleon's body as he fails to block every attack.

"You little...shit...!"

His sword breaks again mid-combo, but even then, another earth serpent instantly delivers a spare. Without even taking his eyes off his opponent, Seiya kicks the sword straight into his hand. This is the price for continuously attacking so his opponent won't even get a chance to breathe. But all of a sudden, a third threat soars over Grandleon's head to attack Seiya: the giant serpent tail! Normal people would have a hard time dealing with an attack from their blind spot, but Seiya deflects it with his blade as if he expected it.

W-wow! He's overpowering Grandleon!

I then hear another metallic *clang*. This time, however, it isn't a platinum sword. As I look at Grandleon, I notice that the claws on his left hand are broken!

"M-my claws...!"

Compared to Seiya's seemingly endless supply of platinum swords, Grandleon's claws are relatively worn. The Beast Emperor suddenly leaps back, creating some distance between them. Both his full-power Jet-Black Nail and his surprise attack thwarted, Grandleon bares his fangs with rage while glaring at Seiya.

"Powers greater than mine even after I surpassed the Dark Lord?! I won't allow it! I won't allow you to exist in this world!"

Spreading the black wings on his back, Grandleon takes to the sky. I rush over to Seiya.

"I-is he running away?!"

"...No."

Grandleon comes to a sudden stop after gaining significant altitude. He then roars so loudly, we can hear him on the surface. The air around him trembles as the lightning flickering around his body increases.

"What in the world...?"

"He's going to focus every drop of power he has left...to kill me."

Seiya sheathes his swords as if he's given up.

"S-Seiya?!"

"I can't use any abilities or magic during Berserk Mode, so I prepared to make up for this shortcoming. The drawback is that it takes time to focus, but it should be perfect against an enemy's most powerful technique."

"But how are you going to attack with your swords sheathed?!"

"Slowly but surely, I'm remembering the Valkyrja techniques of destruction. The Seventh Valkyrja: Break Permission—through granting destructive energy to only material objects, I was able to give the soil an explosive charge."

Seiya taps his foot on the ground three times. Before long, a serpent pops out with a sheath wrapped in cloth.

"This sword was specially crafted. When drawn, the friction will create sparks that ignite the explosive soil inside the sheath, thus creating more power along with the flames. The tremendous energy created will then be used to hit the target."

By the time Seiya finishes his explanation, Grandleon is quietly staring down at us from the sky. The explosive lightning flickering around him is quietly absorbed into his body. He is then swallowed in a blinding ray of light instead.

"Die...! Volt: Sky Strike!"

With the overpowering aura coursing through every vein in his body, Grandleon rapidly descends in our direction like a shooting star followed by a pale ray of light. There's no way we can block that...!

"Seiya! Use the move!"

"No, he needs to be closer."

"B-but at this rate, we'll...!"

"This is all I have left. If I miss, it's over."

Grandleon rapidly approaches at a blinding speed, but even then, Seiya doesn't draw his sword.

W-we're doomed!

The moment my eyes catch sight of Grandleon's Chain Destruction–infused claws...Seiya's hand on the sword's grip twitches.

"Valkyrja Explosion: Crimson Boom...!"

The instantaneous sound of the sword being unsheathed is drowned out by the explosive roar in front of us. The thunderous blow dealt by the Hero with over one million attack power collides into Grandleon, the shooting star.

A tremendous shock wave and radiant light are created when the two extraordinary forces clash, blowing me away.

"N-ngh..."

...I slowly sit up to find Grandleon standing with his back turned to Seiya. Seiya quietly stands with his sword drawn as well. Neither faces the other. They're both completely still. But almost instantly, I hear a crack. The platinum sword in Seiya's hand shatters into ash, and Seiya falls face forward to the ground. Grandleon, on the other hand, reveals only a faint cut on his chest as he turns around.

Th-the attack barely did any damage! It took the full force of Crimson Boom just to cancel out Volt: Sky Strike!

But as the Beast Emperor approaches Seiya to deal the final blow, his chest begins to swell as a glittering red liquid bursts out of the faint cut. Suddenly, Grandleon's torso catches fire. He screams as the flames try to escape from his body. I shiver as the king of the beasts lets out one final cry of agony while the numerous small explosions tear his flesh asunder.

The explosive soil was thrown into his body...!

Though they initially rage out of control, the flames eventually die down to reveal a charred Beast Emperor.

"Seiya!"

I rush over to Seiya and prop him up. His hair color has already returned to normal, which means he isn't in Berserk Mode anymore. He winces in pain, but it looks like he's still conscious. When he finally notices my presence, he instantly snaps to his feet like a whip.

"...What happened to Grandleon?"

"Don't worry! Crimson Boom burned him to a crisp!"

I point in the direction of the body...but Grandleon is nowhere to be found.

"You win...human."

Startled, I look in the direction of the voice. Although his body has been completely charred, he stands behind the queen.

"The wound is fatal... I won't live much longer. But I figured I'd pay you back...before I go."

The beast then grabs a handful of the queen's hair.

"I finally learned...what makes humans suffer the most."

N-no...! Not the queen...!

"It's having what's most important to you...broken!"

I start sprinting for the queen, but when he sees me coming his way, he lets go of the queen's hair.

"...That's right. It's *you*."

Grandleon charges at me with his last bit of strength.

Huh?! Me?! Wh-why?!

It's clear the Beast Emperor doesn't have much power left, but he probably still has enough to kill me. Mere moments before his claws tear through me, a little face pokes out from my chest. It's the earth serpent that Seiya left with me to protect me just in case. Paying no heed to the snake, Grandleon continues driving his claw toward my heart when...

"G-gwah...!"

He groans in agony. Before I even realize it, the earth serpent has latched onto Grandleon's neck with its fangs! He grabs the serpent with both hands and tries to tear it off, but it wraps around him and won't let go! Standing behind me, Seiya says in a neutral voice:

"The earth serpent protecting that woman...is the strongest I can currently create. You no longer have the strength to remove it."

Grandleon's eyes open wide, and he pierces Seiya with a hate-filled glare. He gives up trying to pull off the snake and turns to Seiya to take him to the grave with him...but all of a sudden, he stops. His grip around the earth serpent loosens, and his body droops forward before he lifelessly drops to his knees. Seiya extends a hand in Grandleon's direction.

"...Endless Fall."

Having returned to an earth Spellblade, Seiya unleashes his final attack. Without even touching his opponent himself, earth serpents forcefully drag Grandleon's body underground. The instant he vanishes, the beastkin watching in the distance begin to panic.

"L-Lord Grandleon was killed!"

"The Dark God's power is going to disappear!"

"We're done for…!"

After losing their boss, the beastkin scatter like baby spiders. Seemingly relieved to see that, Seiya drops to a knee. I run over to the battered Hero, place a hand on his stomach, and heal the wound.

"I'm sorry! I'm so sorry…! Because of me, you…!"

Seiya sends me a reproachful gaze.

"Stop crying and don't apologize. You're annoying me."

"But…!"

"We won. That's all that matters. Besides…"

Seiya exhales deeply, then continues:

"I told you in the spirit world I was perfectly prepared, right?"

"Yeah… You're right!"

After I finish closing Seiya's wound, he staggers to his feet.

"At any rate, we need to take the queen somewhere safe…"

But the moment those words come out of his mouth, he goes limp and collapses.

The next day, I find myself standing in Queen Carmilla's old home in the town of Termine. Though the inside is a mess thanks to the beastkin, the furniture is still there for the most part, so Seiya is sleeping in one of the beds. Although I finished healing his wounds yesterday, I still put a cool, damp washrag on his forehead before leaving the room. The queen is talking to a familiar man in the adjacent chamber.

"I can't imagine the pain you went through, Jonde."

"It was nothing compared to what happened to you, my queen."

The pale man speaks as if a wave of emotions has swept over him. I could never forget him. The beastkin turned General Jonde of Termine into an undead and forced him to fight us at the enlistment trial. When the queen notices me there, she introduces us.

"This is Jonde. He was the late king's right-hand man."

The general reverently lowers his head and lets out a bitter laugh.

"Due to unavoidable circumstances, I'm now half-corpse, but I hope you can look past that."

"Y-yeah, I mean…! Of course! It's no problem! Oh-ho-ho-ho!"

I feel so bad for the awful things I did to him at the trial, to the point that I can't look him in the eye. He'd probably punch me in the face if he found out I was that fish.

"The beastkin seem to have escaped from Termine. The Dark God's power has disappeared with Grandleon's death, and their powers have decreased to one-tenth of what they were. They likely feared retaliation and ran."

The beastkin must have gotten pretty cocky, since the Dark God's Blessing had given them powers far greater than any human. They didn't take the surveillance or confinement of humans seriously because they didn't take humans themselves seriously—and lucky for us. The people once kept in captivity are apparently gathering in the town.

The queen sends Jonde a smile.

"They always did call you the Immortal General, after all… It looks like they were right."

The queen jokes, but her expression is brimming with compassion. Tears begin welling in Jonde's sunken eyes. I'm sure he was a knight through and through. He looks away so the queen doesn't see him sob.

"Th-there are probably still numerous people trapped in cells underground! I will go give the soldiers orders to search for and free the remaining prisoners!"

Jonde bows to us once more before leaving the room and closing the door behind him. He may be undead, but he's still a wonderful general. Now that the queen and I are alone, she asks:

"…Are you sure you don't need to be by the Hero's side when he wakes up?"

And the truth just slips off my tongue.

"Um… Honestly, I don't really know how I should act around him, so…"

She gives me a curious look, but I smile.

"I-I'm a terrible goddess! I always mess things up and drag him down with me! Seiya's a human, but he's so much smarter, stronger, and more mature than I am! I mean, he probably would be better without me and—"

"Goddess."

The queen cuts me off midsentence.

"The beastkin thought I was a cold woman who felt no pain, but in reality, I'm a weak person who couldn't even acknowledge her own daughter's death."

The queen turns her eyes to the door of the bedroom in which Seiya is sleeping.

"That man is human, too. He feels grief, and I'm sure, deep down inside, he's in pain."

"'In pain'? Seiya? B-but Seiya doesn't have any memories of the past! Besides, he doesn't care what people say to him. In fact, he gives knuckle sandwiches to anyone who—"

"While that may be true, you cannot expect him not to think about this world's present state, which derives from what happened in his past. Regret, guilt—he will surely be suddenly overwhelmed with negative feelings from time to time. But he knows these feelings won't help him save the world, so he suppresses them by locking them away in the depths of his heart."

The queen's face is overcome with sorrow.

"And that's...a very painful thing."

After relaxing her expression, she sends me a cheerful smile.

"All you need to do is stand by him. Just be by his side in this cruel world. Make a fool of yourself, make mistakes—because that's what's saving him whether you know it or not."

"B-but Seiya doesn't want me around... He thinks I'm..."

The queen rolls her eyes.

"Are you kidding? Even Grandleon noticed..."

"Huh?"

I stare at the queen, unable to understand what she means, but she suddenly places a hand before her mouth as it opens wide.

"O-oh my! I have been so rude to you, haven't I?! Goddess, please forgive me."

"N-no, I don't mind."

"It's strange. I feel so relaxed around you. It must be because you were so kind to me as a fish-person."

"Yeah..."

After sharing a smile, I hop to my feet.

"Well…I'm gonna go check on Seiya!"

"That's a wonderful idea."

After leaving the room, I whisper softly so the queen can't hear me:

"…Thanks, Mom."

I can't believe my eyes when I open the door to the bedroom. Seiya is already sitting up and awake.

"Seiya! You're awake?! You should be slee—"

"Rista. How long was I out?"

"Um… You slept through the night."

"I can't believe I did that…"

Seiya grimly clenches his teeth.

"Once the Demon Lord hears of Grandleon's death, he's going to send his men in droves to invade Termine."

Seiya dons his armor, grabs his sword, and heads straight for the door.

"S-Seiya…!"

He walks outside and places a hand on the garden soil.

"I'm going to spread earth serpents throughout the town."

The ground undulates around his hand. He must be sending dozens— Wait. It's Seiya. He's probably creating hundreds of earth serpents.

"You're awake."

I look over to find Jonde standing behind Seiya. The queen is now positioned by my side as well. Facing Seiya, Jonde says:

"Allow me to express my gratitude to you for defeating Grandleon and saving Termine. However, this would have never happened in the first place if you had defeated the Demon Lord a year ago…"

Jonde grabs Seiya by the back of the neck while his hand is still on the ground.

"Jonde, stop!"

"No! He's not going anywhere until he hears what I have to say!"

The general turns Seiya's head around so the Hero can see the fury in his eyes.

"Why…? Why couldn't you save Princess Tiana?!"

"Jonde…!"

The queen and I both freeze. As a suffocating air reigns over our heads, Seiya places a hand on Jonde's shoulder, and...

Whoosh!

The general is driven into the ground until he's buried up to his knees!

"Huh?!"

Seiya then turns his back to the general and diligently continues making earth serpents.

"Wh-what do you think you're doing?!"

Seiya's earth magic robs Jonde of all mobility, but...

"Hmph!"

He pulls his legs out of the ground with brute force.

"Oh?"

The Hero sounds impressed, but he immediately touches Jonde again.

Whoosh!

"Ahhhhhh!"

This time, he's buried up to his waist.

"Y-you little...!"

I figure there's no way he'll be getting out of this one, but...

"Don't you dare underestimate me, boy!"

...he pulls himself out of the ground once again.

"Oh? Huh."

Seiya places a hand on the general's head as he boldly approaches the Hero.

Bonk! Whoooooosh!

An even louder noise echoes as Jonde's entire body is powerfully sent underground. B-but now that I look carefully, I think I can see his forehead!

"S-Seiya! Help him! His head's the only thing not underground!"

"He's undead. He'll be fine. Leave him."

"I—I can't leave him like this! Pull him out!"

After a few moments pass, Seiya grabs the immortal general's hair in an irritated manner and pulls him out. Jonde is on the verge of tears.

"*Sniffle...!* I-it was so dark...and I couldn't breathe...! It was awful...!"

Seiya curiously stares at him.

"You're undead."

"Suffocating is still painful when you're undead!"

"But I made sure your forehead was sticking out."

"A-are you making fun of me?! I can't breathe through my forehead!"

The queen stares coldly at Seiya, who continues making earth serpents while ignoring Jonde.

"Goddess... I take back what I said earlier. It seems you can't use common sense with this one..."

"Whaaaaaaaaat...?"

Jonde steps away from Seiya so he won't be buried anymore; then he yells:

"It doesn't matter how many of those snakes you make! Once word gets out that Grandleon was killed, Oxerio and the machine corps will be here!"

"'Oxerio'...? 'Machine corps'?"

The queen explains it to me.

"The Machine Emperor Oxerio is a monster who rules the northern continent Barakuda. The Demon Lord created powerful magic weapons known as killing machines, which make up the machine corps. They say there are tens of thousands of them, and they are even more powerful than beastkin."

T-tens of thousands of "killing machines"?!

While I feel I'm about to faint, Seiya doesn't even seem concerned.

"I heard about them from the beastkin while I was gathering information. I've already thought of how to defeat them as well."

"You're still not going to defeat the machine corps with those earth serpents!"

"Who said I was going to use these to fight? They're for scouting and surveillance."

Seiya turns his gaze from Jonde to me as if he's made enough earth serpents.

"Rista, create a gate. It's time to return to the spirit world and prepare for the machine corps."

AFTERWORD

Hello, everyone. Light Tuchihi here. Fun fact: the kanji for my name is 土日月, so the characters themselves could be read as earth (土), sun (日), and moon (月), or as Saturday (土), Sunday (日), and Monday (月). However, it's actually read Light (月) Tuchihi (土日). Anyway, I know it's a little too late to be saying this, but it's a pretty nerdy name, huh? I have no regrets, though.

Moving on… First, I would like to thank you for reading Volume 3 of *The Hero Is Overpowered but Overly Cautious.* This novel, which I started on the novel website KakuYomu, was only able to make it this far thanks to everyone's support. I cannot thank the people who bought the first two volumes enough.

So now, let me briefly talk about Volume 3. The cautious Hero Seiya Ryuuguuin, who saved Gaeabrande in the previous volume, makes an appearance in this volume, of course. Naturally, the useless goddess Rista also makes an appearance, and they still go back and forth with their usual married-couple-like banter. However, if you look at the cover, you can see there is something different about Seiya. The Hero rarely smiles. In fact, it's surprising how little he smiles. You could say he left laughter behind in the womb when he was born. So why is he wearing such a refreshing smile on the cover? Did he win the lottery? Did he eat something good? Did he get a girlfriend? I would love for you to read this volume and find out for yourself.

I hope when you read this story, it will make you laugh, maybe cry, and perhaps feel all kinds of emotions. It's also relatively long compared to the first two volumes, so I hope it feels like a bargain. As a writer, I'm kind of proud of how I handled the second half of the story. I like to think that whoever reads to the end will surely enjoy themselves. (Where does this confidence come from?)

Anyway, I don't have many pages left to write on, so I'm going to make this brief. I would like to thank the following people:

Everyone who worked on this project with me and helped grow this story, Saori Toyota—whose illustrations always go beyond my expectations—and everyone who has supported this series and purchased the novels. Thank you all so very much. I am only able to continue writing because of everyone's support.

While I'm still just a novice writer, I am going to continue working hard to improve so I can make the story funnier and more touching for everyone supporting me. I want to continue creating stories that make people think, *I'm so glad I read that* and *I'm glad I bought this*. It's the least I can do to pay everyone back. And yes, I know this is a little arrogant of me to think.

Before I go, I just want to wish everyone happiness and good health. Let's meet again in the next volume.

Light Tuchihi